Disney FROZEN

COMICS COLLECTION

TRAVEL ARENDELLE

JOE BOOKS LTD

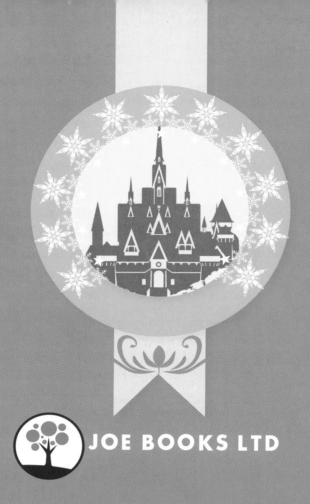

JOE BOOKS LTD

CEO – Jay Firestone
COO – Jody Colero
President – Steve Osgoode
Associate Publisher – Deanna McFadden
Creative Manager – Jason Flores-Holz
Production Manager – Sarah Salomon
Associate Editor – Steffie Davis
Associate Designer – Nicole Dalcin
Publishing Assistant – Emma Hambly
Sales and Marketing Assistant – Samantha Carr

Disney Frozen Comics Collection, September 2017. ISBN 978-1-77275-332-5. Published by Joe Books Ltd. 489 College Street, Suite 203, Toronto, Ontario, M6G 1A5.
Printed in Canada.

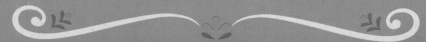

CONTENTS

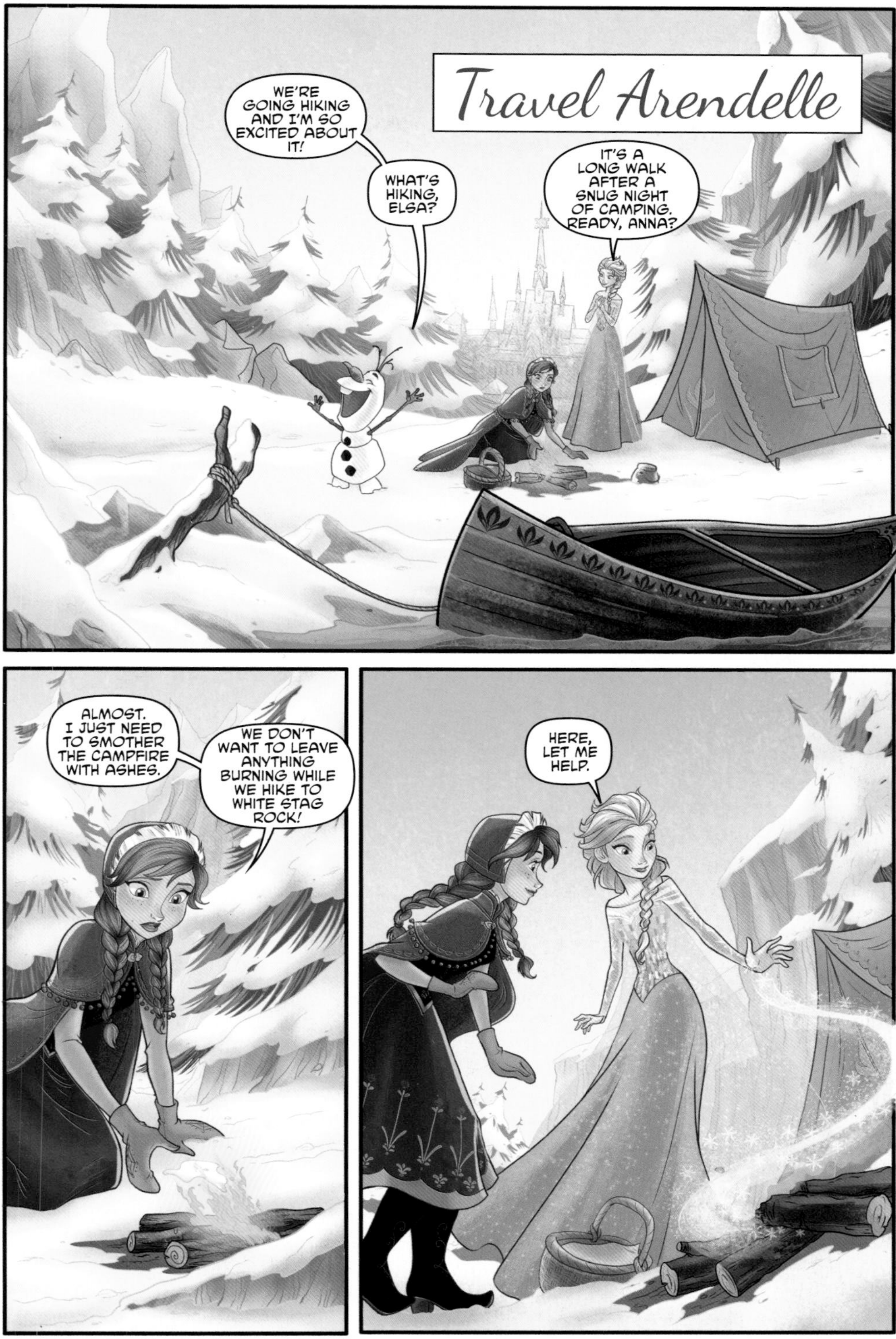

Travel Arendelle
WE'RE GOING HIKING AND I'M SO EXCITED ABOUT IT!
WHAT'S HIKING, ELSA?
IT'S A LONG WALK AFTER A SNUG NIGHT OF CAMPING. READY, ANNA?
ALMOST. I JUST NEED TO SMOTHER THE CAMPFIRE WITH ASHES.
WE DON'T WANT TO LEAVE ANYTHING BURNING WHILE WE HIKE TO WHITE STAG ROCK!
HERE, LET ME HELP.

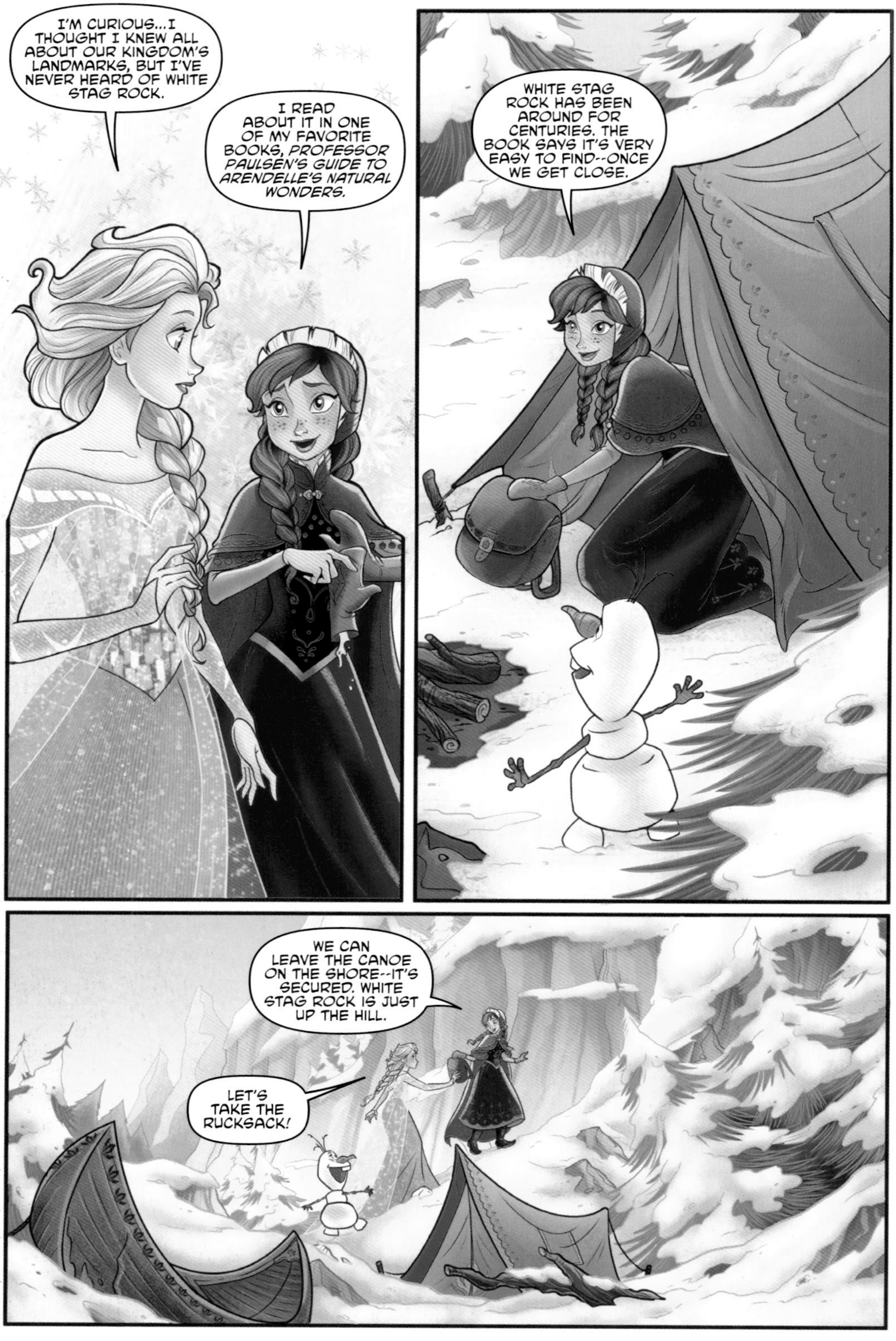
I'M CURIOUS...I THOUGHT I KNEW ALL ABOUT OUR KINGDOM'S LANDMARKS, BUT I'VE NEVER HEARD OF WHITE STAG ROCK.
I READ ABOUT IT IN ONE OF MY FAVORITE BOOKS, *PROFESSOR PAULSEN'S GUIDE TO ARENDELLE'S NATURAL WONDERS.*
WHITE STAG ROCK HAS BEEN AROUND FOR CENTURIES. THE BOOK SAYS IT'S VERY EASY TO FIND--ONCE WE GET CLOSE.
WE CAN LEAVE THE CANOE ON THE SHORE--IT'S SECURED. WHITE STAG ROCK IS JUST UP THE HILL.
LET'S TAKE THE RUCKSACK!

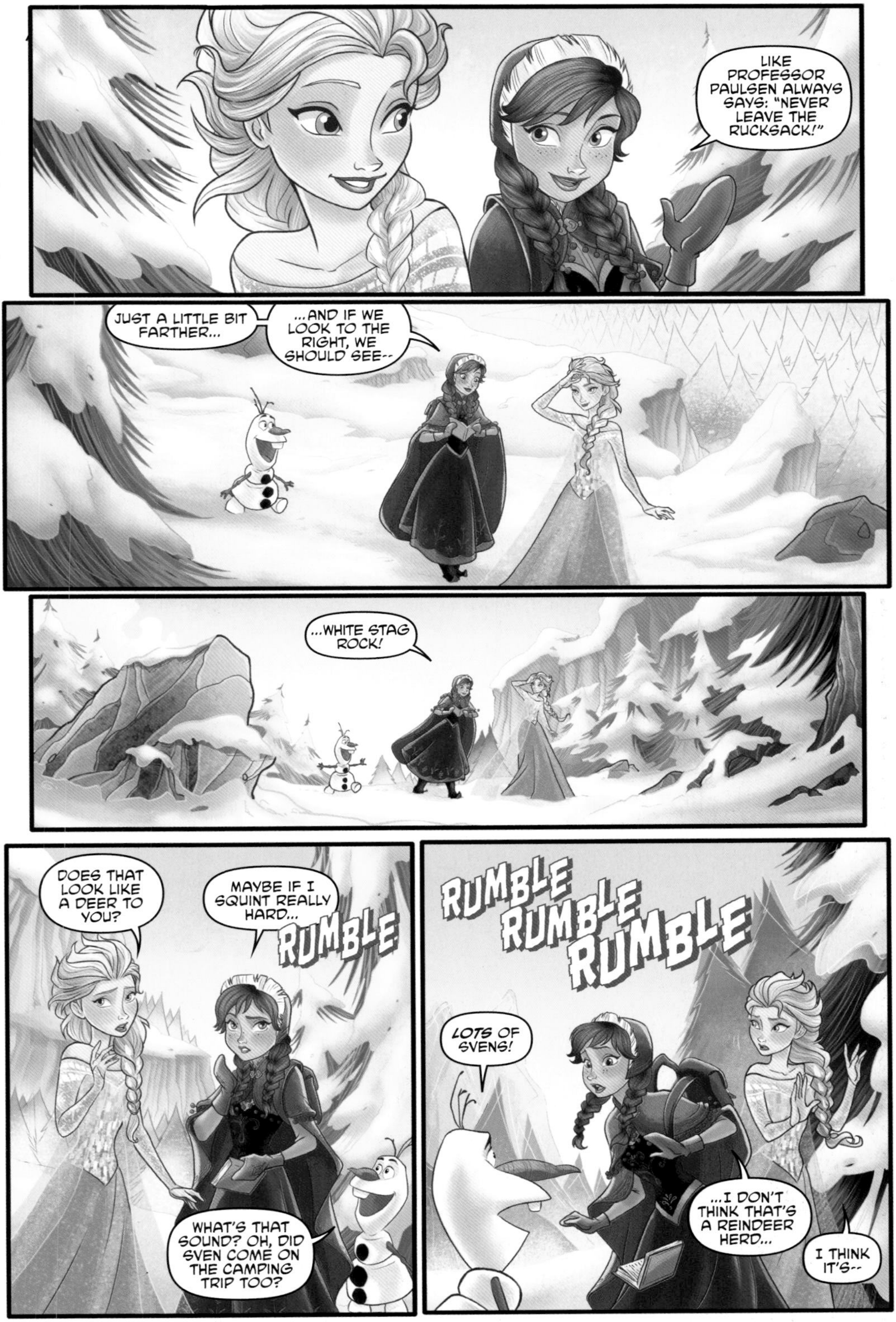
LIKE PROFESSOR PAULSEN ALWAYS SAYS: "NEVER LEAVE THE RUCKSACK!"
JUST A LITTLE BIT FARTHER...
...AND IF WE LOOK TO THE RIGHT, WE SHOULD SEE--
...WHITE STAG ROCK!
DOES THAT LOOK LIKE A DEER TO YOU?
MAYBE IF I SQUINT REALLY HARD...
RUMBLE
WHAT'S THAT SOUND? OH, DID SVEN COME ON THE CAMPING TRIP TOO?
RUMBLE RUMBLE RUMBLE
LOTS OF SVENS!
...I DON'T THINK THAT'S A REINDEER HERD...
I THINK IT'S--

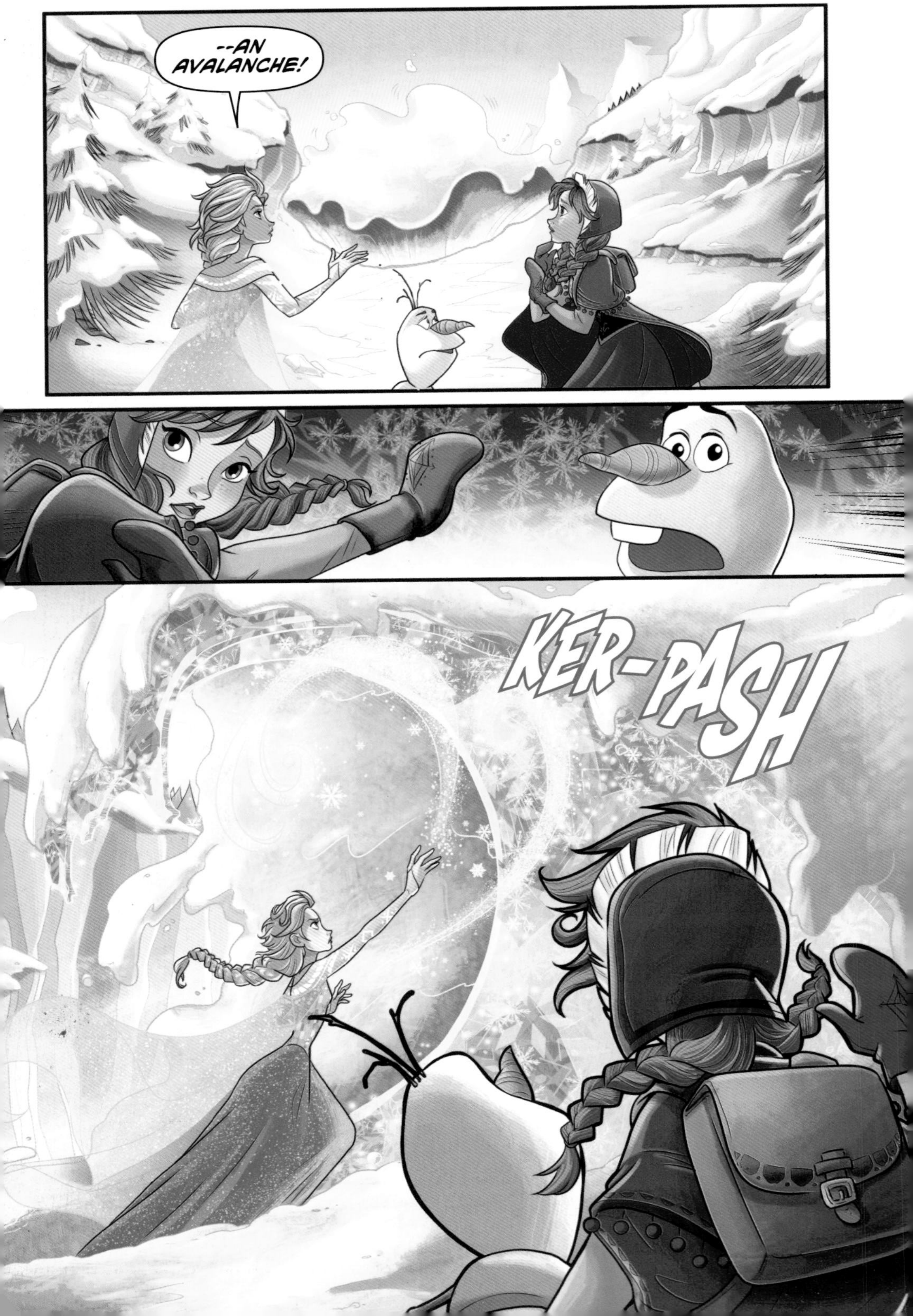
--AN AVALANCHE!
KER-PASH

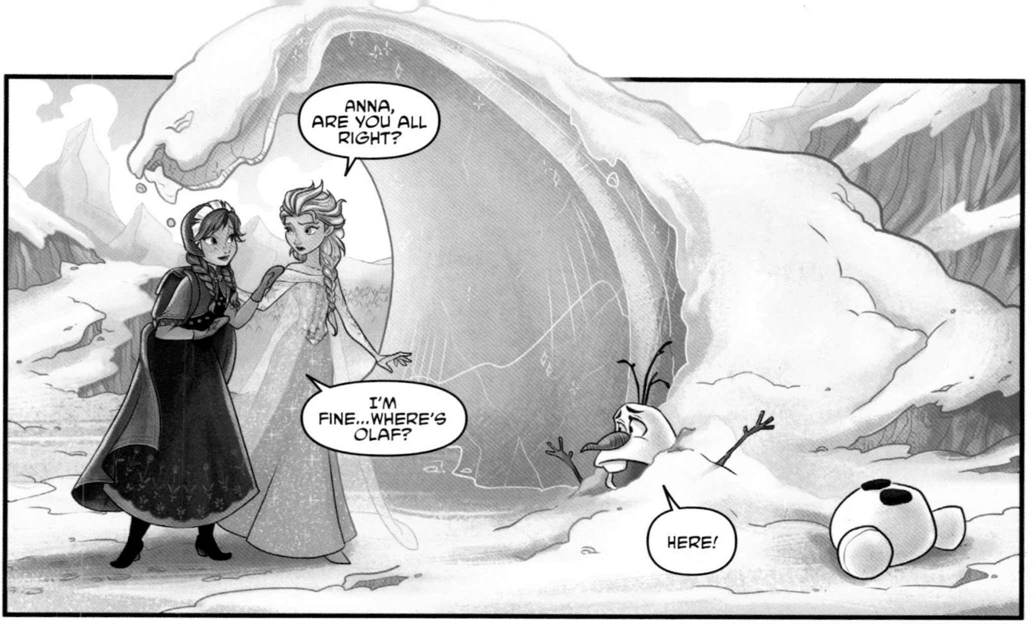
ANNA, ARE YOU ALL RIGHT?
I'M FINE...WHERE'S OLAF?
HERE!

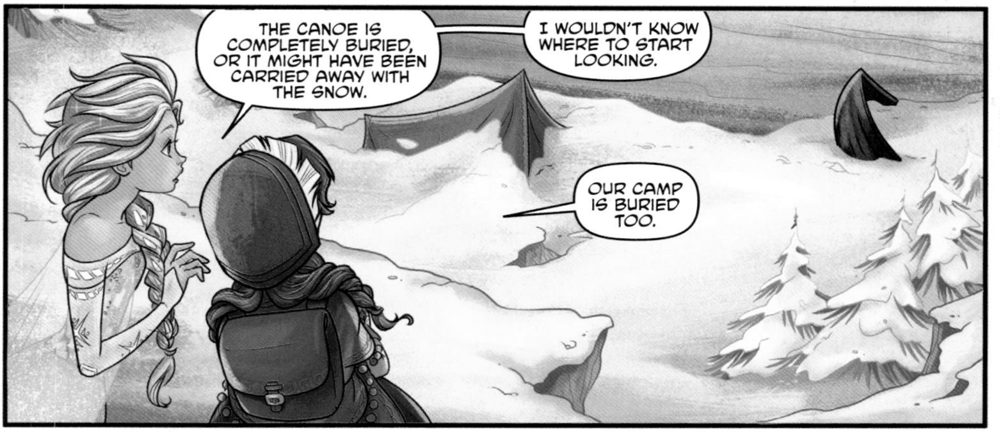
THE CANOE IS COMPLETELY BURIED, OR IT MIGHT HAVE BEEN CARRIED AWAY WITH THE SNOW.
I WOULDN'T KNOW WHERE TO START LOOKING.
OUR CAMP IS BURIED TOO.

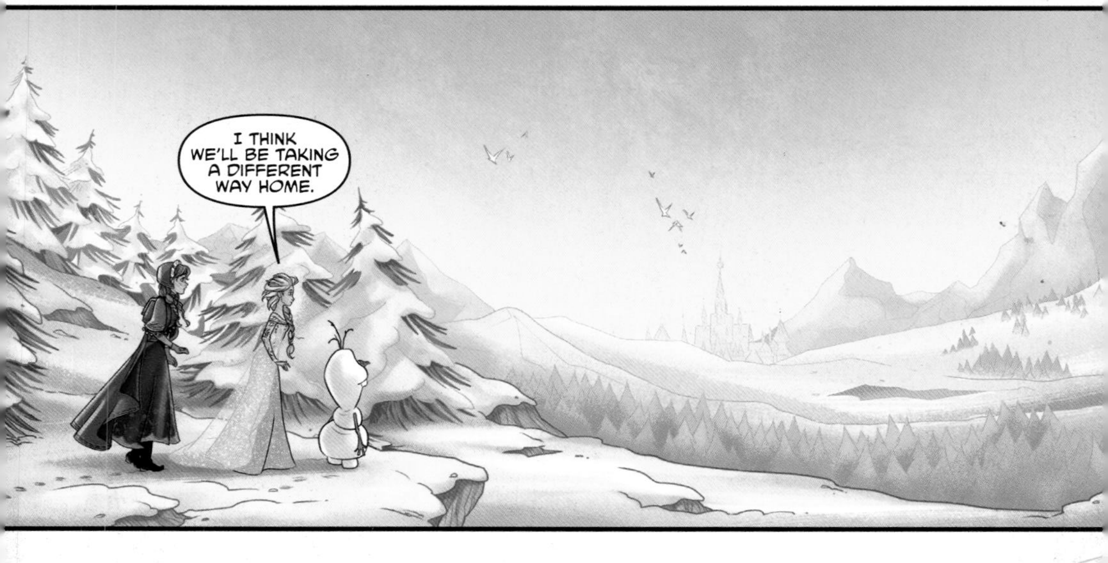
I THINK WE'LL BE TAKING A DIFFERENT WAY HOME.

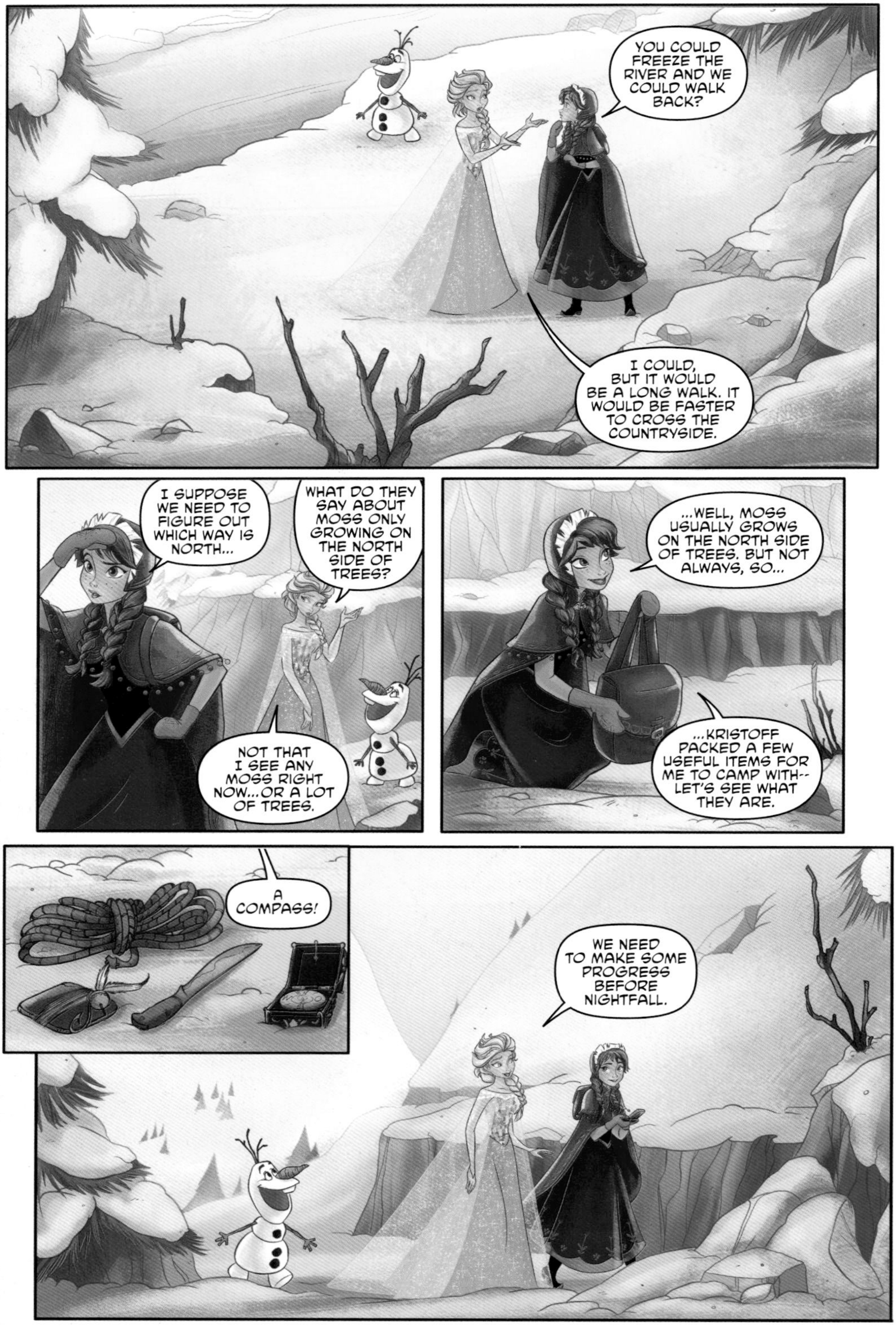

YOU COULD FREEZE THE RIVER AND WE COULD WALK BACK?
I COULD, BUT IT WOULD BE A LONG WALK. IT WOULD BE FASTER TO CROSS THE COUNTRYSIDE.
I SUPPOSE WE NEED TO FIGURE OUT WHICH WAY IS NORTH...
WHAT DO THEY SAY ABOUT MOSS ONLY GROWING ON THE NORTH SIDE OF TREES?
NOT THAT I SEE ANY MOSS RIGHT NOW...OR A LOT OF TREES.
...WELL, MOSS USUALLY GROWS ON THE NORTH SIDE OF TREES. BUT NOT ALWAYS, SO...
...KRISTOFF PACKED A FEW USEFUL ITEMS FOR ME TO CAMP WITH-- LET'S SEE WHAT THEY ARE.
A COMPASS!
WE NEED TO MAKE SOME PROGRESS BEFORE NIGHTFALL.

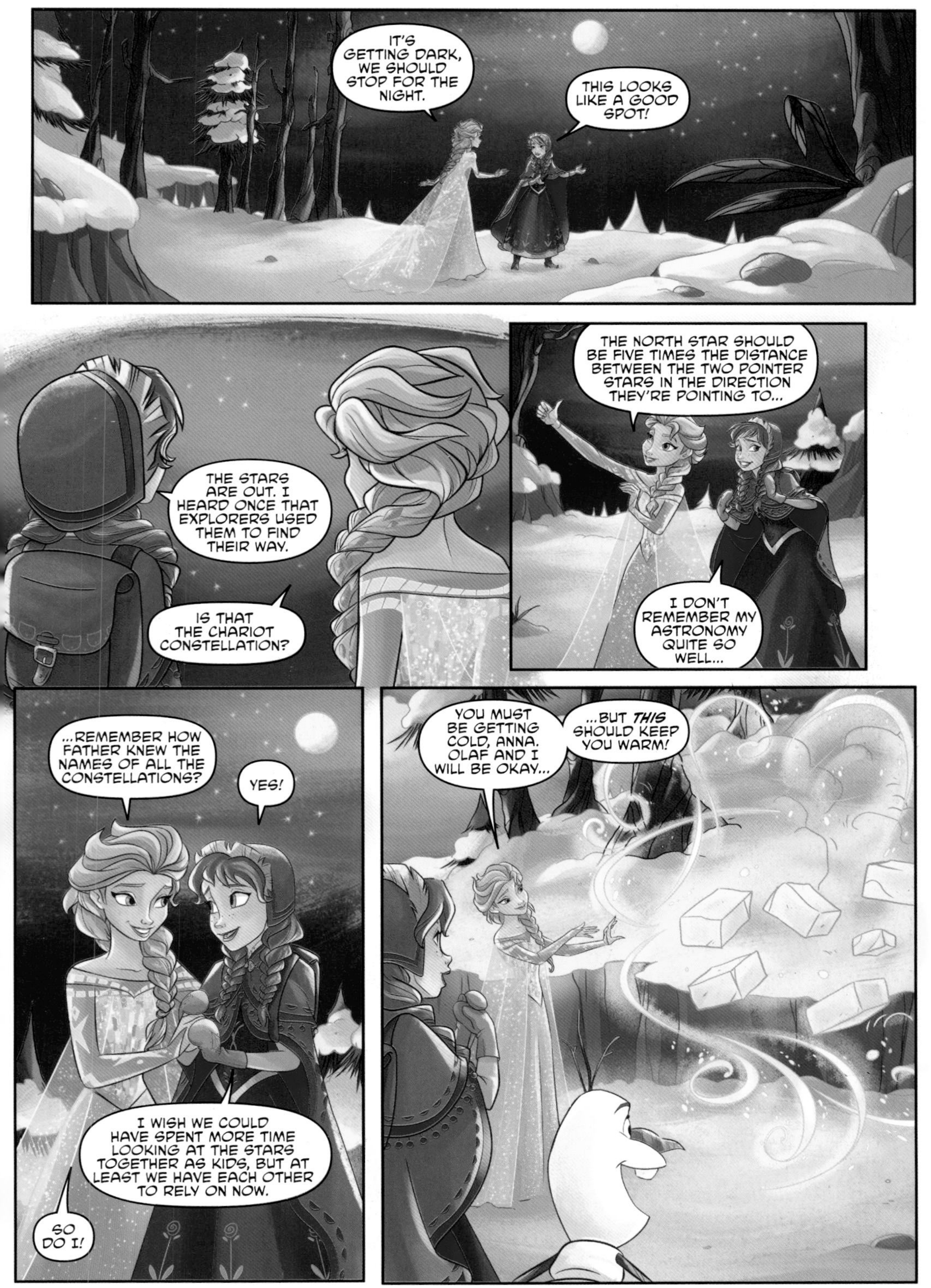
IT'S GETTING DARK, WE SHOULD STOP FOR THE NIGHT.
THIS LOOKS LIKE A GOOD SPOT!
THE STARS ARE OUT. I HEARD ONCE THAT EXPLORERS USED THEM TO FIND THEIR WAY.
IS THAT THE CHARIOT CONSTELLATION?
THE NORTH STAR SHOULD BE FIVE TIMES THE DISTANCE BETWEEN THE TWO POINTER STARS IN THE DIRECTION THEY'RE POINTING TO...
I DON'T REMEMBER MY ASTRONOMY QUITE SO WELL...
...REMEMBER HOW FATHER KNEW THE NAMES OF ALL THE CONSTELLATIONS?
YES!
I WISH WE COULD HAVE SPENT MORE TIME LOOKING AT THE STARS TOGETHER AS KIDS, BUT AT LEAST WE HAVE EACH OTHER TO RELY ON NOW.
SO DO I!
YOU MUST BE GETTING COLD, ANNA. OLAF AND I WILL BE OKAY...
...BUT *THIS* SHOULD KEEP YOU WARM!

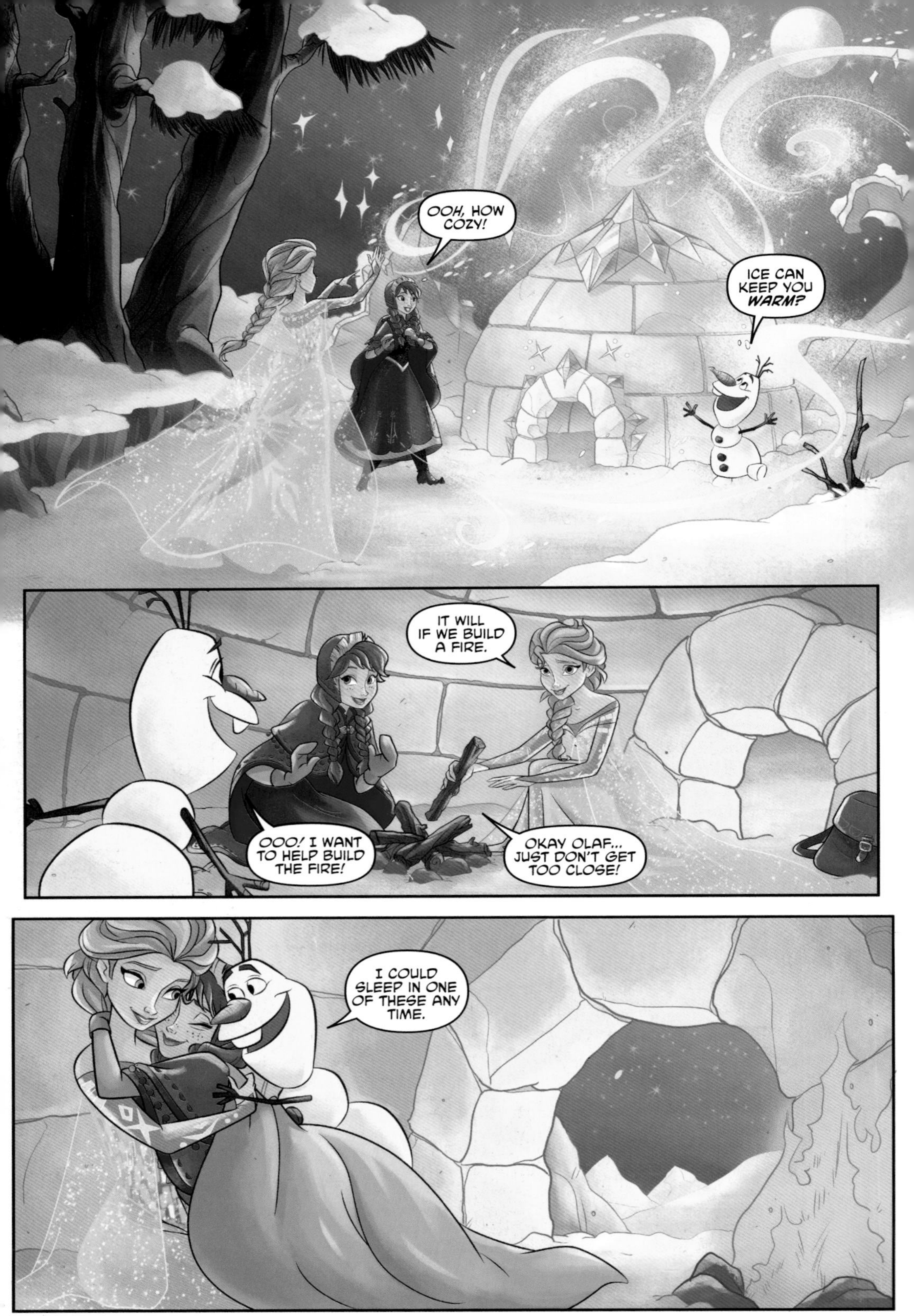
OOH, HOW COZY!
ICE CAN KEEP YOU *WARM*?
IT WILL IF WE BUILD A FIRE.
OOO! I WANT TO HELP BUILD THE FIRE!
OKAY OLAF... JUST DON'T GET TOO CLOSE!
I COULD SLEEP IN ONE OF THESE ANY TIME.

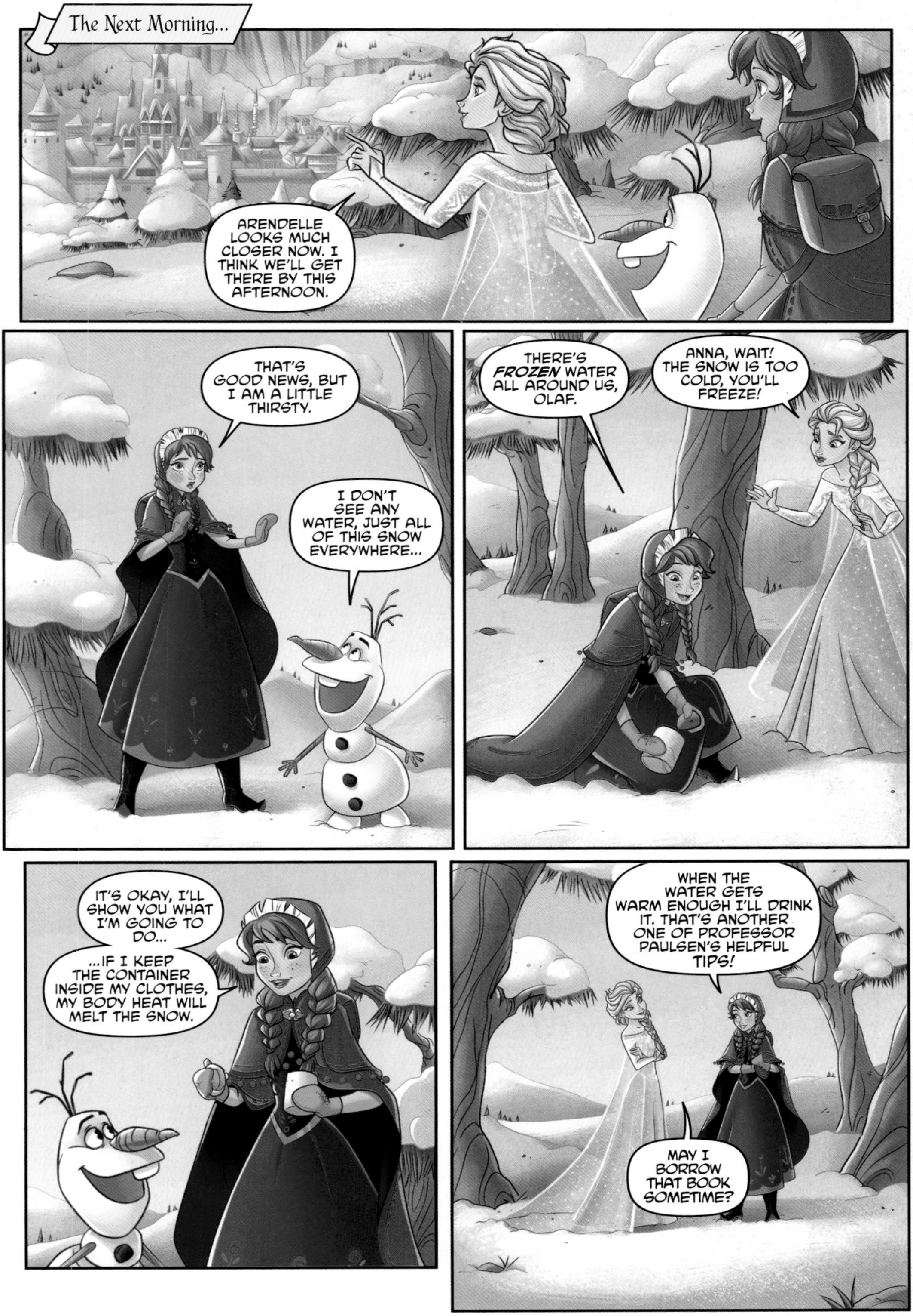
The Next Morning...
ARENDELLE LOOKS MUCH CLOSER NOW. I THINK WE'LL GET THERE BY THIS AFTERNOON.
THAT'S GOOD NEWS, BUT I AM A LITTLE THIRSTY.
I DON'T SEE ANY WATER, JUST ALL OF THIS SNOW EVERYWHERE...
THERE'S *FROZEN* WATER ALL AROUND US, OLAF.
ANNA, WAIT! THE SNOW IS TOO COLD, YOU'LL FREEZE!
IT'S OKAY, I'LL SHOW YOU WHAT I'M GOING TO DO...
...IF I KEEP THE CONTAINER INSIDE MY CLOTHES, MY BODY HEAT WILL MELT THE SNOW.
WHEN THE WATER GETS WARM ENOUGH I'LL DRINK IT. THAT'S ANOTHER ONE OF PROFESSOR PAULSEN'S HELPFUL TIPS!
MAY I BORROW THAT BOOK SOMETIME?

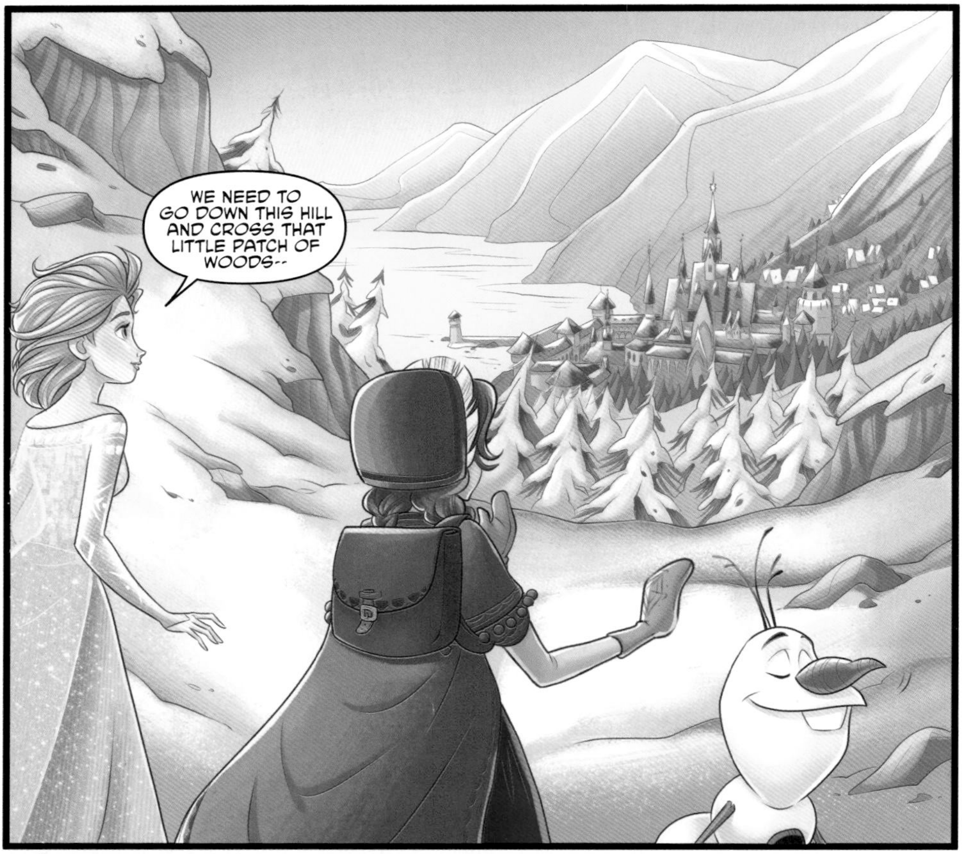
WE NEED TO GO DOWN THIS HILL AND CROSS THAT LITTLE PATCH OF WOODS--

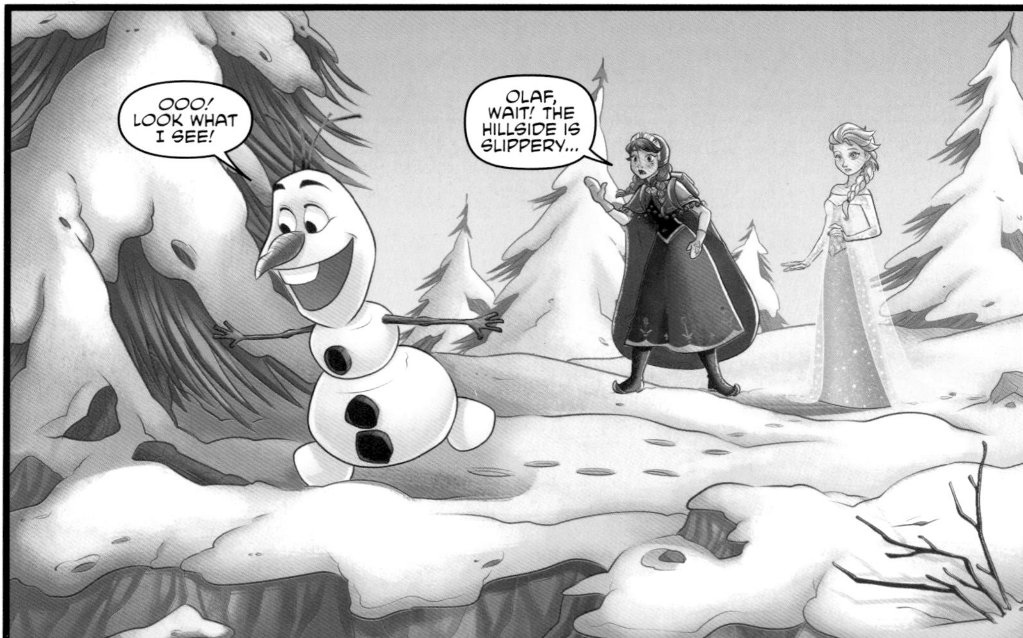
OOO! LOOK WHAT I SEE!
OLAF, WAIT! THE HILLSIDE IS SLIPPERY...

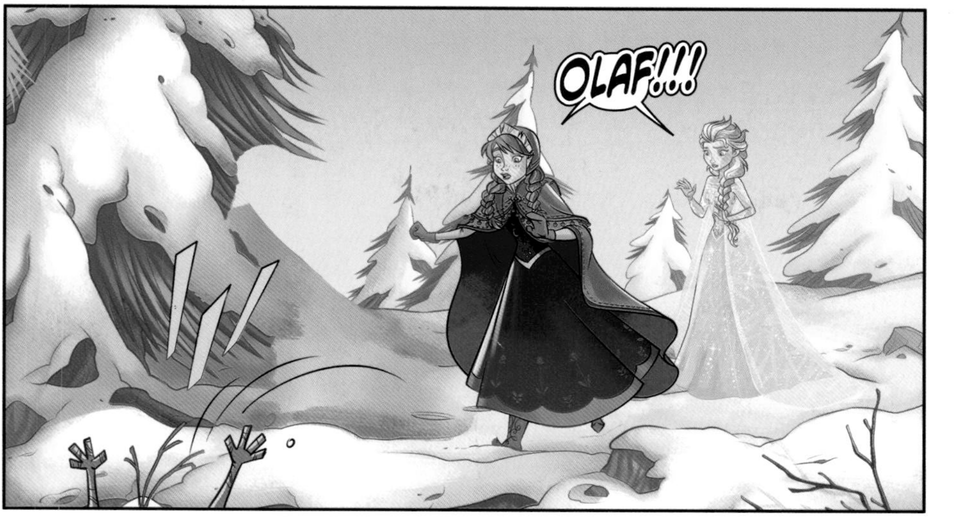
OLAF!!!

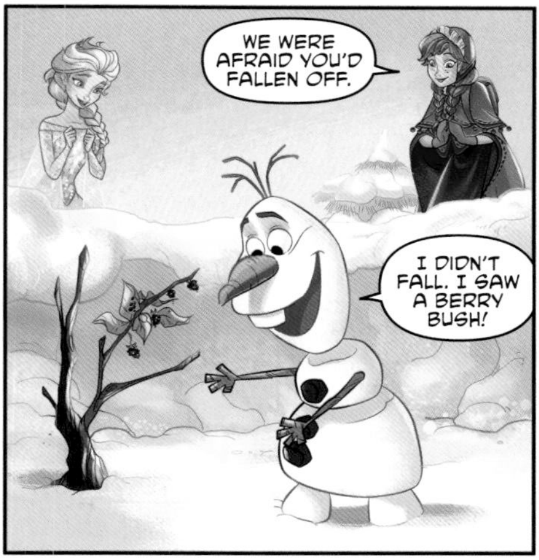
WE WERE AFRAID YOU'D FALLEN OFF.
I DIDN'T FALL. I SAW A BERRY BUSH!

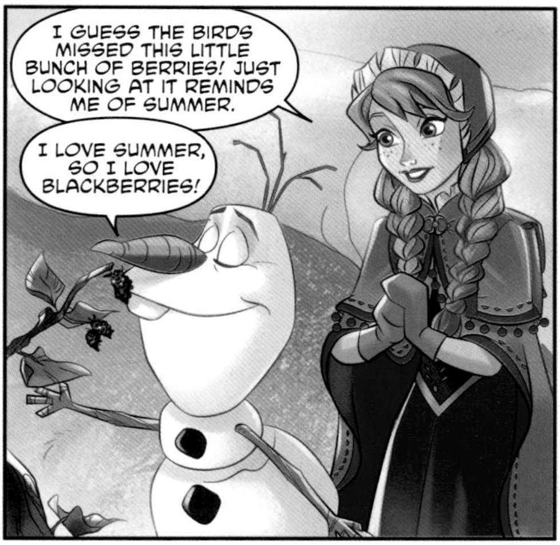
I GUESS THE BIRDS MISSED THIS LITTLE BUNCH OF BERRIES! JUST LOOKING AT IT REMINDS ME OF SUMMER.
I LOVE SUMMER, SO I LOVE BLACKBERRIES!

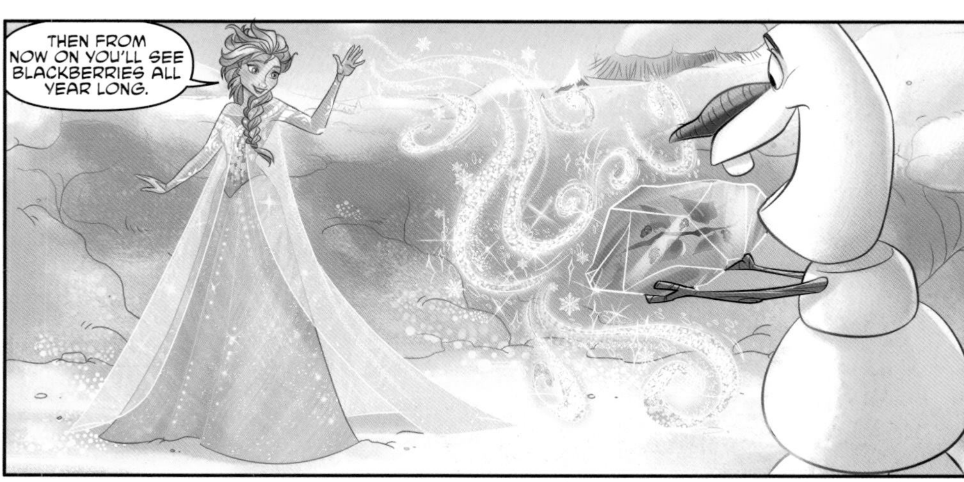
THEN FROM NOW ON YOU'LL SEE BLACKBERRIES ALL YEAR LONG.

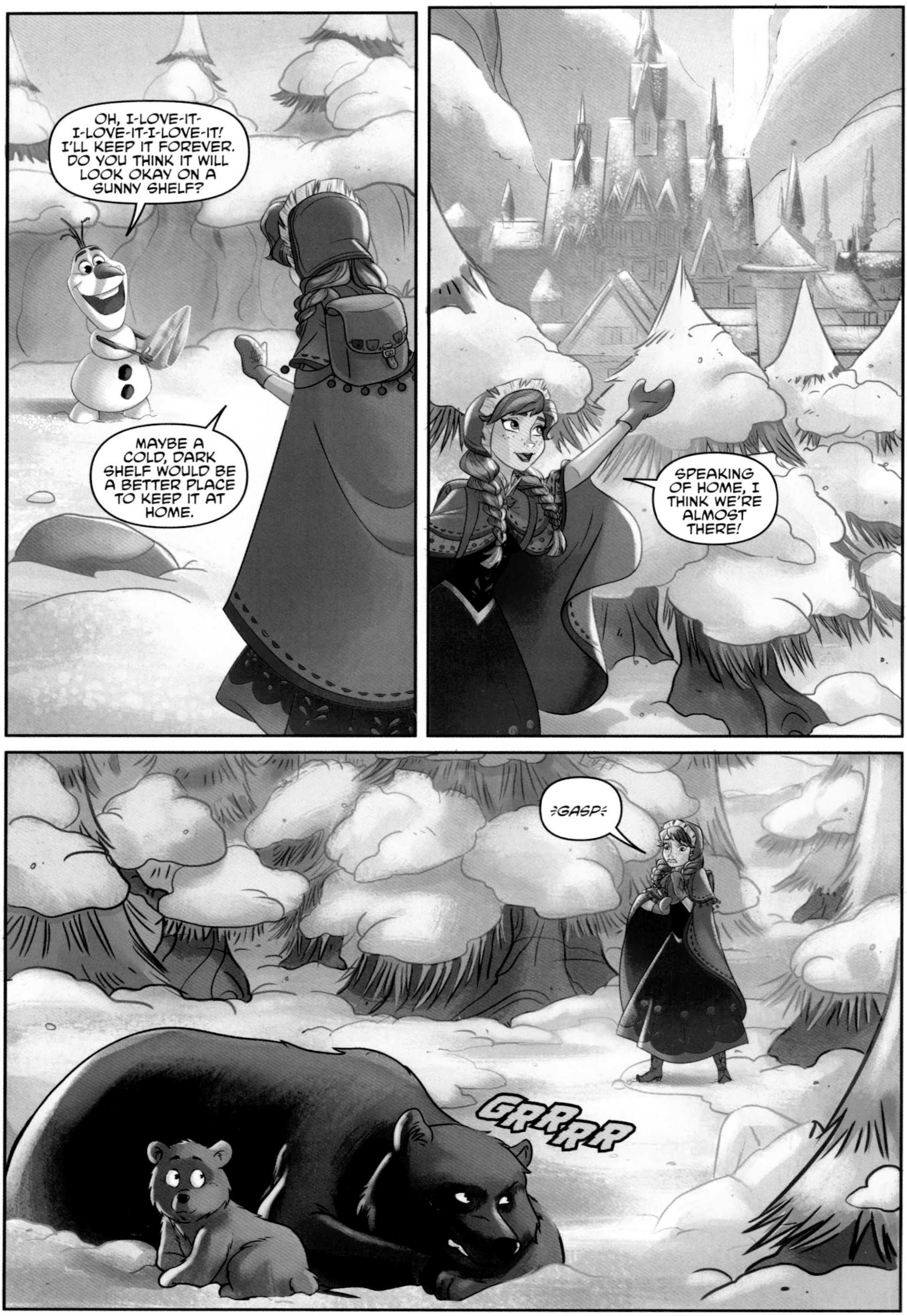
OH, I-LOVE-IT-I-LOVE-IT-I-LOVE-IT! I'LL KEEP IT FOREVER. DO YOU THINK IT WILL LOOK OKAY ON A SUNNY SHELF?
MAYBE A COLD, DARK SHELF WOULD BE A BETTER PLACE TO KEEP IT AT HOME.
SPEAKING OF HOME, I THINK WE'RE ALMOST THERE!
GASP
GRRRR

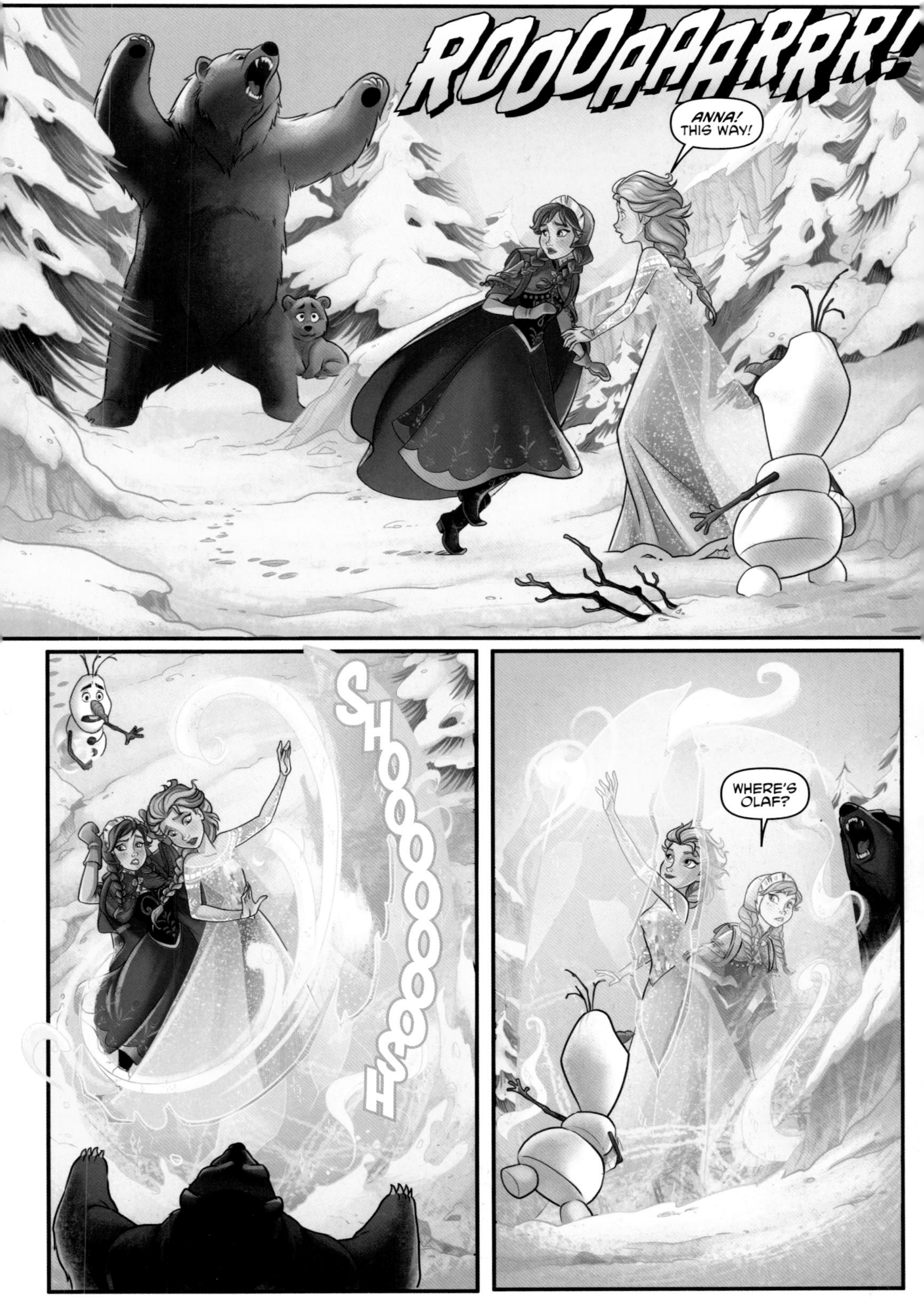
ROOOAAARRRR!
ANNA! THIS WAY!
SHOOOOOOOSH
WHERE'S OLAF?

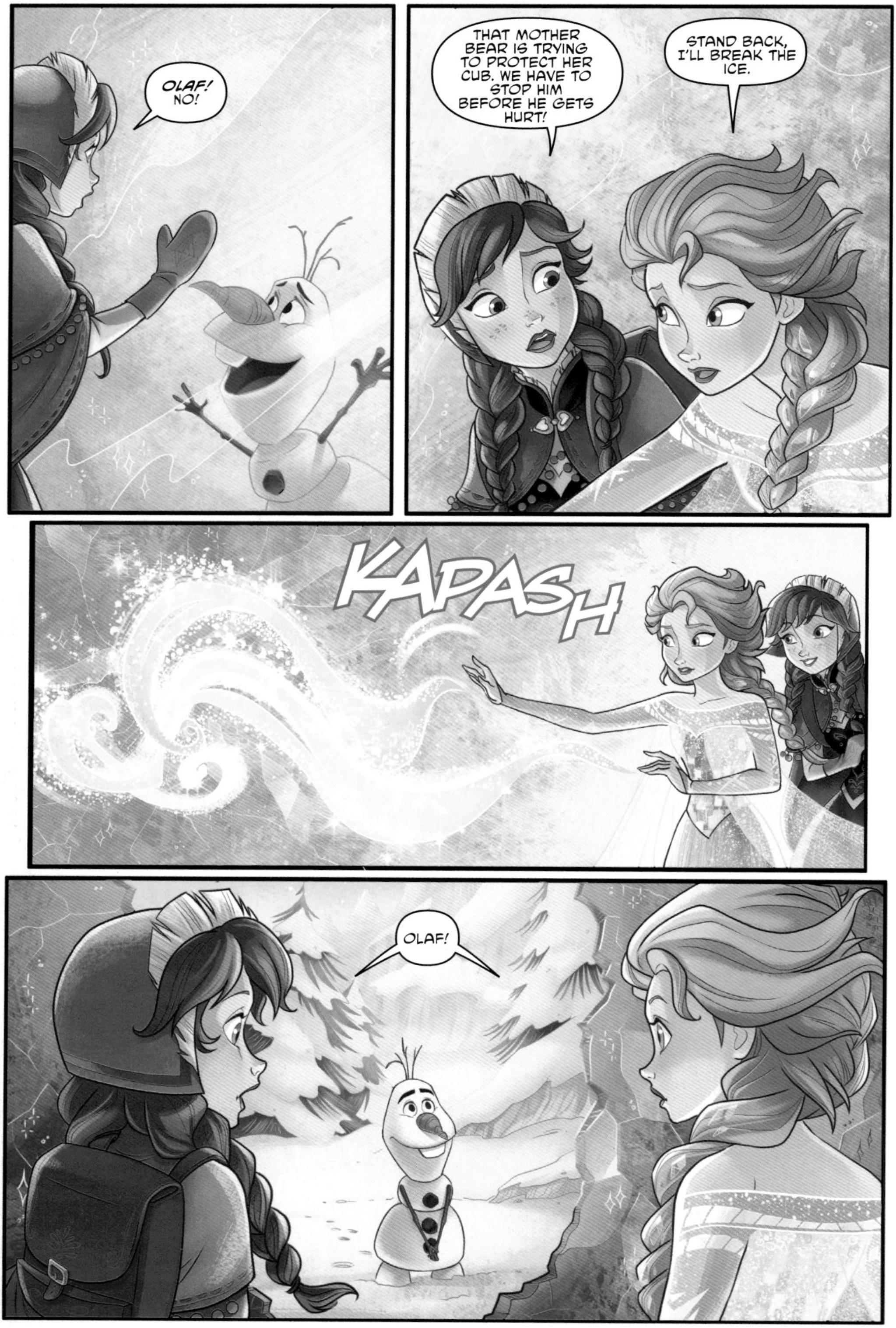
OLAF! NO!
THAT MOTHER BEAR IS TRYING TO PROTECT HER CUB. WE HAVE TO STOP HIM BEFORE HE GETS HURT!
STAND BACK, I'LL BREAK THE ICE.
KAPASH
OLAF!

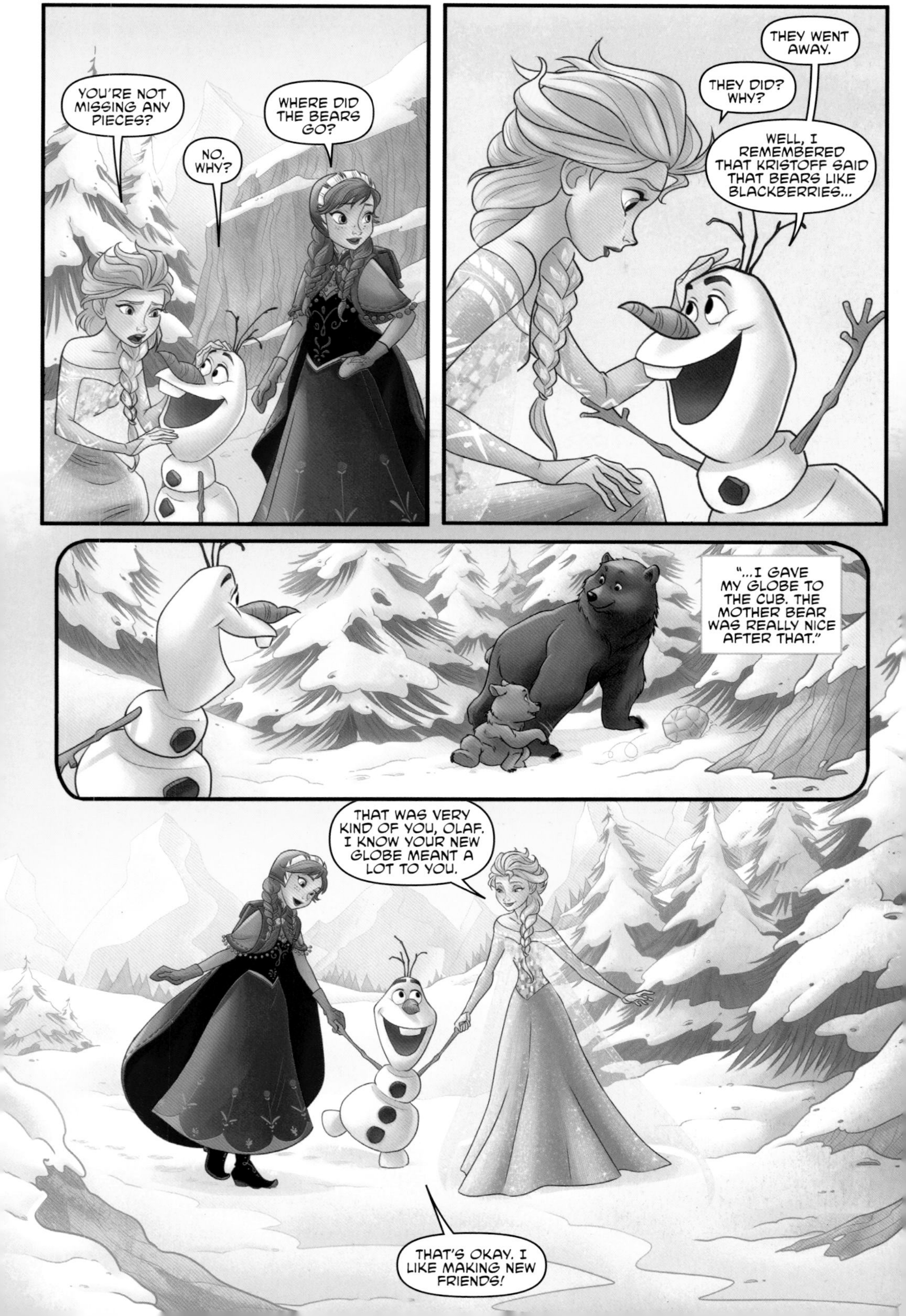
YOU'RE NOT MISSING ANY PIECES?
NO. WHY?
WHERE DID THE BEARS GO?
THEY WENT AWAY.
THEY DID? WHY?
WELL, I REMEMBERED THAT KRISTOFF SAID THAT BEARS LIKE BLACKBERRIES...
"...I GAVE MY GLOBE TO THE CUB. THE MOTHER BEAR WAS REALLY NICE AFTER THAT."
THAT WAS VERY KIND OF YOU, OLAF. I KNOW YOUR NEW GLOBE MEANT A LOT TO YOU.
THAT'S OKAY. I LIKE MAKING NEW FRIENDS!

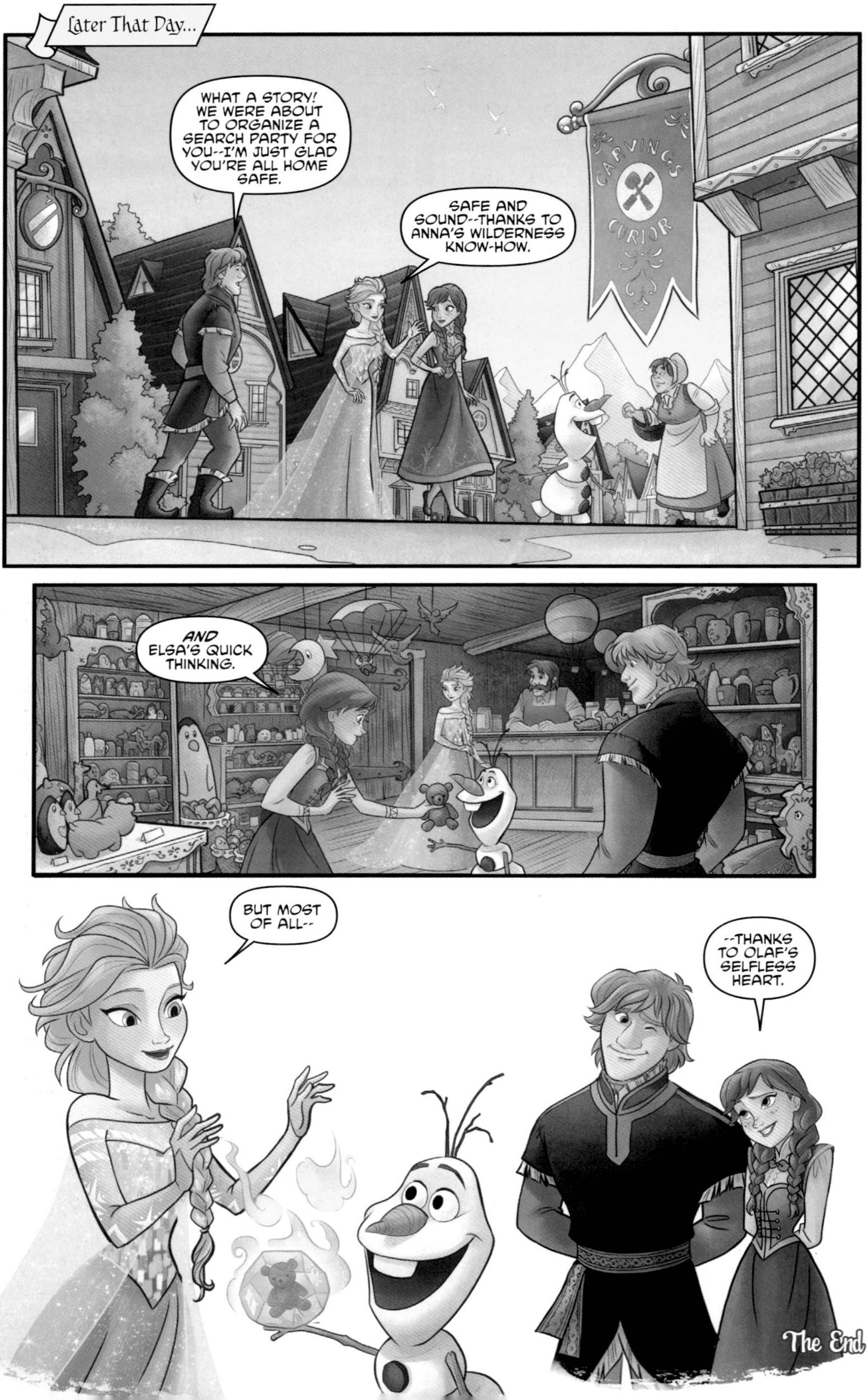
Later That Day...
WHAT A STORY! WE WERE ABOUT TO ORGANIZE A SEARCH PARTY FOR YOU--I'M JUST GLAD YOU'RE ALL HOME SAFE.
SAFE AND SOUND--THANKS TO ANNA'S WILDERNESS KNOW-HOW.
CARVINGS CURIOS
AND ELSA'S QUICK THINKING.
BUT MOST OF ALL--
--THANKS TO OLAF'S SELFLESS HEART.
The End

The Shifting Shores of Sankershus

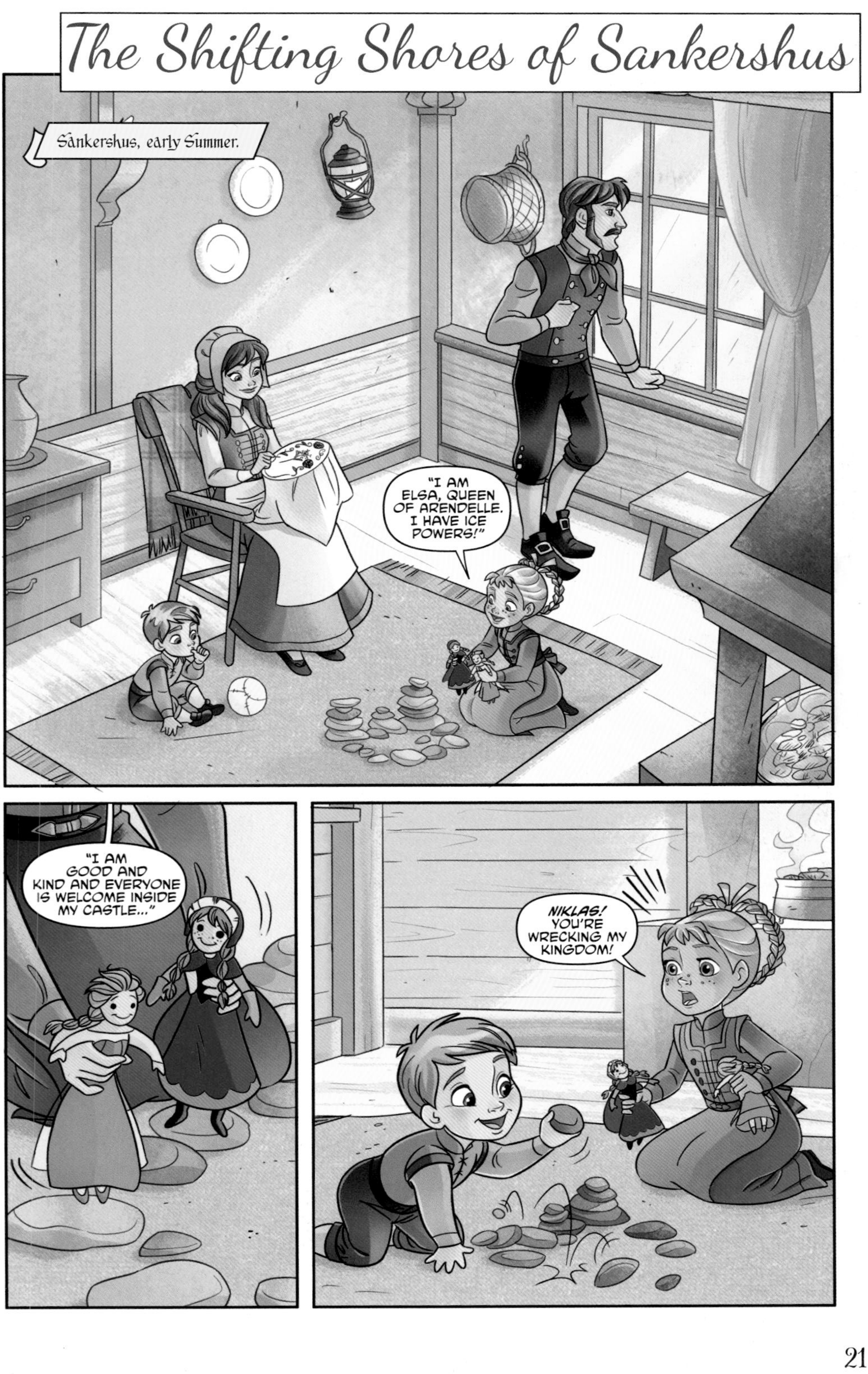

Sankershus, early Summer.
"I AM ELSA, QUEEN OF ARENDELLE. I HAVE ICE POWERS!"
"I AM GOOD AND KIND AND EVERYONE IS WELCOME INSIDE MY CASTLE..."
NIKLAS! YOU'RE WRECKING MY KINGDOM!

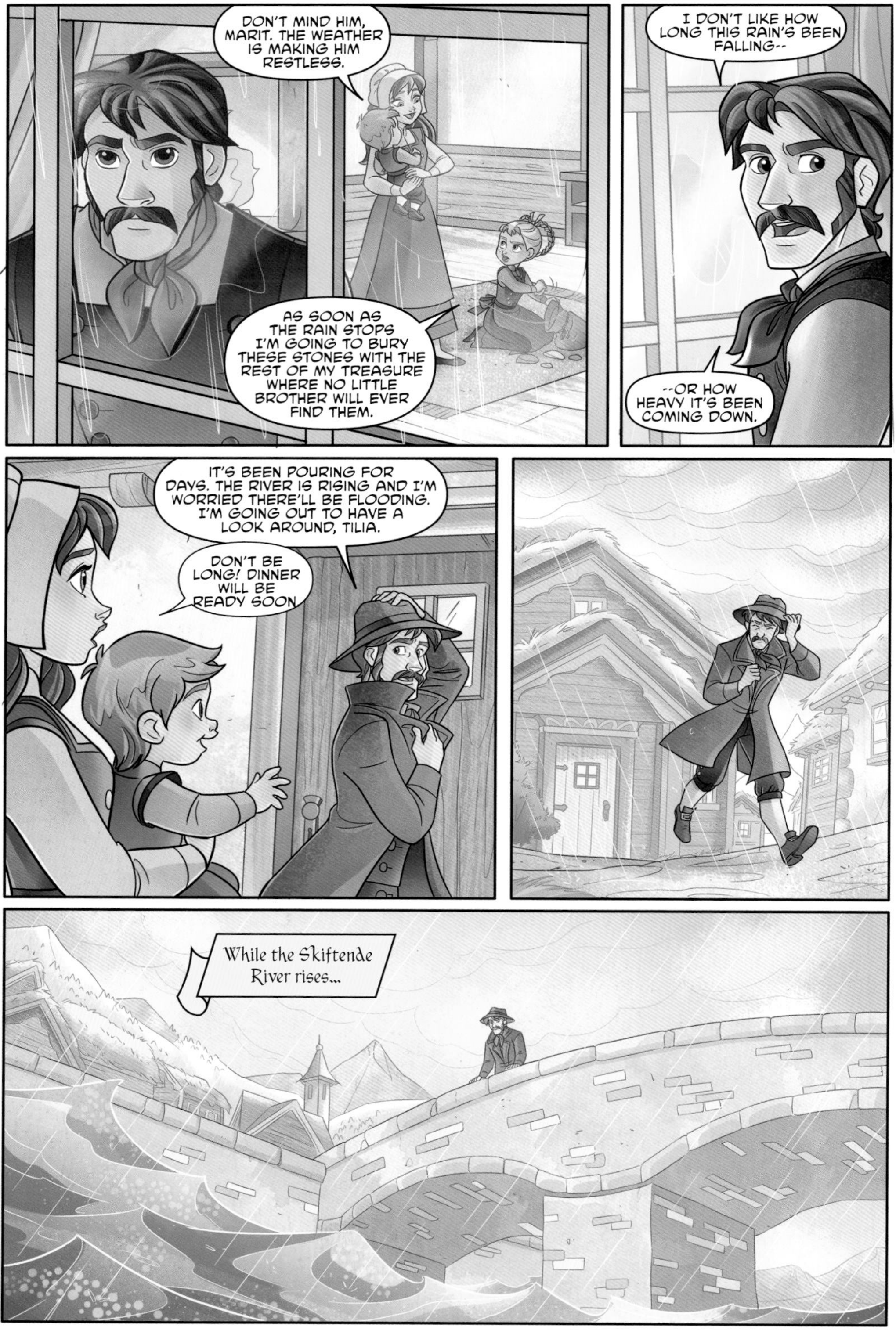
DON'T MIND HIM, MARIT. THE WEATHER IS MAKING HIM RESTLESS.
AS SOON AS THE RAIN STOPS I'M GOING TO BURY THESE STONES WITH THE REST OF MY TREASURE WHERE NO LITTLE BROTHER WILL EVER FIND THEM.
I DON'T LIKE HOW LONG THIS RAIN'S BEEN FALLING--
--OR HOW HEAVY IT'S BEEN COMING DOWN.
IT'S BEEN POURING FOR DAYS. THE RIVER IS RISING AND I'M WORRIED THERE'LL BE FLOODING. I'M GOING OUT TO HAVE A LOOK AROUND, TILIA.
DON'T BE LONG! DINNER WILL BE READY SOON
While the Skiftende River rises...

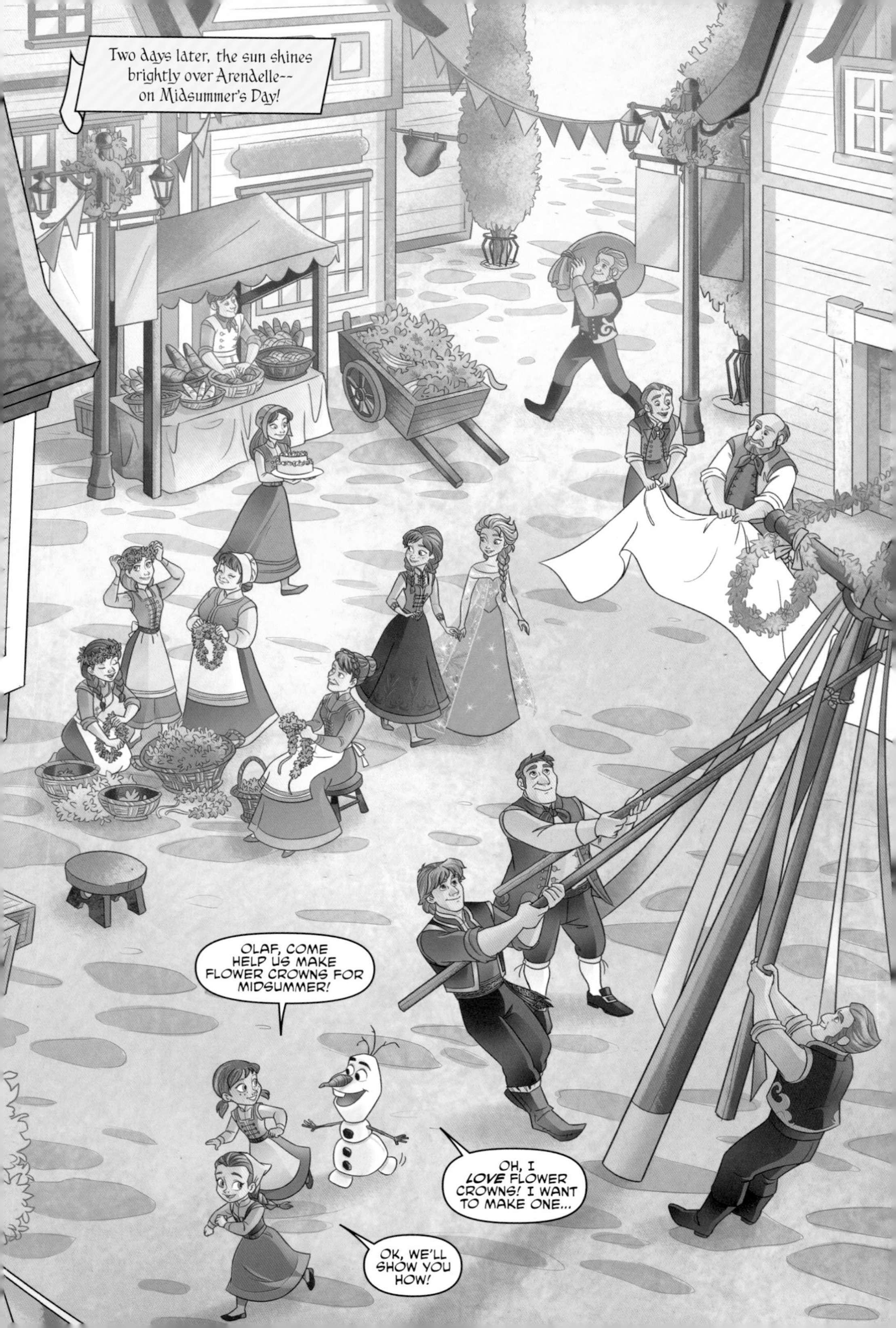
Two days later, the sun shines brightly over Arendelle-- on Midsummer's Day!
OLAF, COME HELP US MAKE FLOWER CROWNS FOR MIDSUMMER!
OH, I *LOVE* FLOWER CROWNS! I WANT TO MAKE ONE...
OK, WE'LL SHOW YOU HOW!

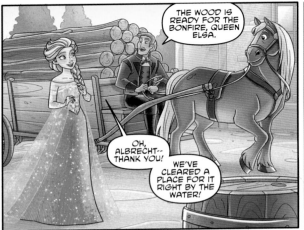

THE WOOD IS READY FOR THE BONFIRE, QUEEN ELSA.

OH, ALBRECHT-- THANK YOU! WE'VE CLEARED A PLACE FOR IT RIGHT BY THE WATER!

WHAT DO YOU THINK OF THE WREATHS THIS YEAR, PRINCESS ANNA?

GORGEOUS! ARE THOSE HYACINTHS, ELKE?

MMM-HMM...

ELSA! ANNA! CAN YOU COME TO THE DOCK?

WHAT IS IT, KRISTOFF?

I JUST THOUGHT YOU MIGHT LIKE TO SEE THE BOATS!

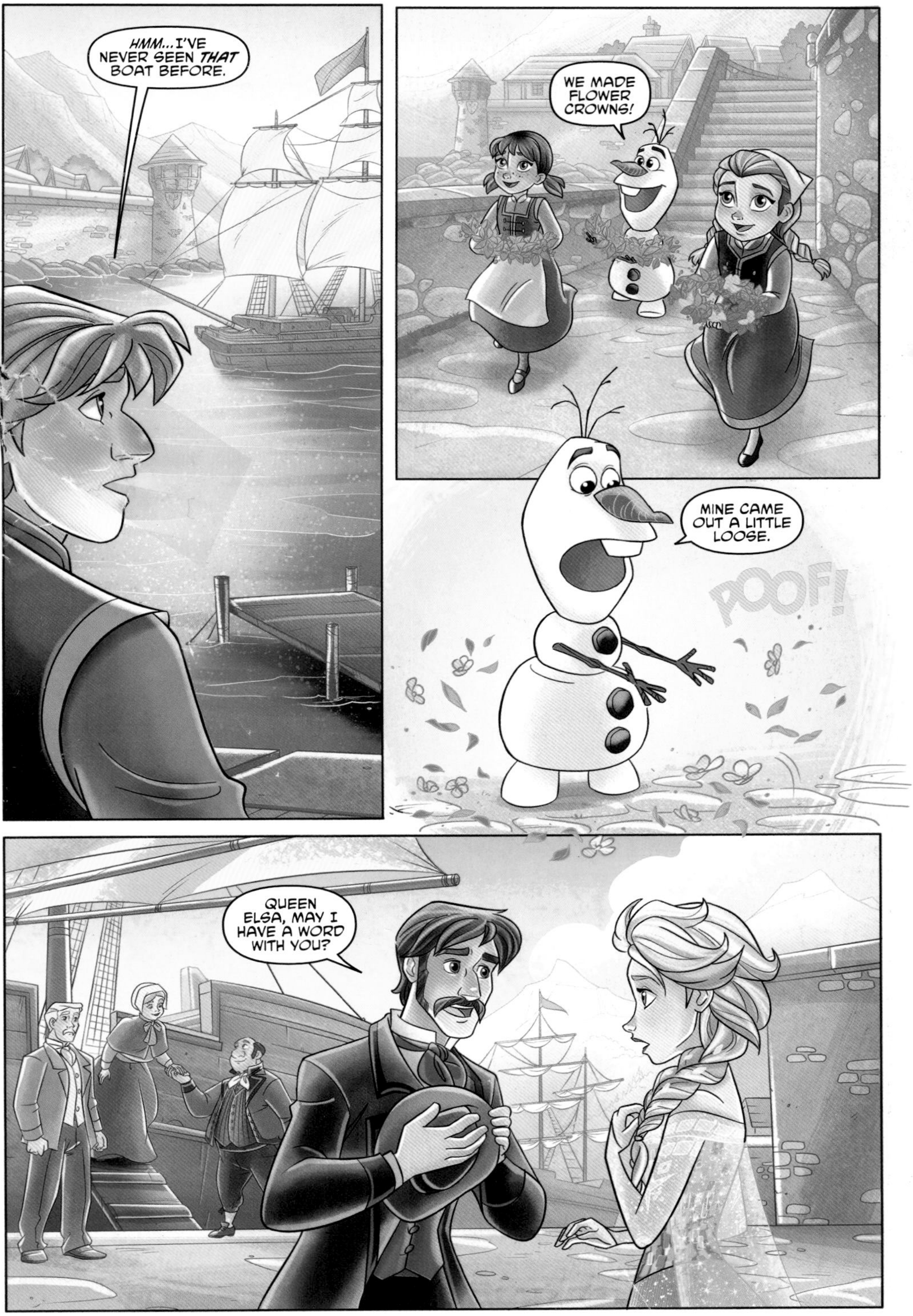
HMM...I'VE NEVER SEEN *THAT* BOAT BEFORE.
WE MADE FLOWER CROWNS!
MINE CAME OUT A LITTLE LOOSE.
POOF!
QUEEN ELSA, MAY I HAVE A WORD WITH YOU?

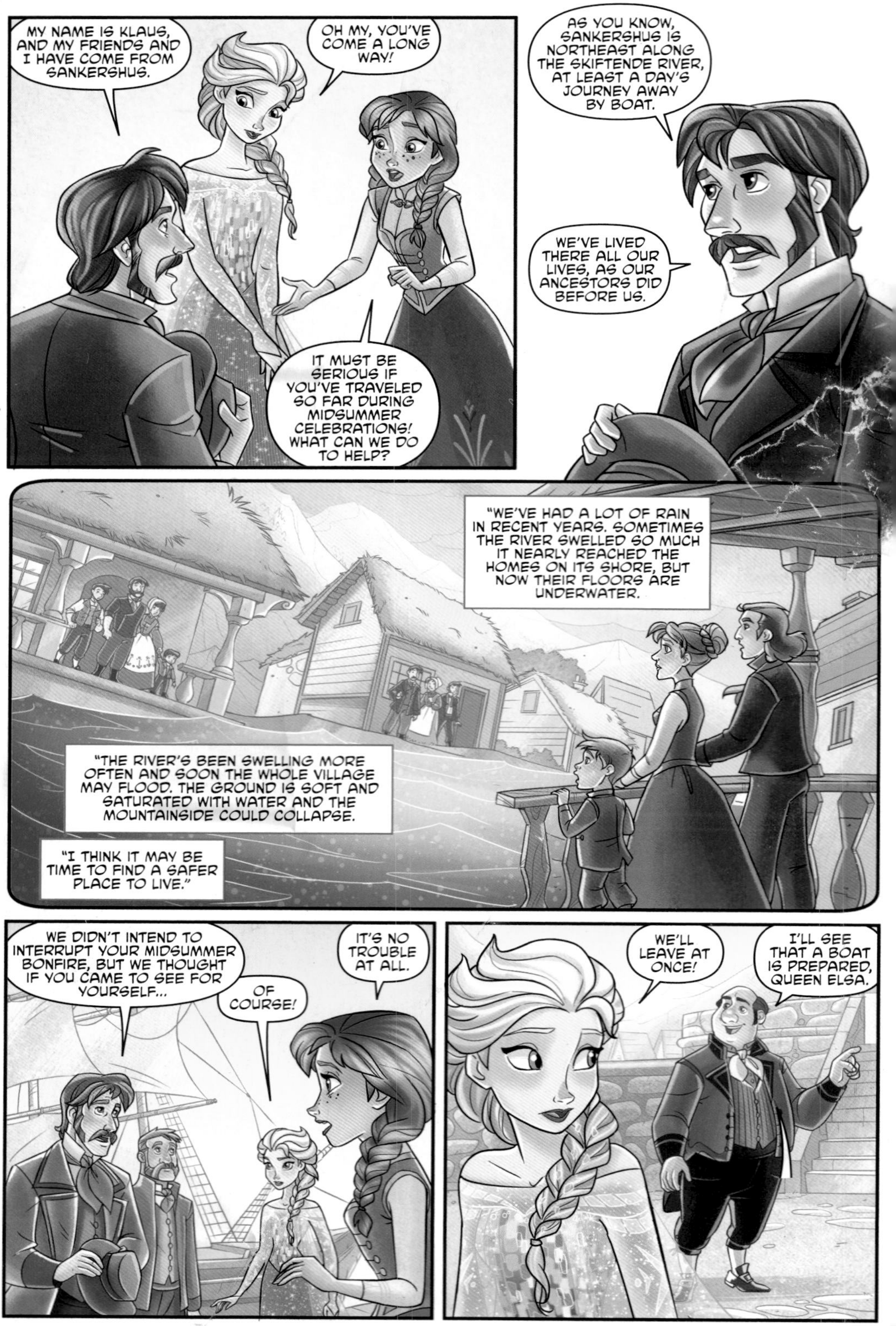
MY NAME IS KLAUS, AND MY FRIENDS AND I HAVE COME FROM SANKERSHUS.
OH MY, YOU'VE COME A LONG WAY!
IT MUST BE SERIOUS IF YOU'VE TRAVELED SO FAR DURING MIDSUMMER CELEBRATIONS! WHAT CAN WE DO TO HELP?
AS YOU KNOW, SANKERSHUS IS NORTHEAST ALONG THE SKIFTENDE RIVER, AT LEAST A DAY'S JOURNEY AWAY BY BOAT.
WE'VE LIVED THERE ALL OUR LIVES, AS OUR ANCESTORS DID BEFORE US.
"WE'VE HAD A LOT OF RAIN IN RECENT YEARS. SOMETIMES THE RIVER SWELLED SO MUCH IT NEARLY REACHED THE HOMES ON ITS SHORE, BUT NOW THEIR FLOORS ARE UNDERWATER.
"THE RIVER'S BEEN SWELLING MORE OFTEN AND SOON THE WHOLE VILLAGE MAY FLOOD. THE GROUND IS SOFT AND SATURATED WITH WATER AND THE MOUNTAINSIDE COULD COLLAPSE.
"I THINK IT MAY BE TIME TO FIND A SAFER PLACE TO LIVE."
WE DIDN'T INTEND TO INTERRUPT YOUR MIDSUMMER BONFIRE, BUT WE THOUGHT IF YOU CAME TO SEE FOR YOURSELF...
OF COURSE!
IT'S NO TROUBLE AT ALL.
WE'LL LEAVE AT ONCE!
I'LL SEE THAT A BOAT IS PREPARED, QUEEN ELSA.

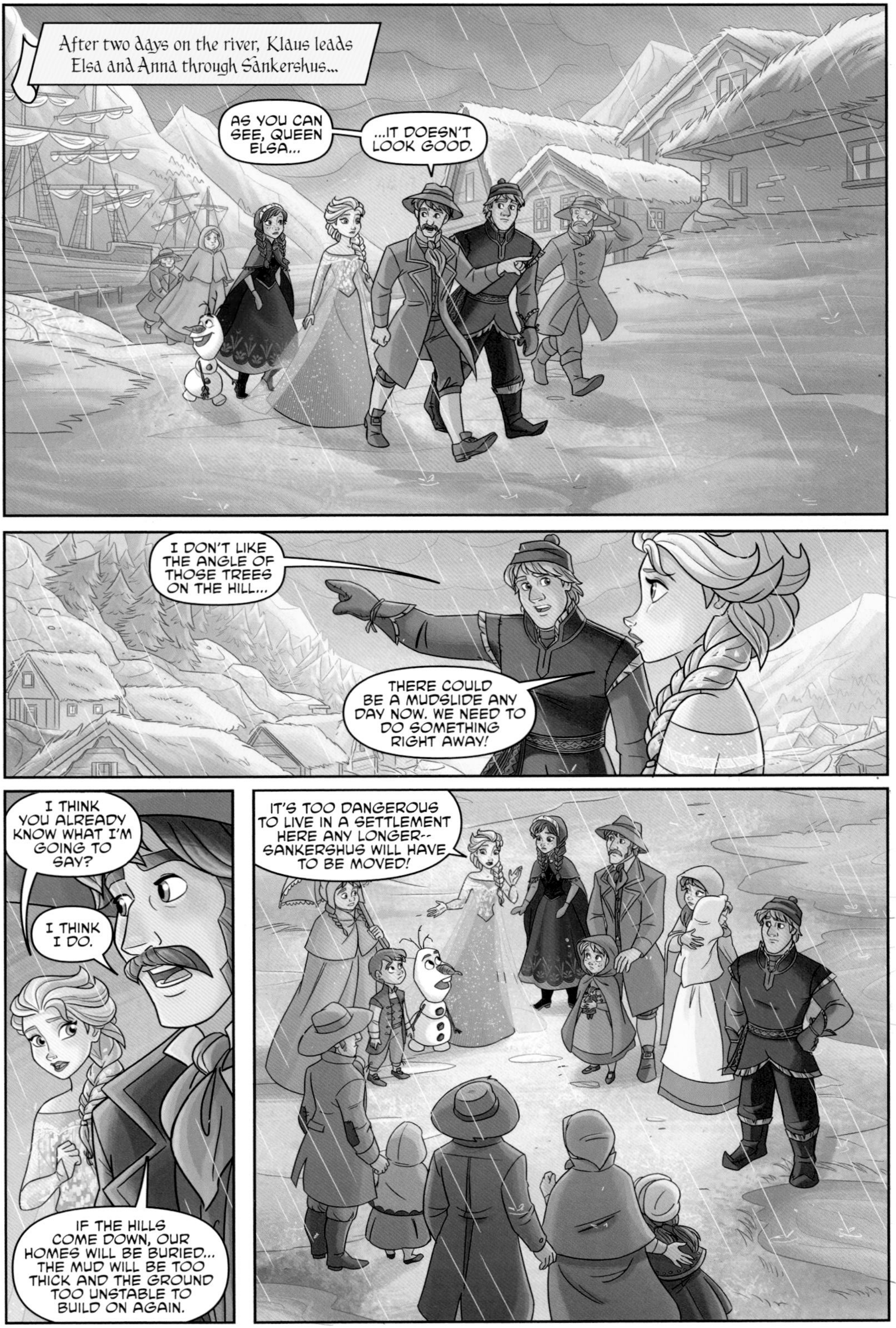
After two days on the river, Klaus leads Elsa and Anna through Sankershus...
AS YOU CAN SEE, QUEEN ELSA...
...IT DOESN'T LOOK GOOD.
I DON'T LIKE THE ANGLE OF THOSE TREES ON THE HILL...
THERE COULD BE A MUDSLIDE ANY DAY NOW. WE NEED TO DO SOMETHING RIGHT AWAY!
I THINK YOU ALREADY KNOW WHAT I'M GOING TO SAY?
I THINK I DO.
IF THE HILLS COME DOWN, OUR HOMES WILL BE BURIED... THE MUD WILL BE TOO THICK AND THE GROUND TOO UNSTABLE TO BUILD ON AGAIN.
IT'S TOO DANGEROUS TO LIVE IN A SETTLEMENT HERE ANY LONGER-- SANKERSHUS WILL HAVE TO BE MOVED!

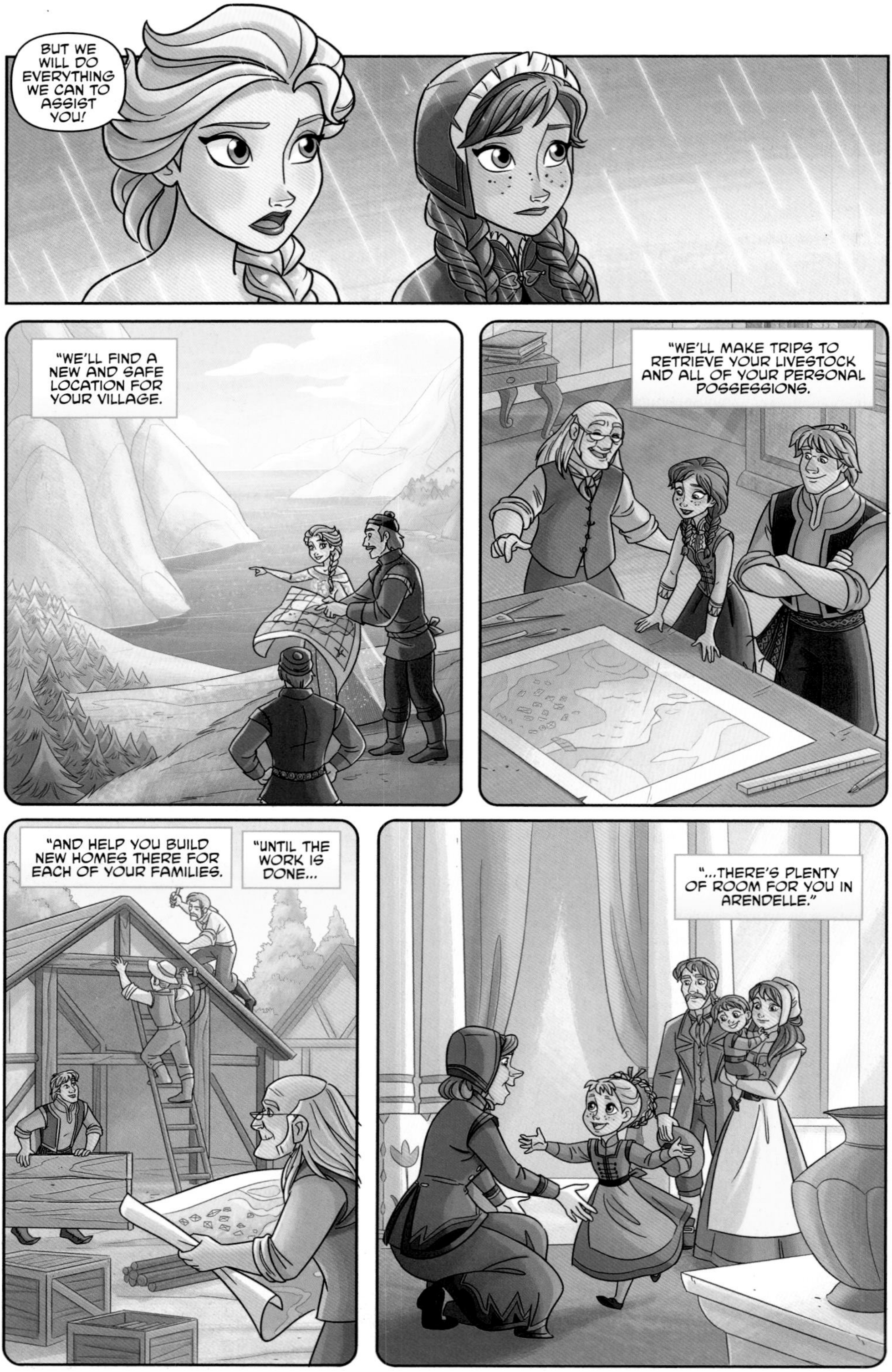
BUT WE WILL DO EVERYTHING WE CAN TO ASSIST YOU!
"WE'LL FIND A NEW AND SAFE LOCATION FOR YOUR VILLAGE.
"WE'LL MAKE TRIPS TO RETRIEVE YOUR LIVESTOCK AND ALL OF YOUR PERSONAL POSSESSIONS.
"AND HELP YOU BUILD NEW HOMES THERE FOR EACH OF YOUR FAMILIES.
"UNTIL THE WORK IS DONE...
"...THERE'S PLENTY OF ROOM FOR YOU IN ARENDELLE."

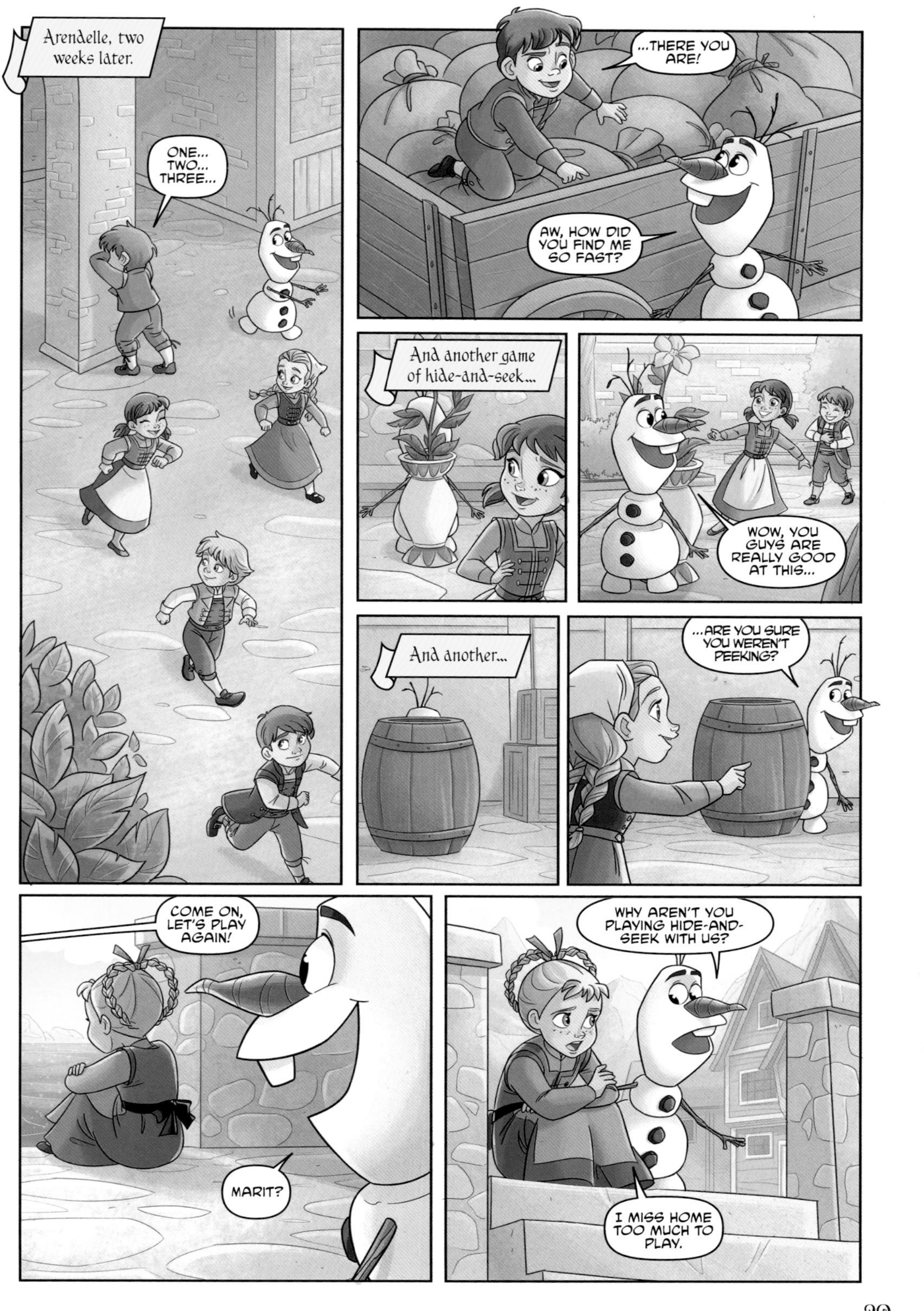

Arendelle, two weeks later.
ONE... TWO... THREE...
...THERE YOU ARE!
AW, HOW DID YOU FIND ME SO FAST?
And another game of hide-and-seek...
WOW, YOU GUYS ARE REALLY GOOD AT THIS...
And another...
...ARE YOU SURE YOU WEREN'T PEEKING?
COME ON, LET'S PLAY AGAIN!
MARIT?
WHY AREN'T YOU PLAYING HIDE-AND-SEEK WITH US?
I MISS HOME TOO MUCH TO PLAY.

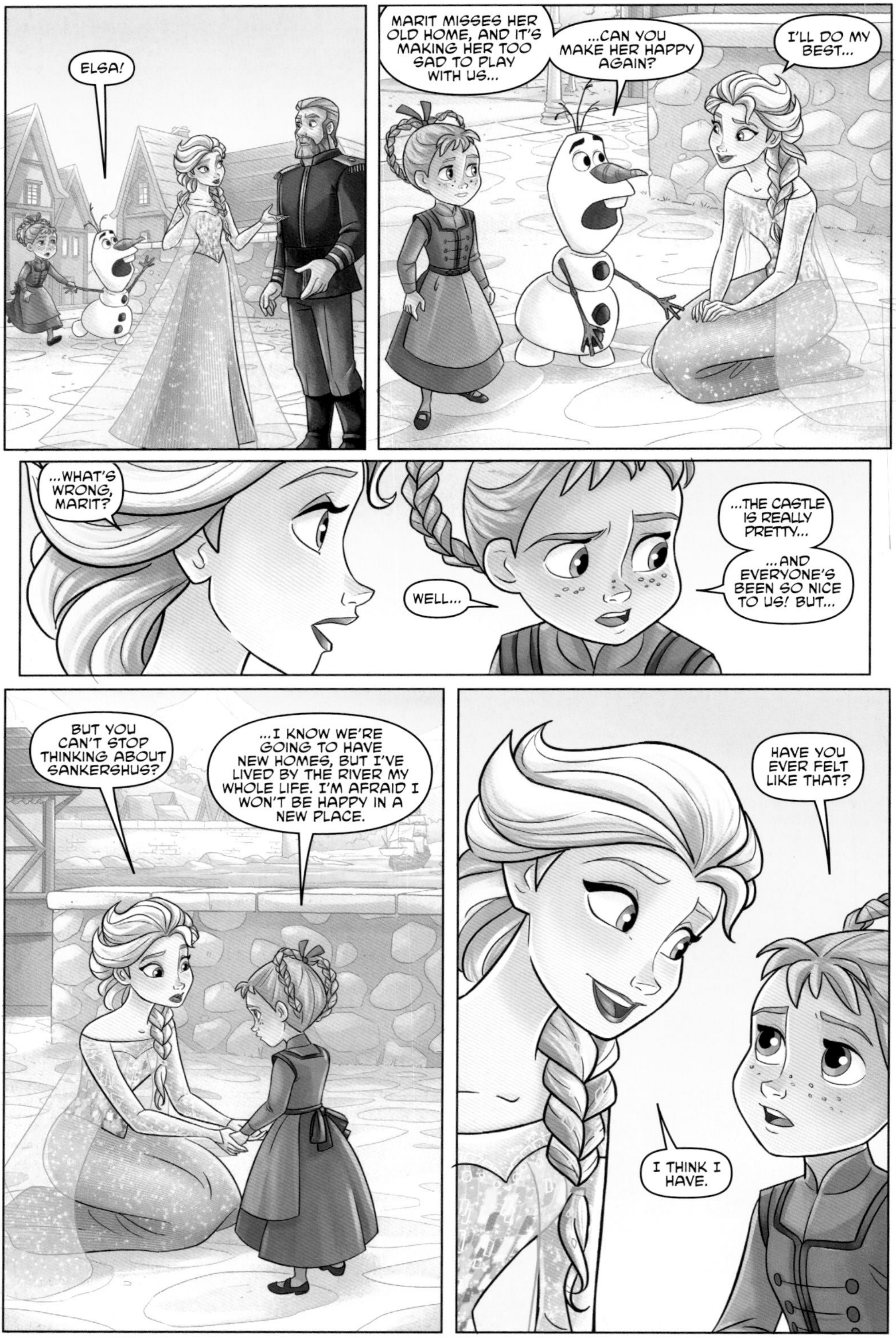
ELSA!
MARIT MISSES HER OLD HOME, AND IT'S MAKING HER TOO SAD TO PLAY WITH US...
...CAN YOU MAKE HER HAPPY AGAIN?
I'LL DO MY BEST...
...WHAT'S WRONG, MARIT?
WELL...
...THE CASTLE IS REALLY PRETTY...
...AND EVERYONE'S BEEN SO NICE TO US! BUT...
BUT YOU CAN'T STOP THINKING ABOUT SANKERSHUS?
...I KNOW WE'RE GOING TO HAVE NEW HOMES, BUT I'VE LIVED BY THE RIVER MY WHOLE LIFE. I'M AFRAID I WON'T BE HAPPY IN A NEW PLACE.
HAVE YOU EVER FELT LIKE THAT?
I THINK I HAVE.

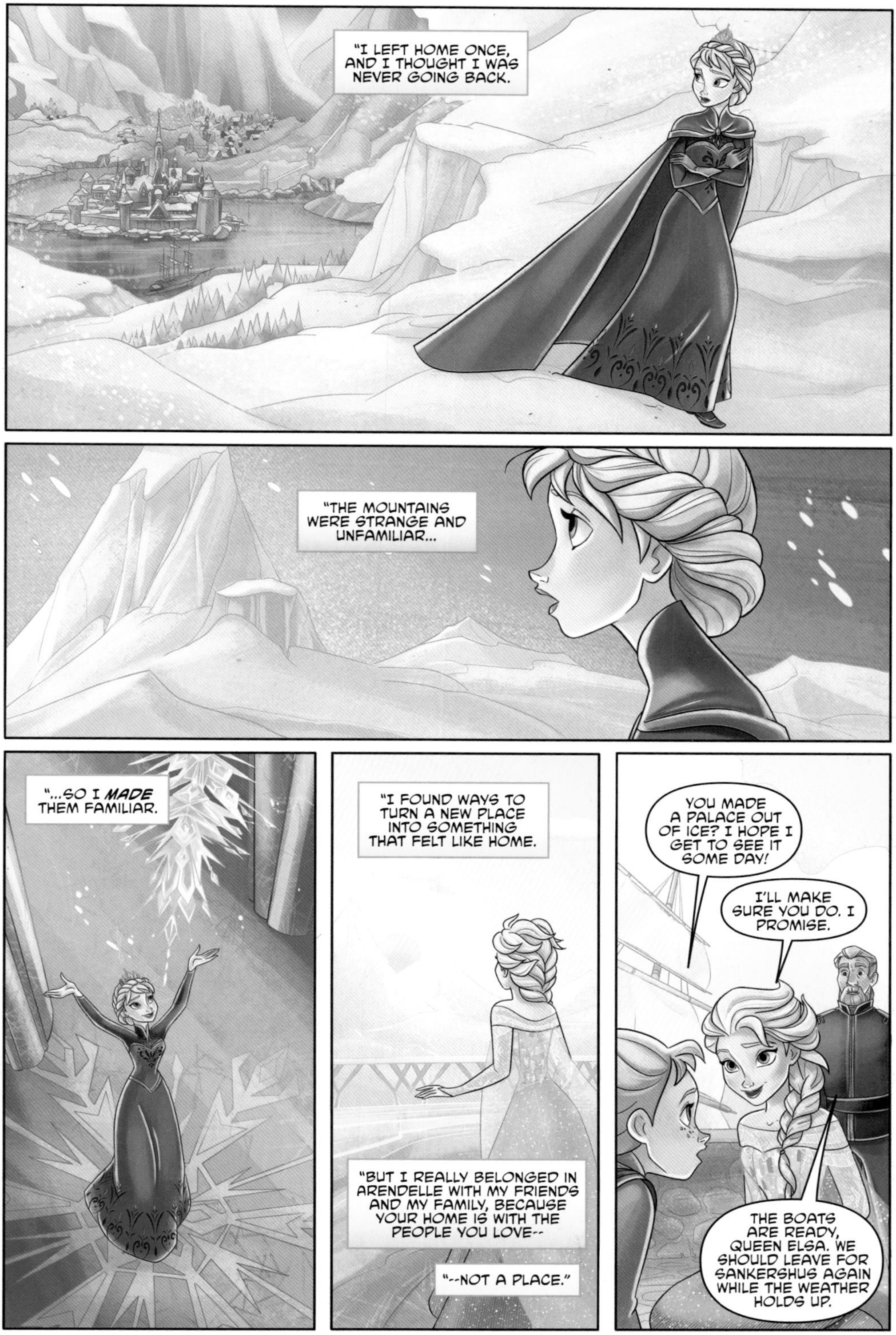
"I LEFT HOME ONCE, AND I THOUGHT I WAS NEVER GOING BACK.
"THE MOUNTAINS WERE STRANGE AND UNFAMILIAR...
"...SO I *MADE* THEM FAMILIAR.
"I FOUND WAYS TO TURN A NEW PLACE INTO SOMETHING THAT FELT LIKE HOME.
"BUT I REALLY BELONGED IN ARENDELLE WITH MY FRIENDS AND MY FAMILY, BECAUSE YOUR HOME IS WITH THE PEOPLE YOU LOVE--
"--NOT A PLACE."
YOU MADE A PALACE OUT OF ICE? I HOPE I GET TO SEE IT SOME DAY!
I'LL MAKE SURE YOU DO. I PROMISE.
THE BOATS ARE READY, QUEEN ELSA. WE SHOULD LEAVE FOR SANKERSHUS AGAIN WHILE THE WEATHER HOLDS UP.

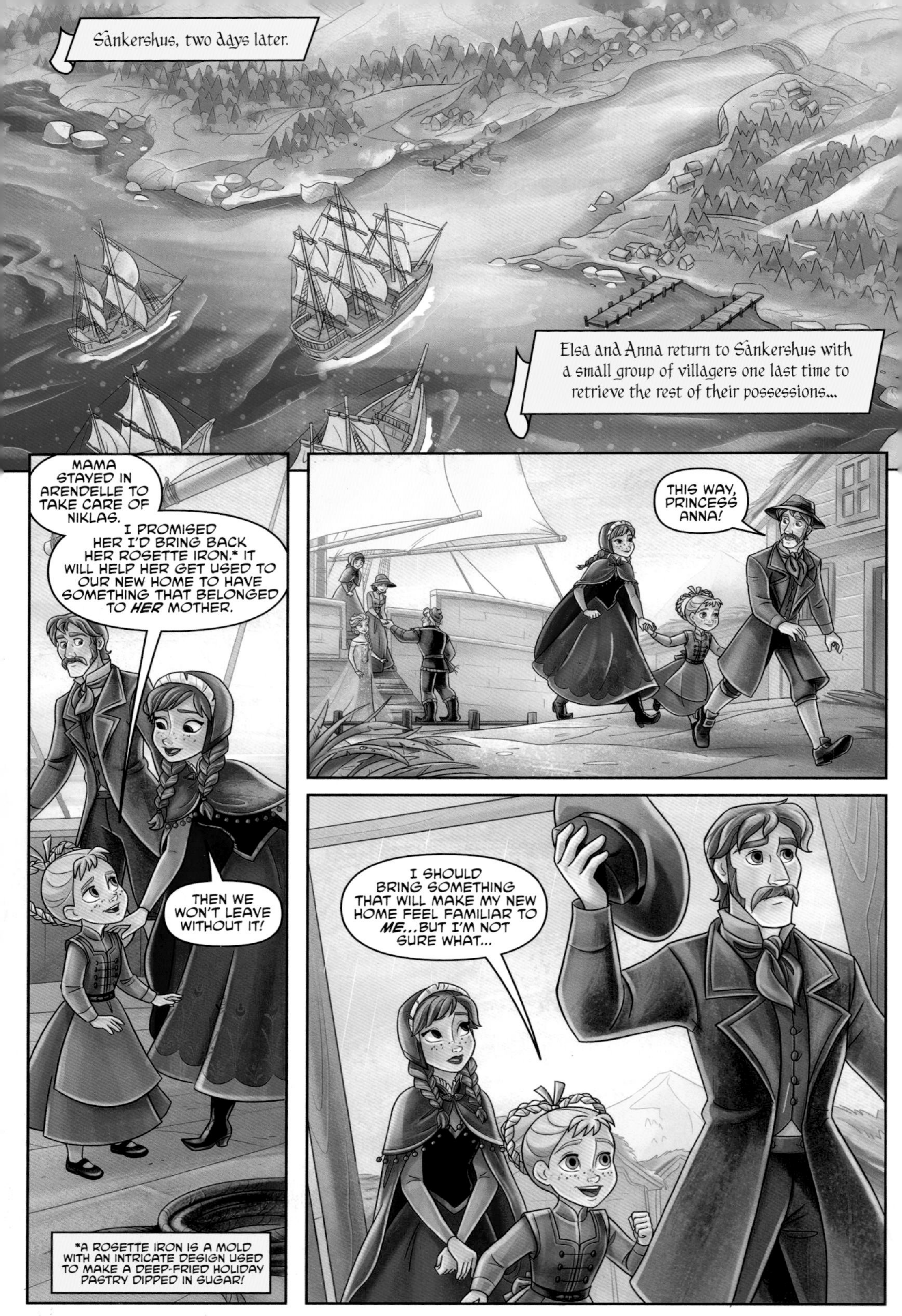
Sânkershus, two days later.
Elsa and Anna return to Sânkershus with a small group of villagers one last time to retrieve the rest of their possessions...
MAMA STAYED IN ARENDELLE TO TAKE CARE OF NIKLAS.
I PROMISED HER I'D BRING BACK HER ROSETTE IRON.* IT WILL HELP HER GET USED TO OUR NEW HOME TO HAVE SOMETHING THAT BELONGED TO *HER* MOTHER.
THEN WE WON'T LEAVE WITHOUT IT!
*A ROSETTE IRON IS A MOLD WITH AN INTRICATE DESIGN USED TO MAKE A DEEP-FRIED HOLIDAY PASTRY DIPPED IN SUGAR!
THIS WAY, PRINCESS ANNA!
I SHOULD BRING SOMETHING THAT WILL MAKE MY NEW HOME FEEL FAMILIAR TO *ME*...BUT I'M NOT SURE WHAT...

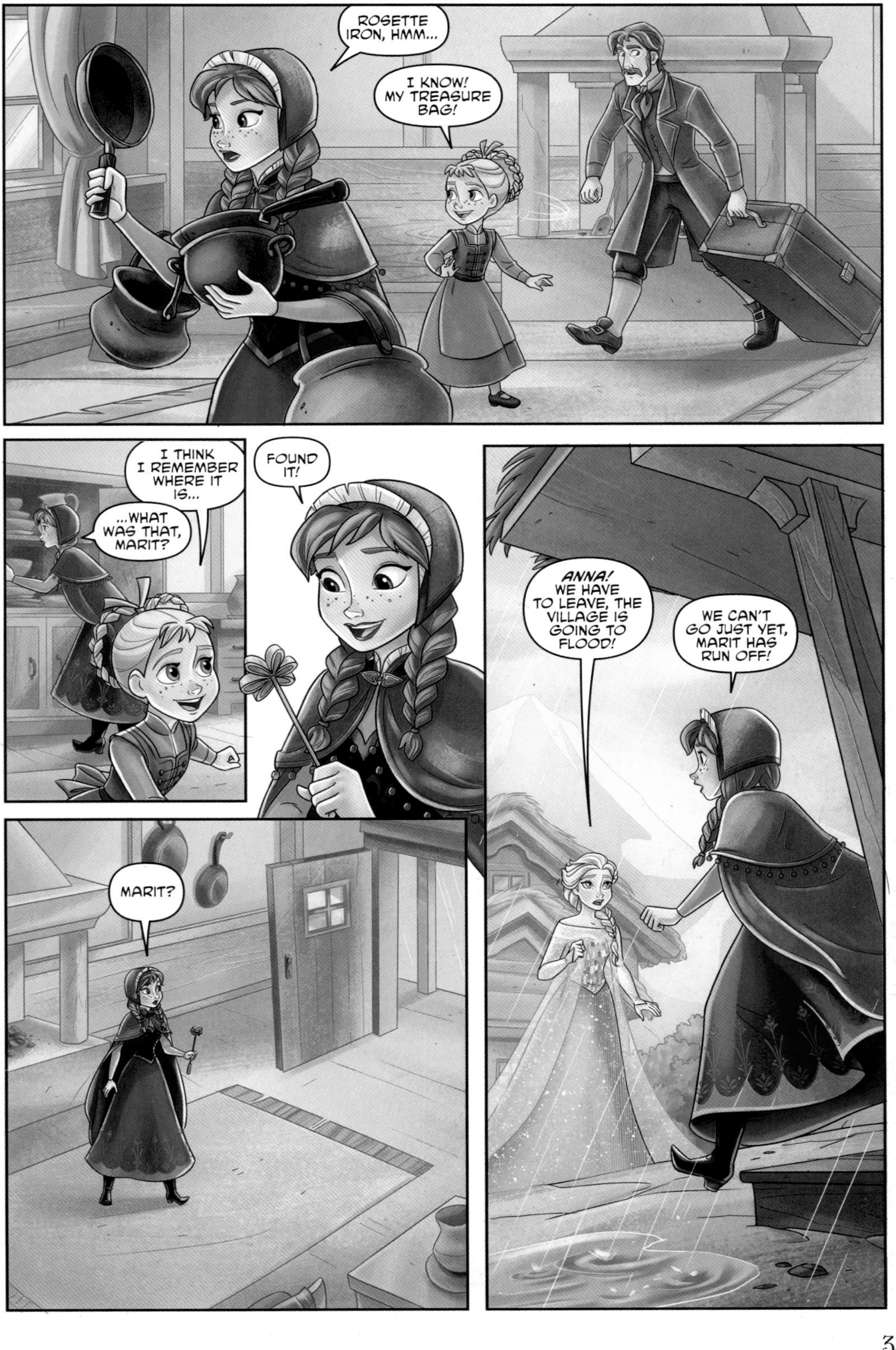
ROSETTE IRON, HMM...
I KNOW! MY TREASURE BAG!
I THINK I REMEMBER WHERE IT IS...
...WHAT WAS THAT, MARIT?
FOUND IT!
MARIT?
ANNA! WE HAVE TO LEAVE, THE VILLAGE IS GOING TO FLOOD!
WE CAN'T GO JUST YET, MARIT HAS RUN OFF!

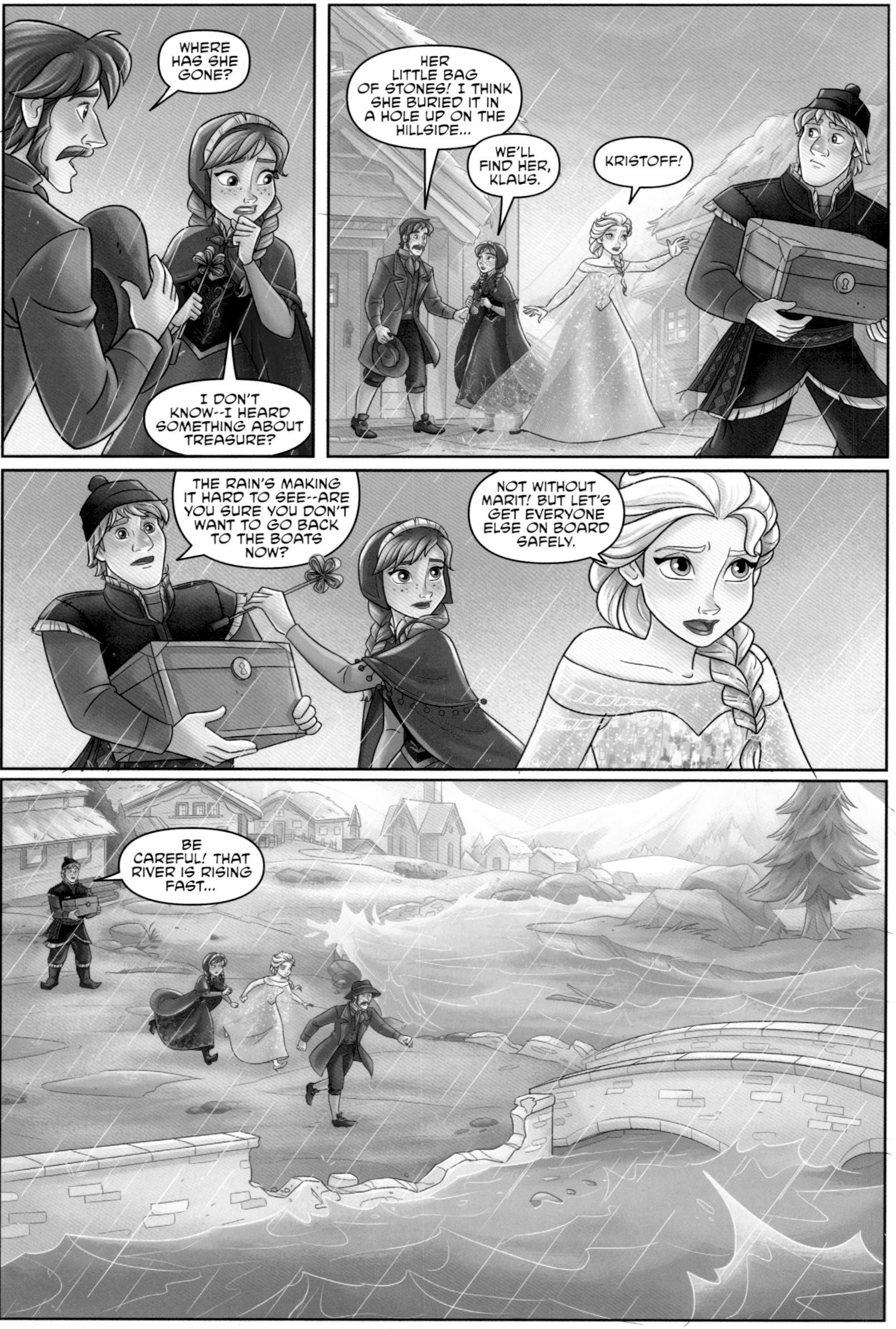
WHERE HAS SHE GONE?
I DON'T KNOW--I HEARD SOMETHING ABOUT TREASURE?
HER LITTLE BAG OF STONES! I THINK SHE BURIED IT IN A HOLE UP ON THE HILLSIDE...
WE'LL FIND HER, KLAUS.
KRISTOFF!
THE RAIN'S MAKING IT HARD TO SEE--ARE YOU SURE YOU DON'T WANT TO GO BACK TO THE BOATS NOW?
NOT WITHOUT MARIT! BUT LET'S GET EVERYONE ELSE ON BOARD SAFELY.
BE CAREFUL! THAT RIVER IS RISING FAST...

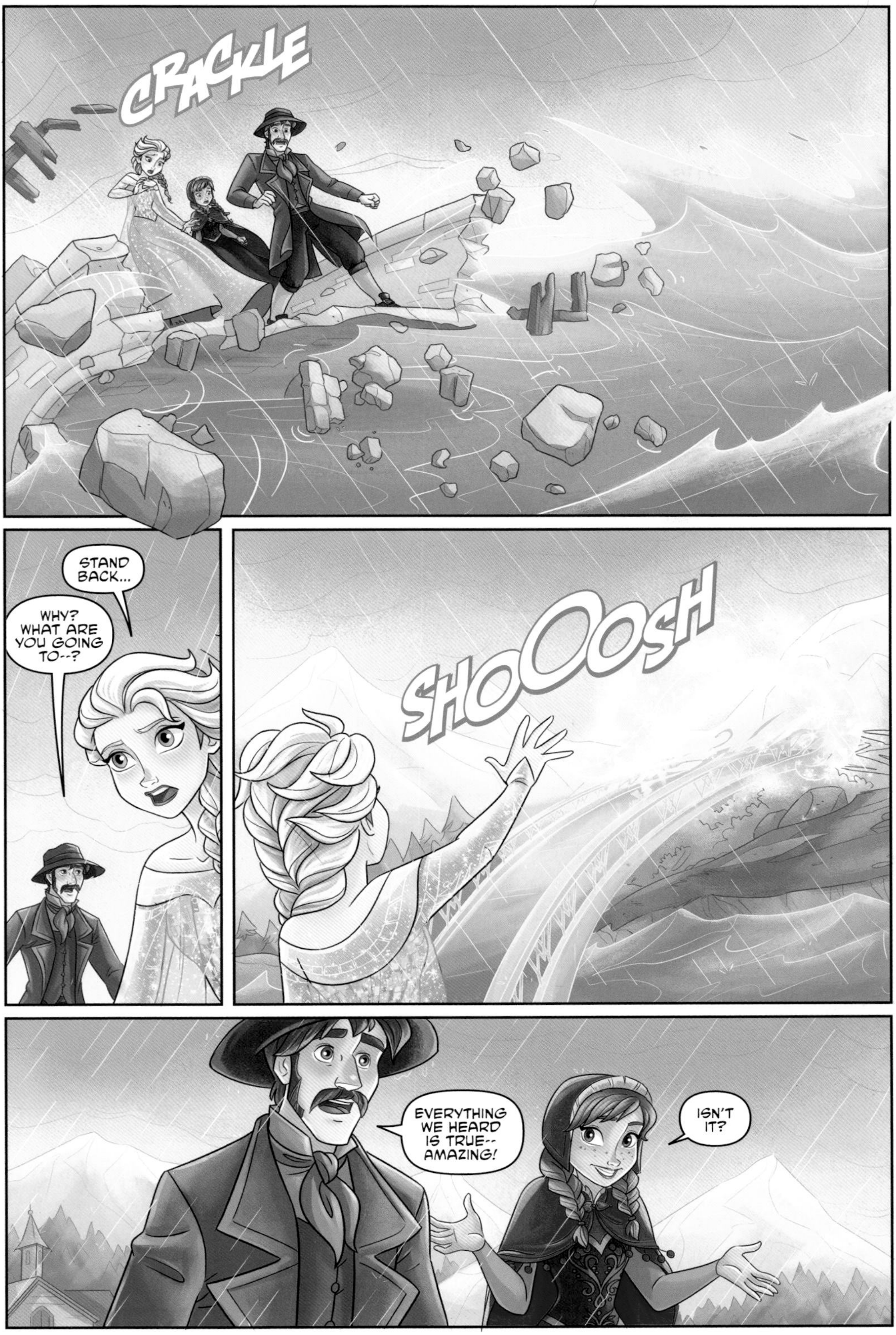
CRACKLE
STAND BACK...
WHY? WHAT ARE YOU GOING TO--?
SHOOOSH
EVERYTHING WE HEARD IS TRUE-- AMAZING!
ISN'T IT?

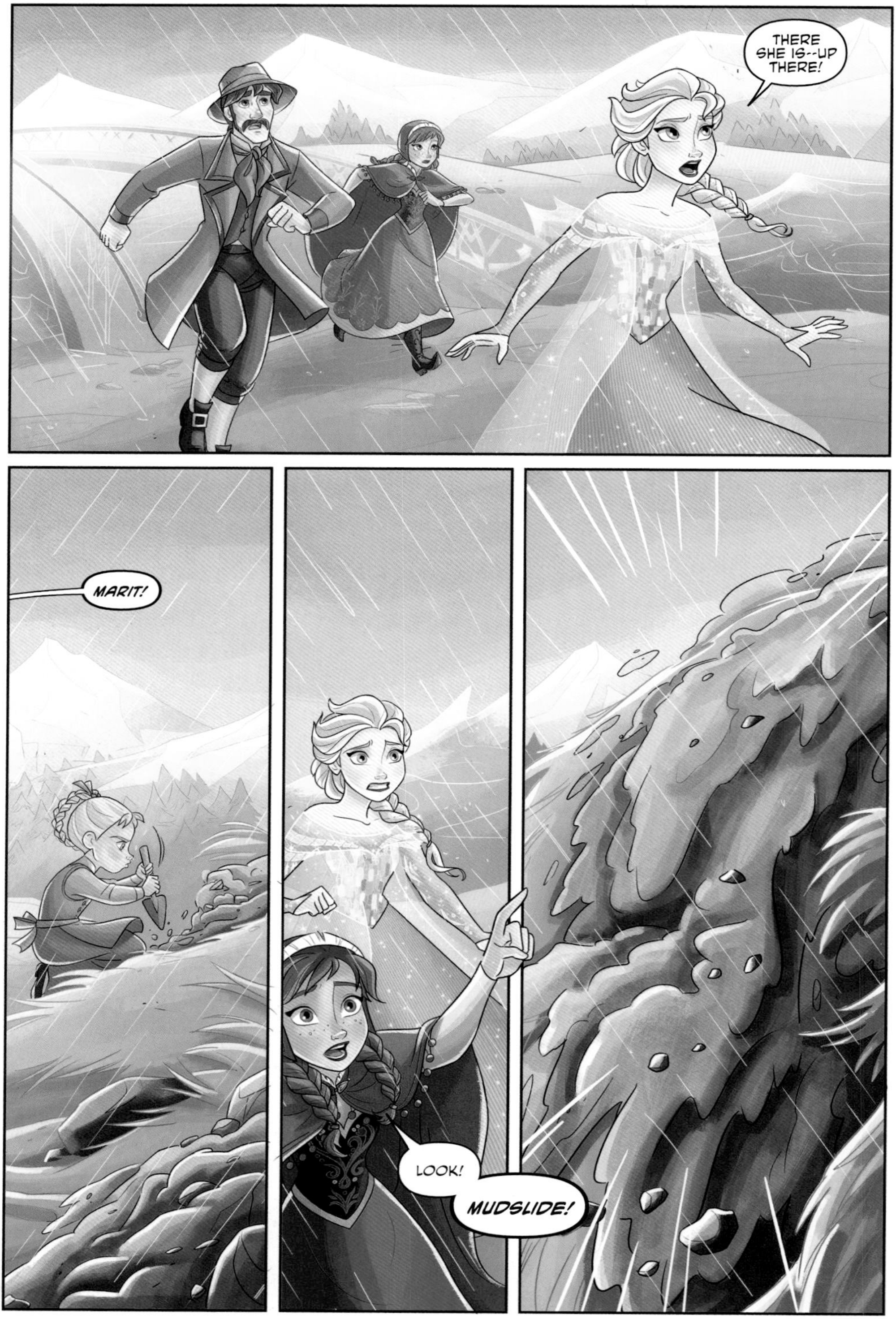
THERE SHE IS--UP THERE!
MARIT!
LOOK!
MUDSLIDE!

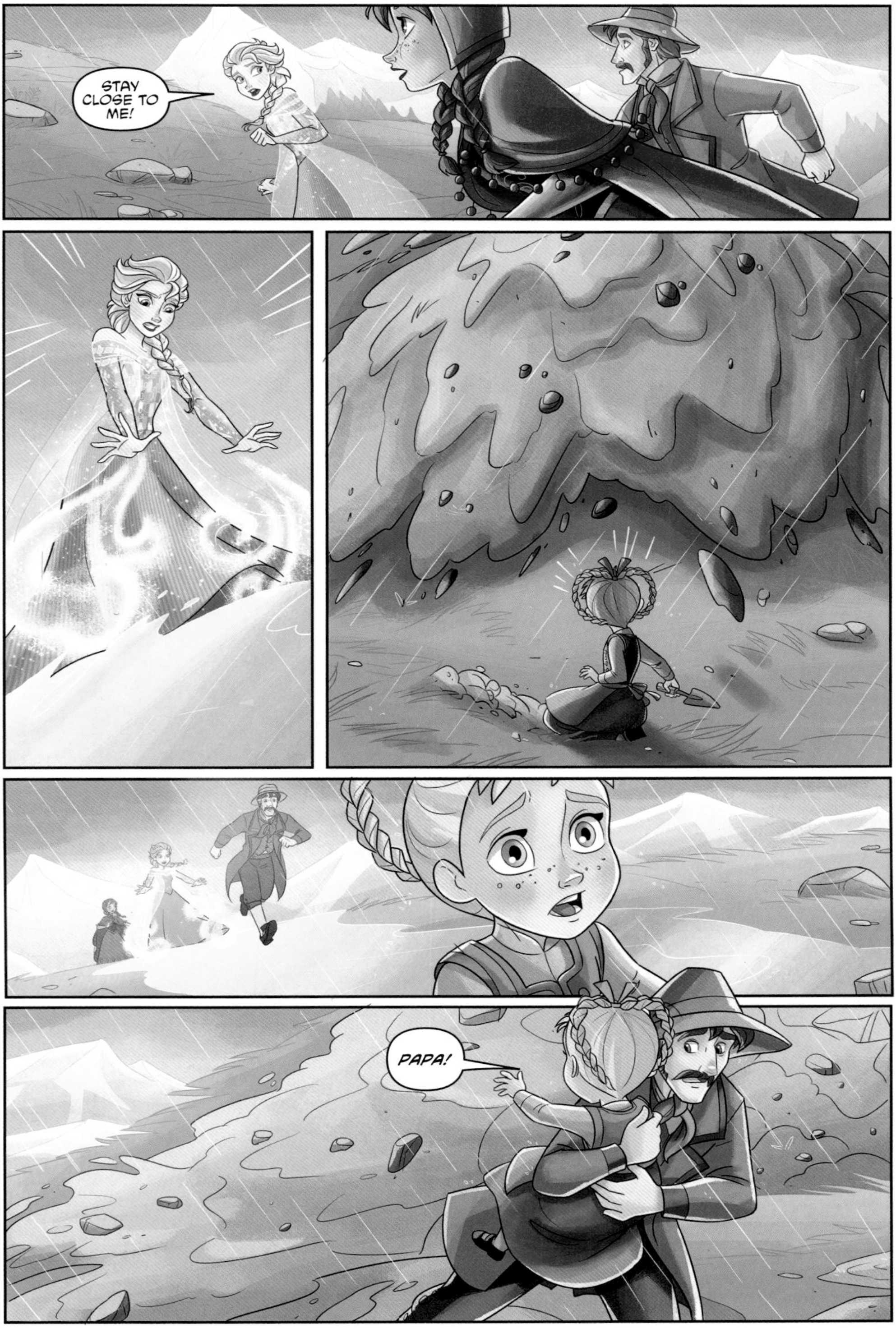
STAY CLOSE TO ME!
PAPA!

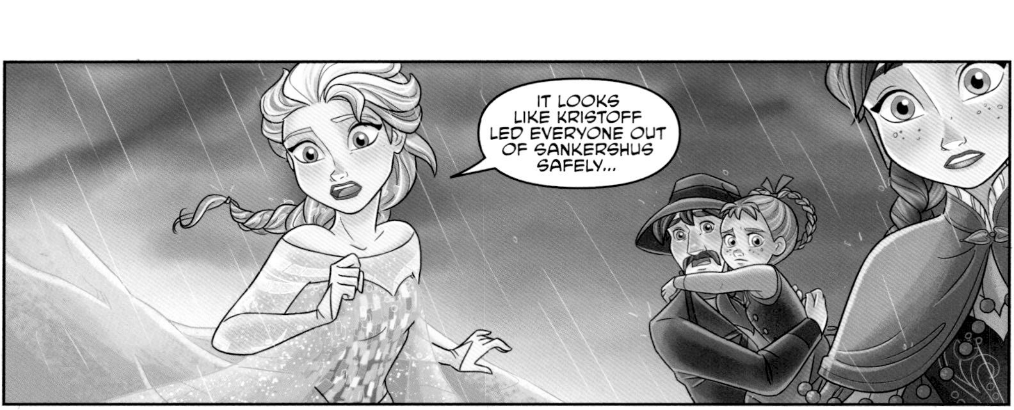
IT LOOKS LIKE KRISTOFF LED EVERYONE OUT OF SANKERSHUS SAFELY...

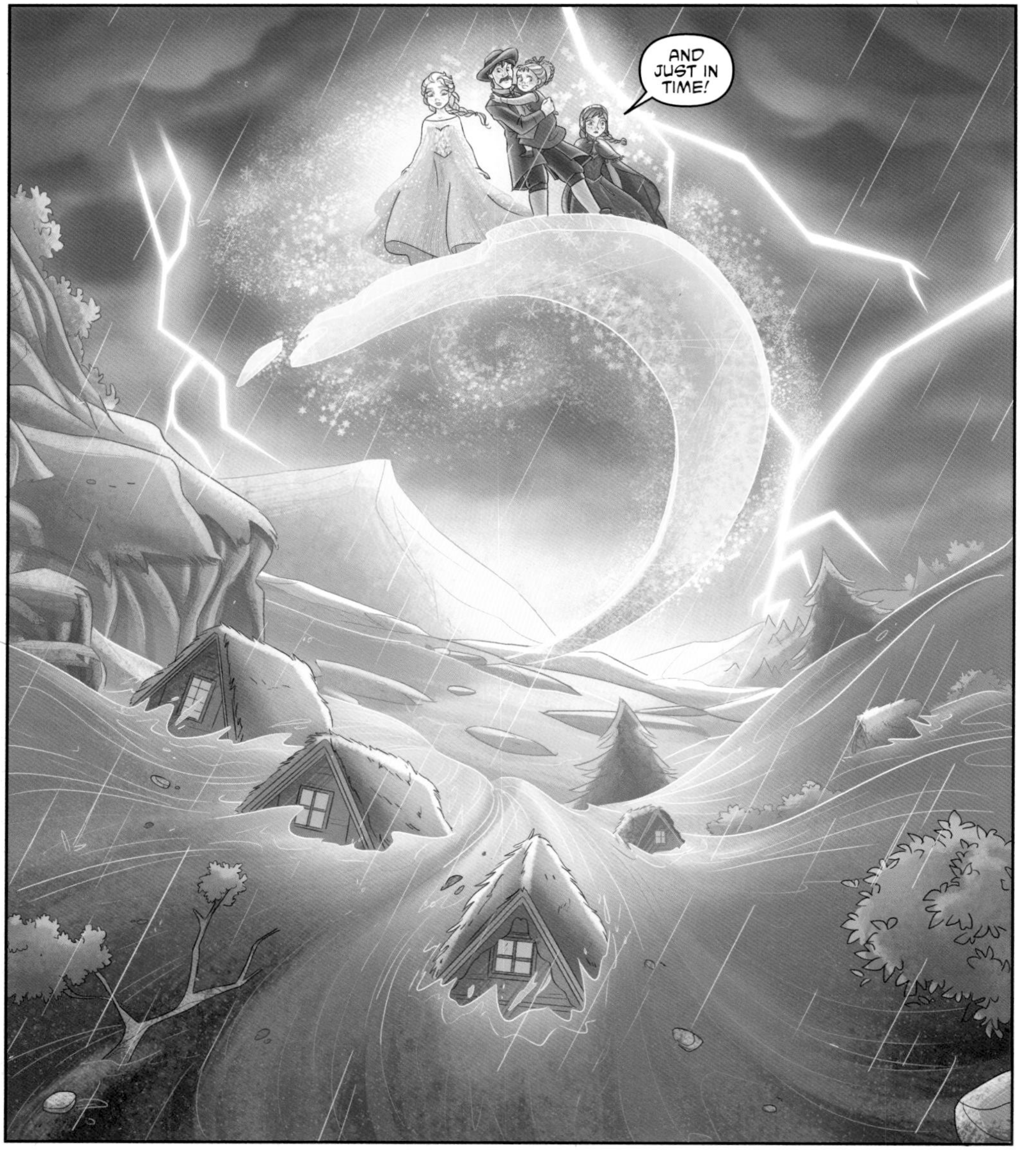
AND JUST IN TIME!

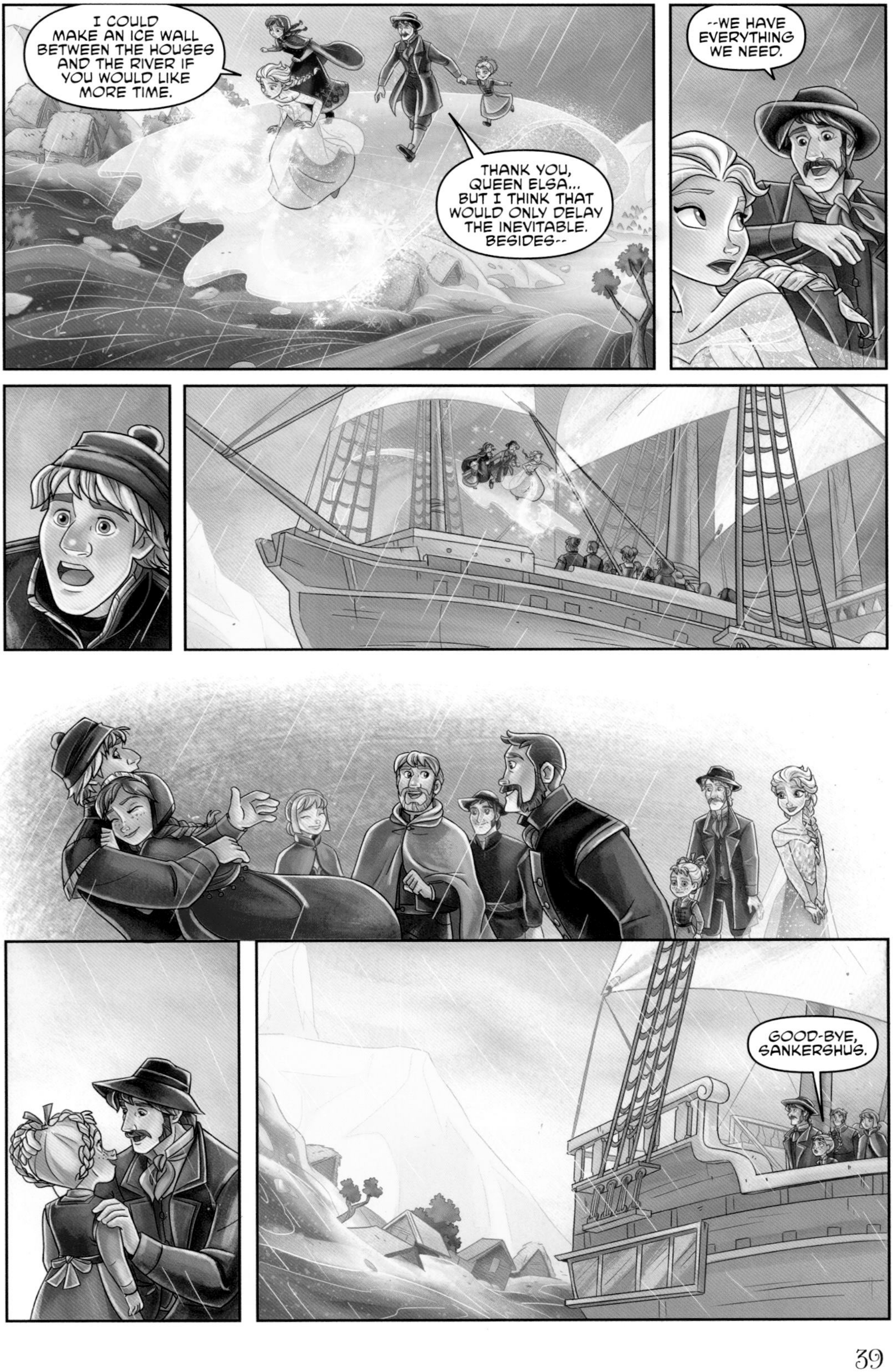
I COULD MAKE AN ICE WALL BETWEEN THE HOUSES AND THE RIVER IF YOU WOULD LIKE MORE TIME.
THANK YOU, QUEEN ELSA... BUT I THINK THAT WOULD ONLY DELAY THE INEVITABLE. BESIDES--
--WE HAVE EVERYTHING WE NEED.
GOOD-BYE, SANKERSHUS.

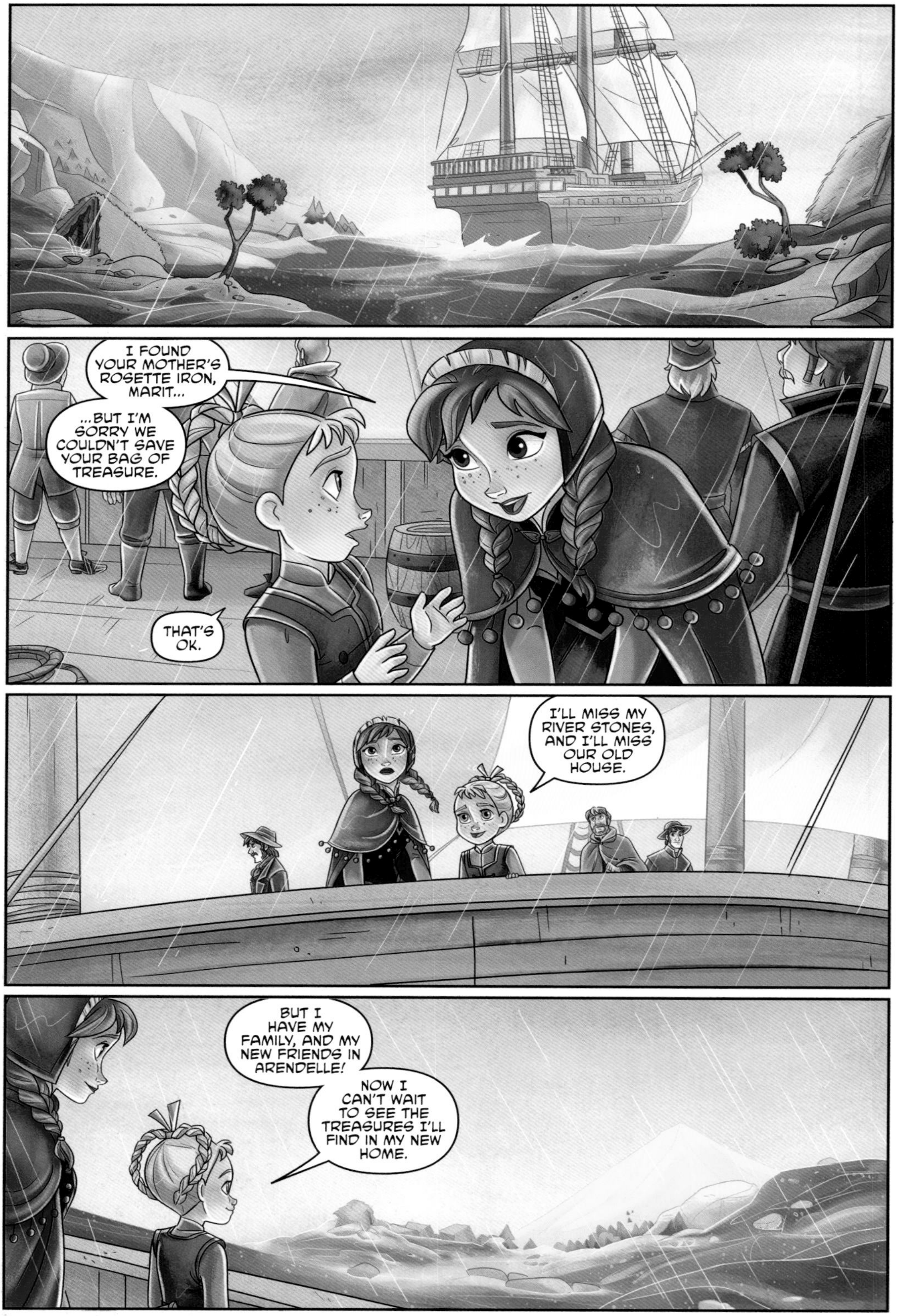
I FOUND YOUR MOTHER'S ROSETTE IRON, MARIT...
...BUT I'M SORRY WE COULDN'T SAVE YOUR BAG OF TREASURE.
THAT'S OK.
I'LL MISS MY RIVER STONES, AND I'LL MISS OUR OLD HOUSE.
BUT I HAVE MY FAMILY, AND MY NEW FRIENDS IN ARENDELLE!
NOW I CAN'T WAIT TO SEE THE TREASURES I'LL FIND IN MY NEW HOME.

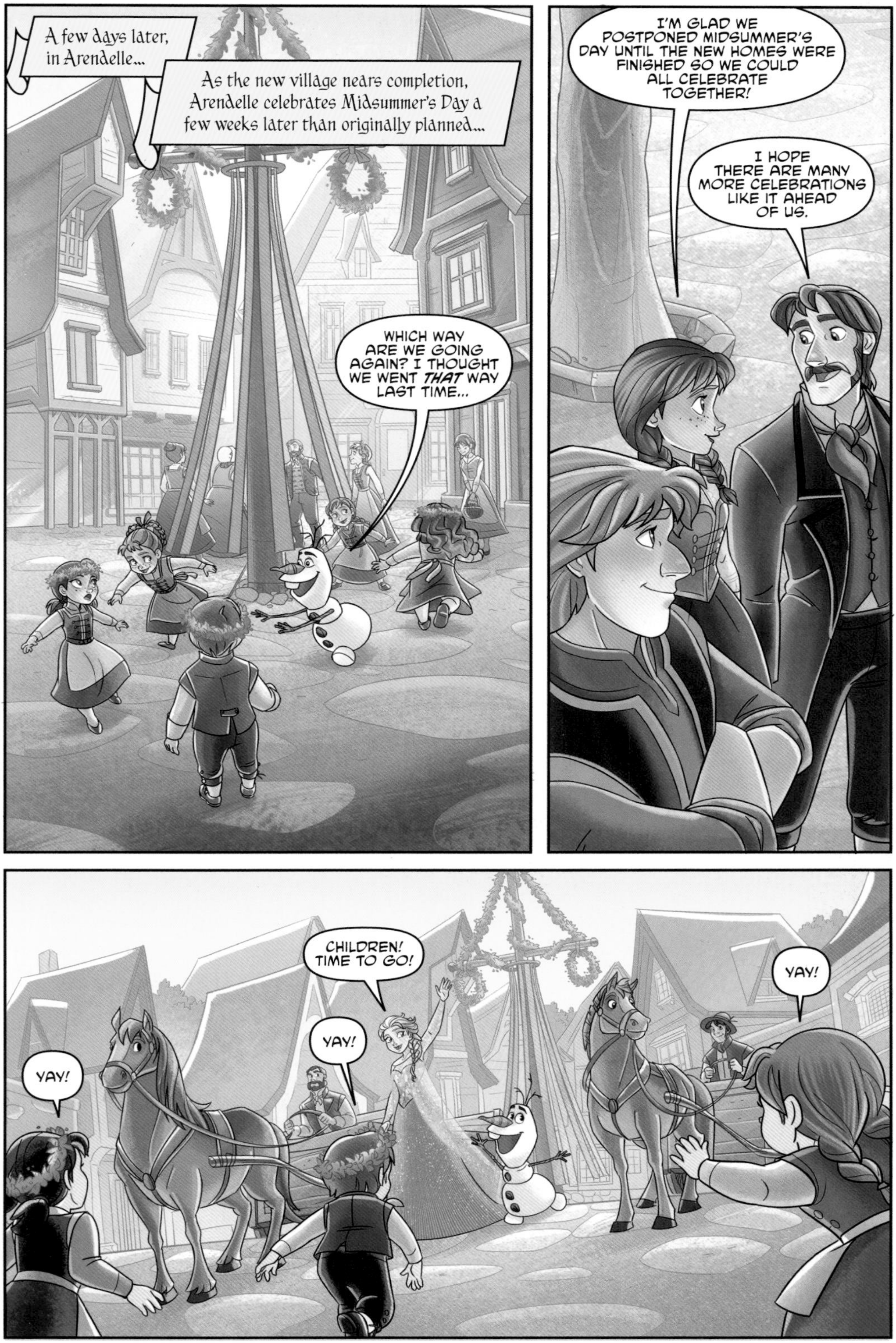
A few days later, in Arendelle...
As the new village nears completion, Arendelle celebrates Midsummer's Day a few weeks later than originally planned...
WHICH WAY ARE WE GOING AGAIN? I THOUGHT WE WENT *THAT* WAY LAST TIME...
I'M GLAD WE POSTPONED MIDSUMMER'S DAY UNTIL THE NEW HOMES WERE FINISHED SO WE COULD ALL CELEBRATE TOGETHER!
I HOPE THERE ARE MANY MORE CELEBRATIONS LIKE IT AHEAD OF US.
CHILDREN! TIME TO GO!
YAY!
YAY!
YAY!

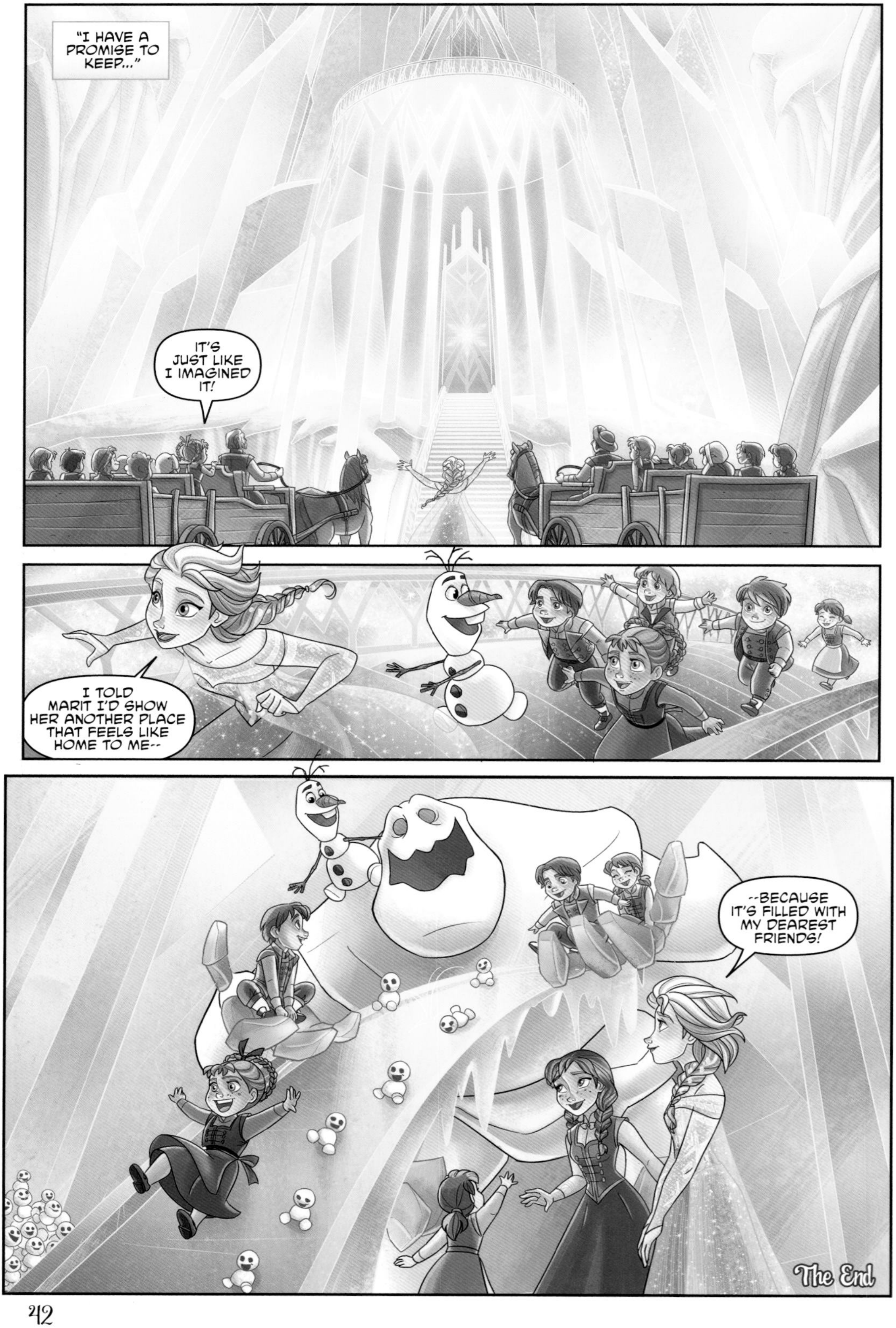
"I HAVE A PROMISE TO KEEP..."
IT'S JUST LIKE I IMAGINED IT!
I TOLD MARIT I'D SHOW HER ANOTHER PLACE THAT FEELS LIKE HOME TO ME--
--BECAUSE IT'S FILLED WITH MY DEAREST FRIENDS!
The End

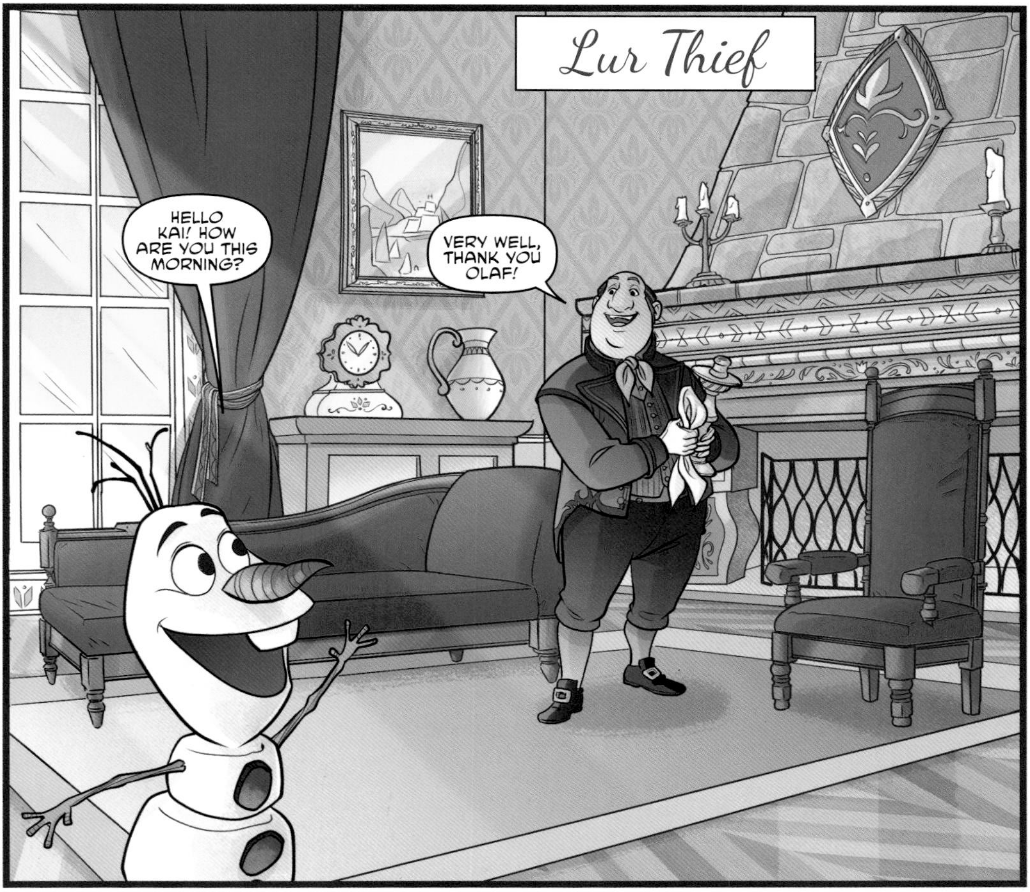
Fur Thief
HELLO KAI! HOW ARE YOU THIS MORNING?
VERY WELL, THANK YOU OLAF!

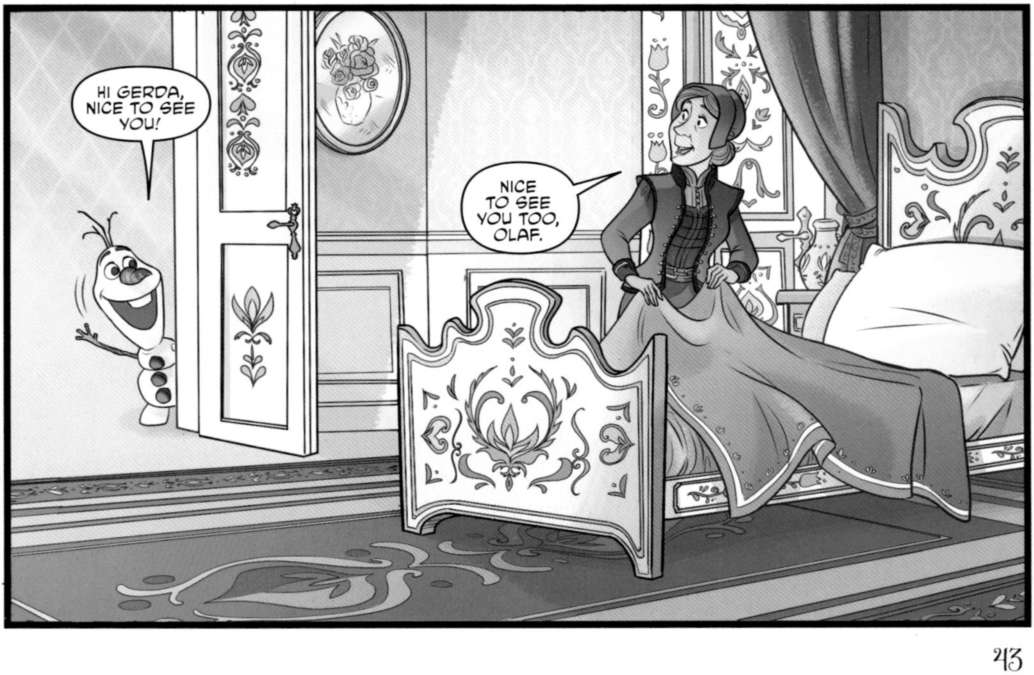
HI GERDA, NICE TO SEE YOU!
NICE TO SEE YOU TOO, OLAF.

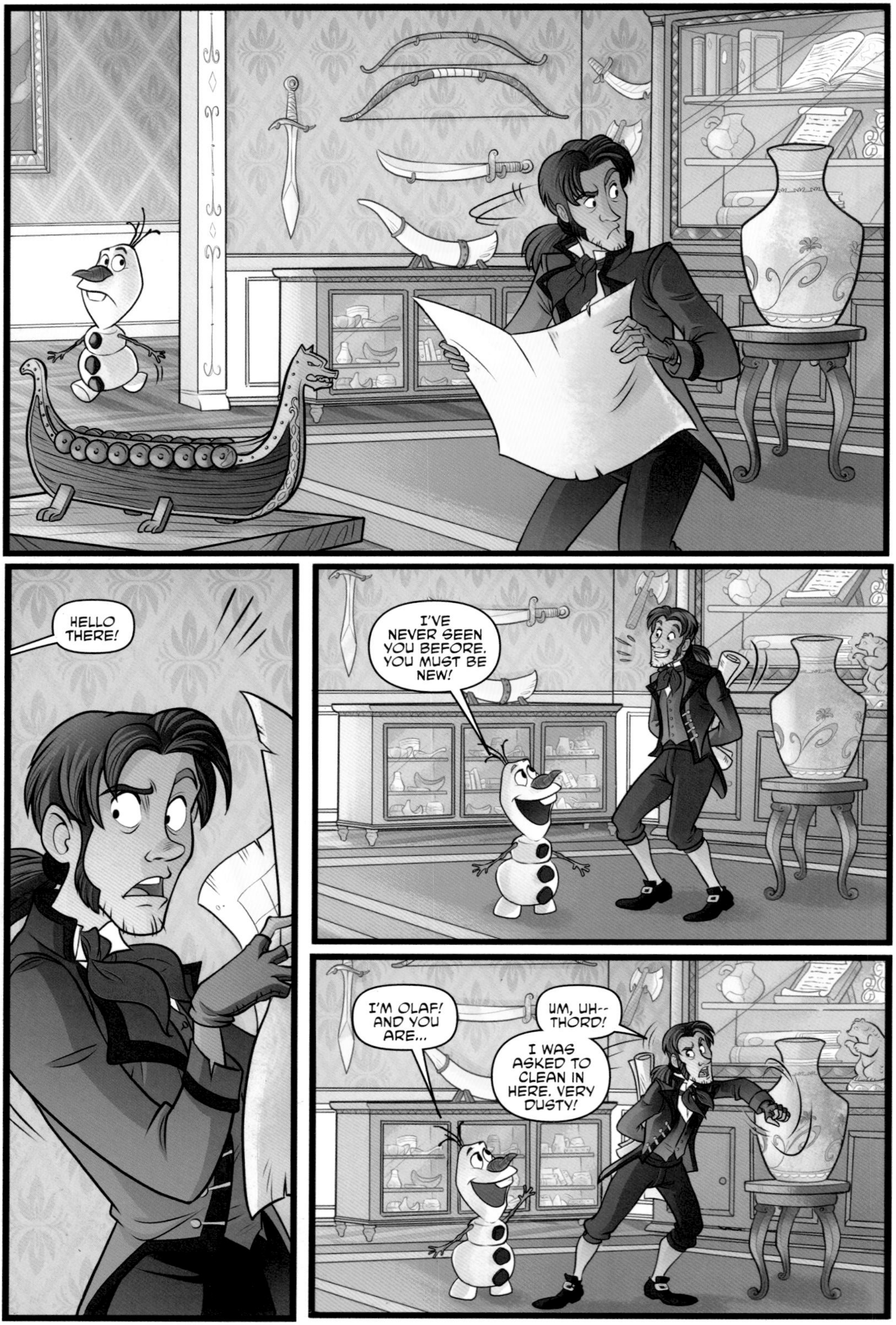
HELLO THERE!
I'VE NEVER SEEN YOU BEFORE. YOU MUST BE NEW!
I'M OLAF! AND YOU ARE...
UM, UH-- THORD!
I WAS ASKED TO CLEAN IN HERE. VERY DUSTY!

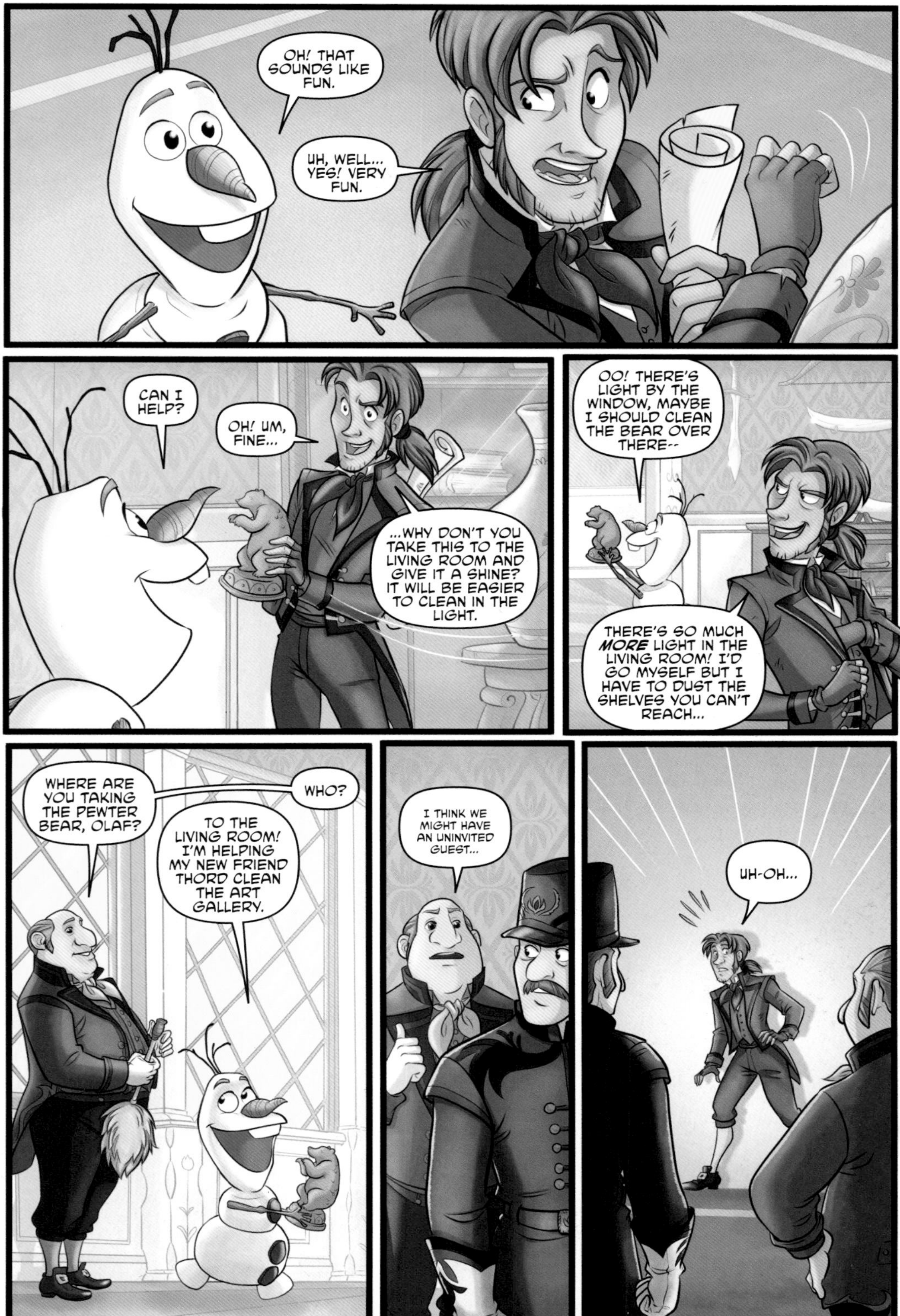
OH! THAT SOUNDS LIKE FUN.
UH, WELL... YES! VERY FUN.
CAN I HELP?
OH! UM, FINE...
...WHY DON'T YOU TAKE THIS TO THE LIVING ROOM AND GIVE IT A SHINE? IT WILL BE EASIER TO CLEAN IN THE LIGHT.
OO! THERE'S LIGHT BY THE WINDOW, MAYBE I SHOULD CLEAN THE BEAR OVER THERE--
THERE'S SO MUCH MORE LIGHT IN THE LIVING ROOM! I'D GO MYSELF BUT I HAVE TO DUST THE SHELVES YOU CAN'T REACH...
WHERE ARE YOU TAKING THE PEWTER BEAR, OLAF?
TO THE LIVING ROOM! I'M HELPING MY NEW FRIEND THORD CLEAN THE ART GALLERY.
WHO?
I THINK WE MIGHT HAVE AN UNINVITED GUEST...
UH-OH...

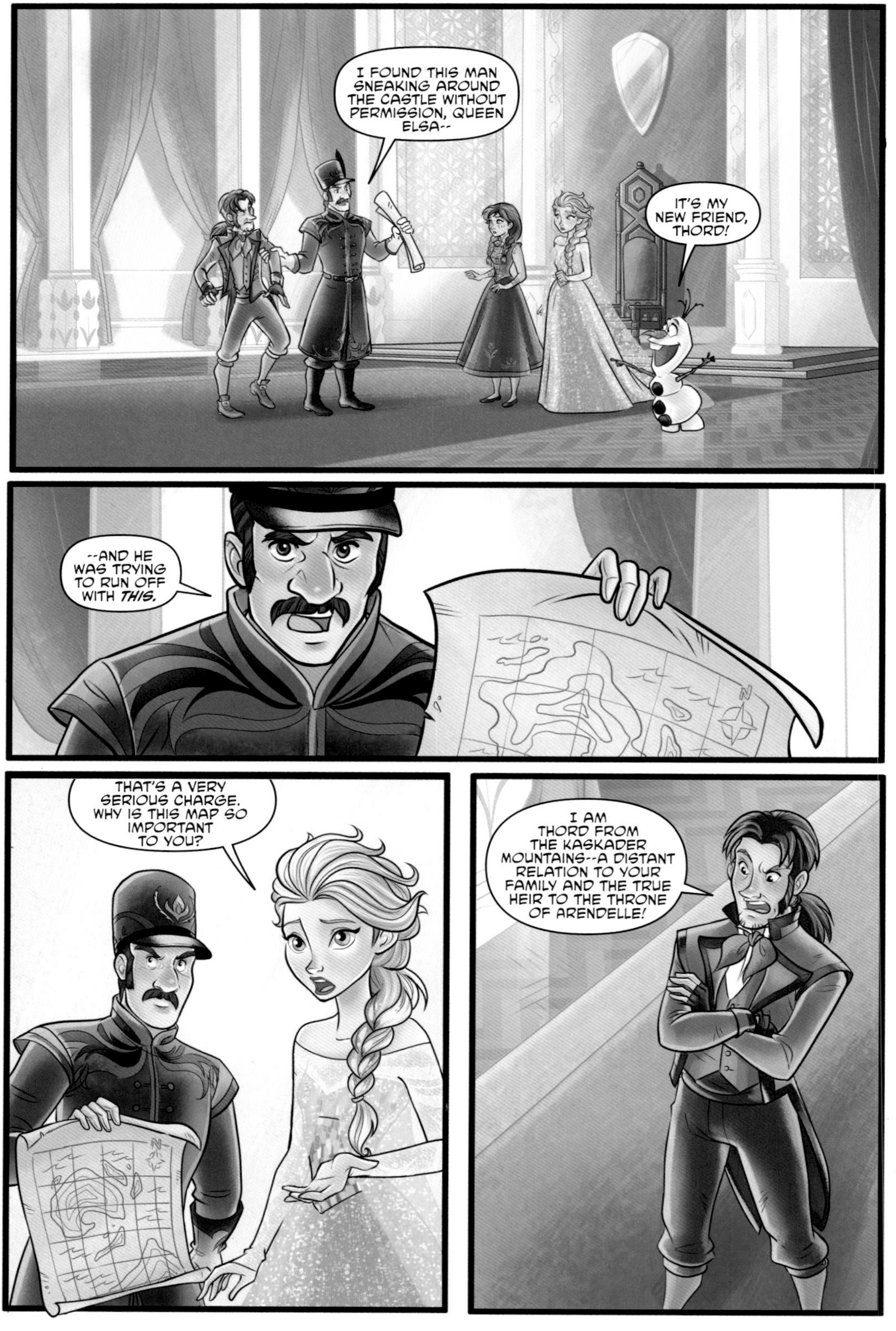
I FOUND THIS MAN SNEAKING AROUND THE CASTLE WITHOUT PERMISSION, QUEEN ELSA--
IT'S MY NEW FRIEND, THORD!
--AND HE WAS TRYING TO RUN OFF WITH *THIS.*
THAT'S A VERY SERIOUS CHARGE. WHY IS THIS MAP SO IMPORTANT TO YOU?
I AM THORD FROM THE KASKADER MOUNTAINS--A DISTANT RELATION TO YOUR FAMILY AND THE TRUE HEIR TO THE THRONE OF ARENDELLE!

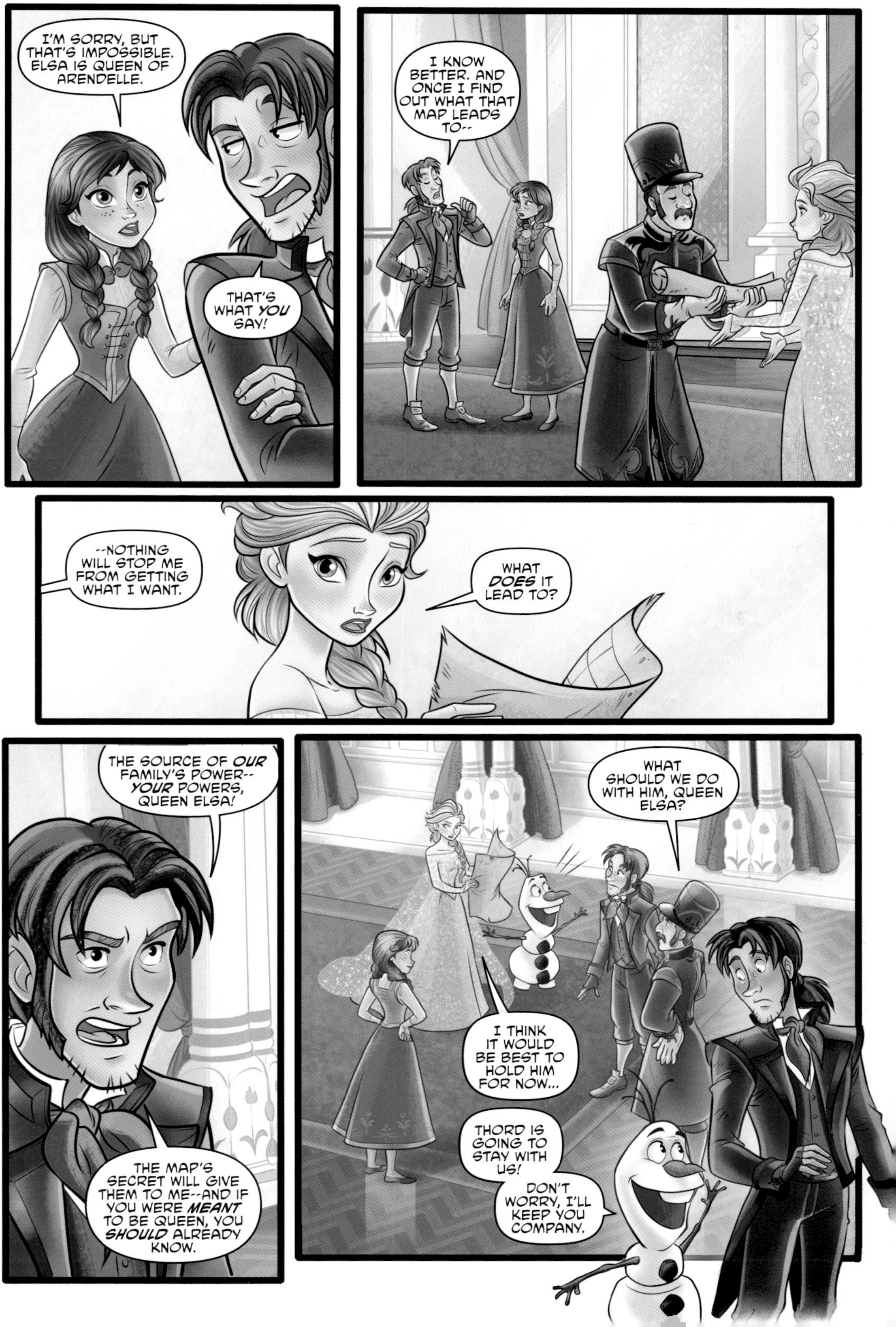
I'M SORRY, BUT THAT'S IMPOSSIBLE. ELSA IS QUEEN OF ARENDELLE.
THAT'S WHAT *YOU* SAY!
I KNOW BETTER. AND ONCE I FIND OUT WHAT THAT MAP LEADS TO--
--NOTHING WILL STOP ME FROM GETTING WHAT I WANT.
WHAT *DOES* IT LEAD TO?
THE SOURCE OF *OUR* FAMILY'S POWER-- *YOUR* POWERS, QUEEN ELSA!
THE MAP'S SECRET WILL GIVE THEM TO ME--AND IF YOU WERE *MEANT* TO BE QUEEN, YOU *SHOULD* ALREADY KNOW.
WHAT SHOULD WE DO WITH HIM, QUEEN ELSA?
I THINK IT WOULD BE BEST TO HOLD HIM FOR NOW...
THORD IS GOING TO STAY WITH US!
DON'T WORRY, I'LL KEEP YOU COMPANY.

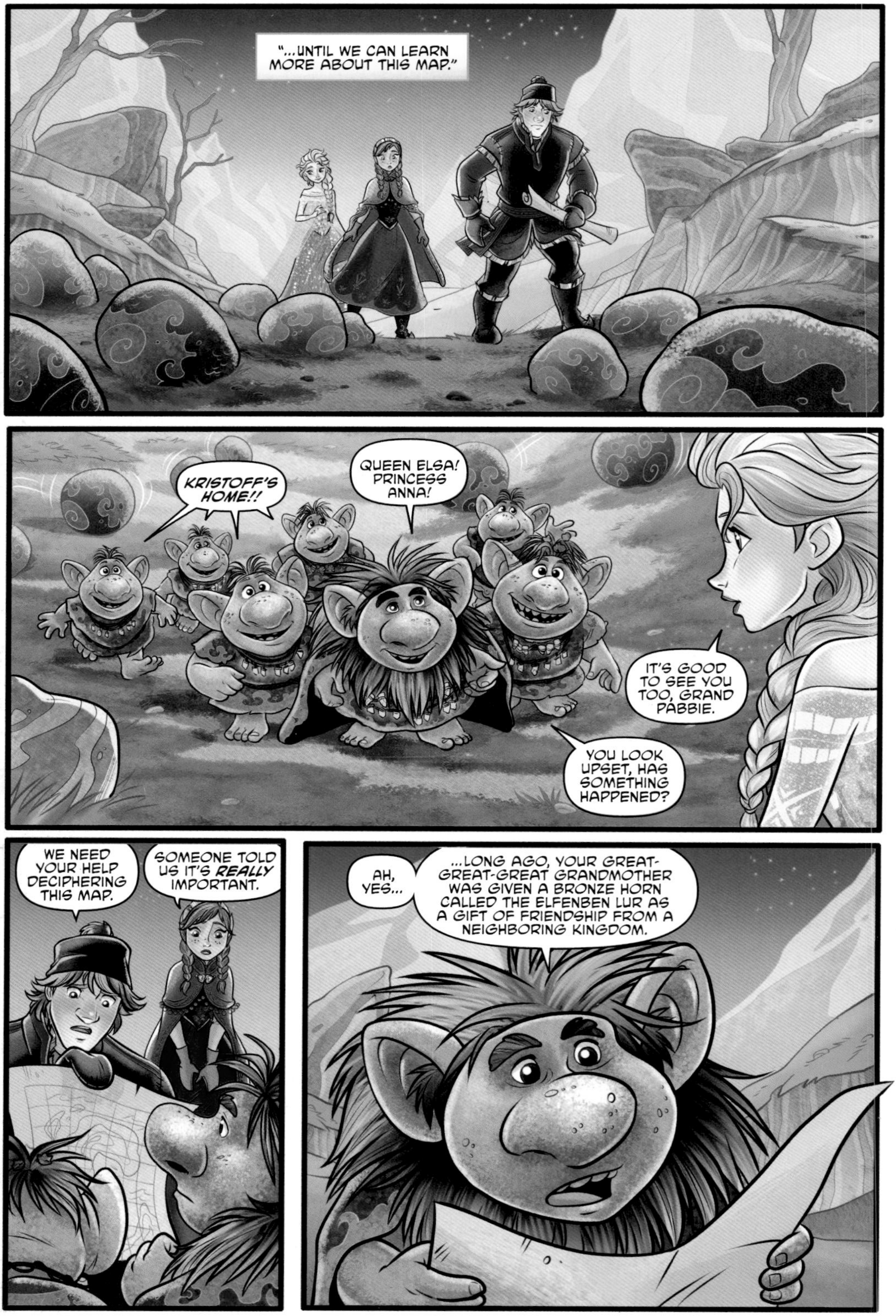
"...UNTIL WE CAN LEARN MORE ABOUT THIS MAP."
KRISTOFF'S HOME!!
QUEEN ELSA! PRINCESS ANNA!
IT'S GOOD TO SEE YOU TOO, GRAND PABBIE.
YOU LOOK UPSET, HAS SOMETHING HAPPENED?
WE NEED YOUR HELP DECIPHERING THIS MAP.
SOMEONE TOLD US IT'S *REALLY* IMPORTANT.
AH, YES...
...LONG AGO, YOUR GREAT-GREAT-GREAT GRANDMOTHER WAS GIVEN A BRONZE HORN CALLED THE ELFENBEN LUR AS A GIFT OF FRIENDSHIP FROM A NEIGHBORING KINGDOM.

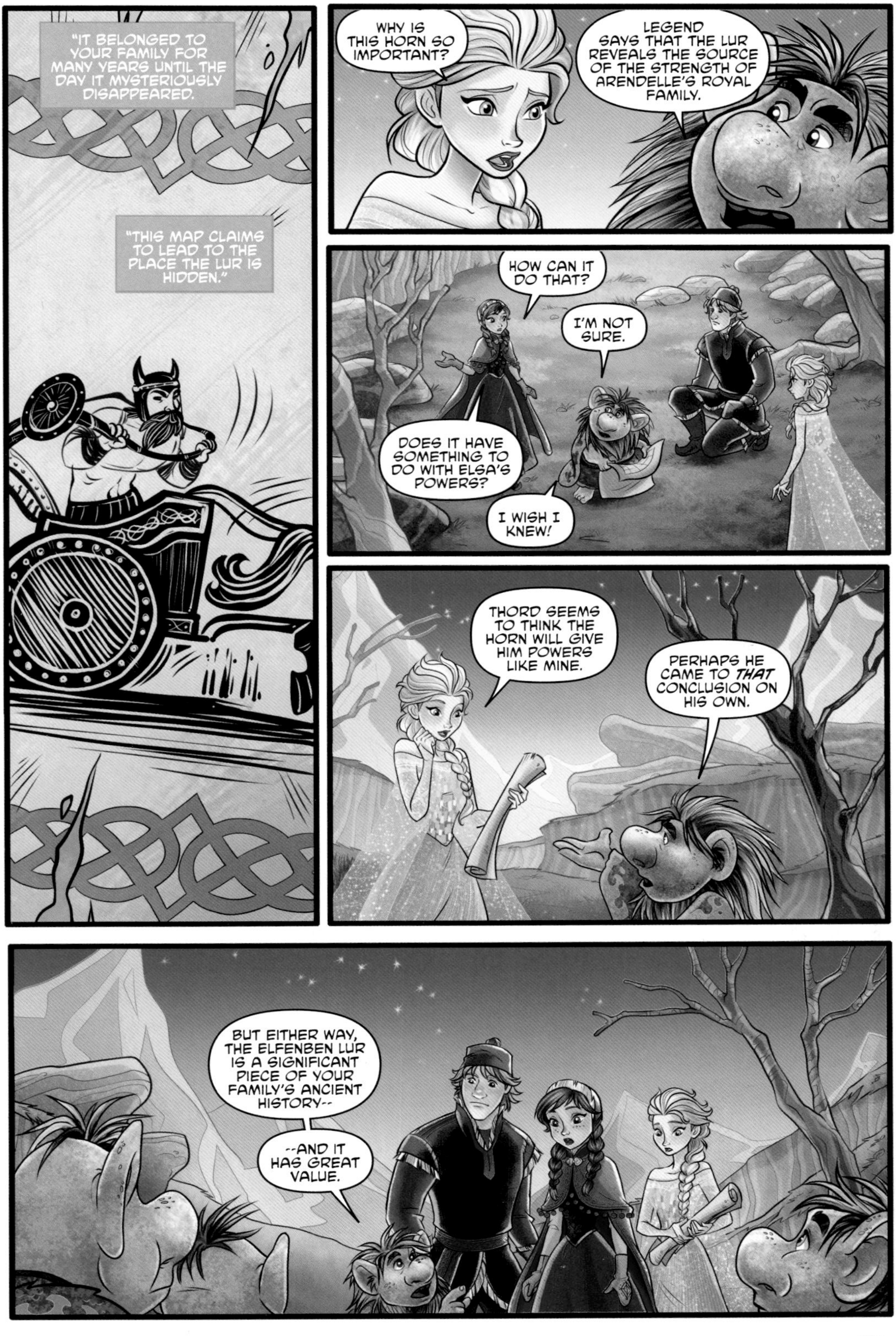
"IT BELONGED TO YOUR FAMILY FOR MANY YEARS UNTIL THE DAY IT MYSTERIOUSLY DISAPPEARED.
"THIS MAP CLAIMS TO LEAD TO THE PLACE THE LUR IS HIDDEN."
WHY IS THIS HORN SO IMPORTANT?
LEGEND SAYS THAT THE LUR REVEALS THE SOURCE OF THE STRENGTH OF ARENDELLE'S ROYAL FAMILY.
HOW CAN IT DO THAT?
I'M NOT SURE.
DOES IT HAVE SOMETHING TO DO WITH ELSA'S POWERS?
I WISH I KNEW!
THORD SEEMS TO THINK THE HORN WILL GIVE HIM POWERS LIKE MINE.
PERHAPS HE CAME TO *THAT* CONCLUSION ON HIS OWN.
BUT EITHER WAY, THE ELFENBEN LUR IS A SIGNIFICANT PIECE OF YOUR FAMILY'S ANCIENT HISTORY--
--AND IT HAS GREAT VALUE.

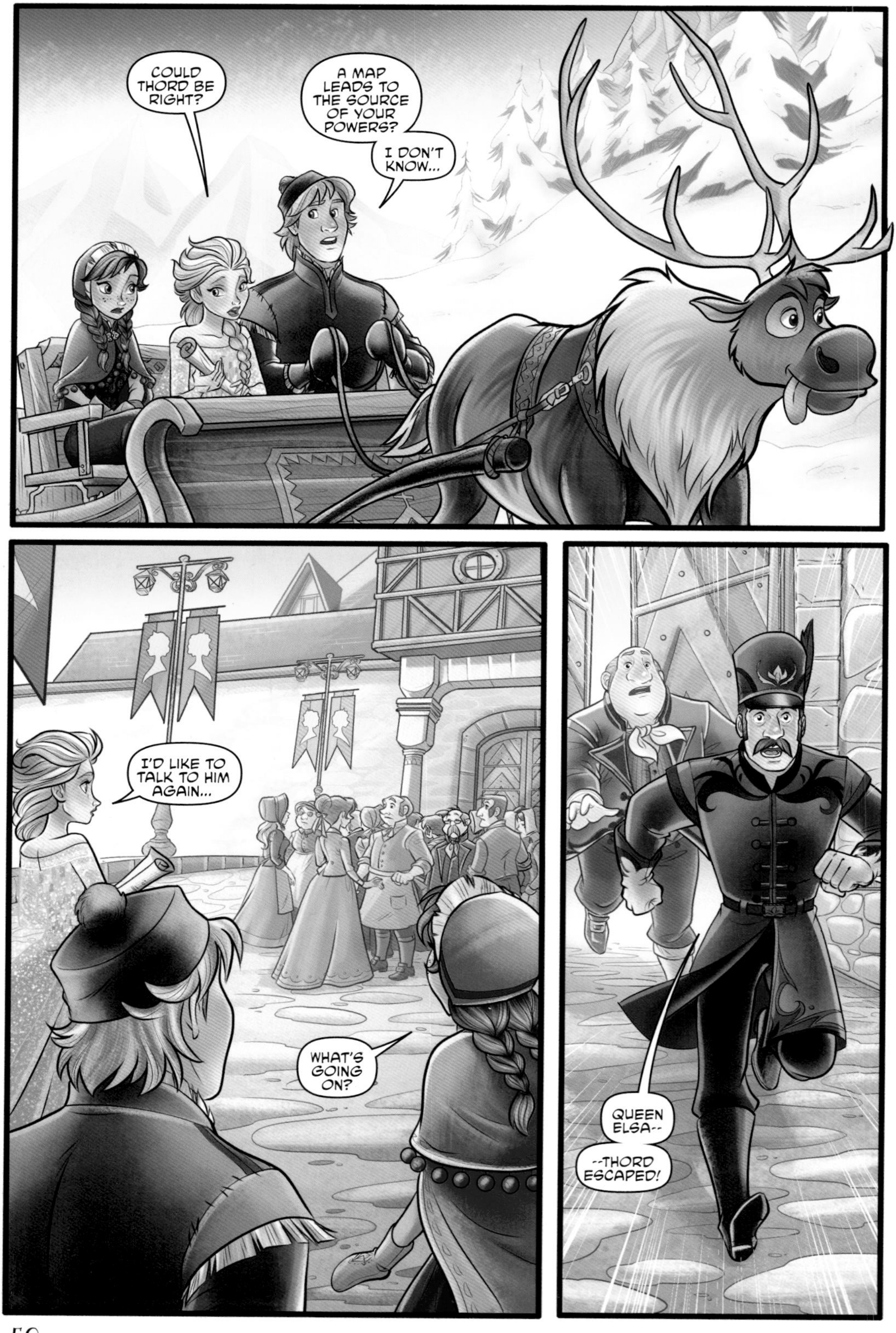
COULD THORD BE RIGHT?
A MAP LEADS TO THE SOURCE OF YOUR POWERS?
I DON'T KNOW...
I'D LIKE TO TALK TO HIM AGAIN...
WHAT'S GOING ON?
QUEEN ELSA--
--THORD ESCAPED!

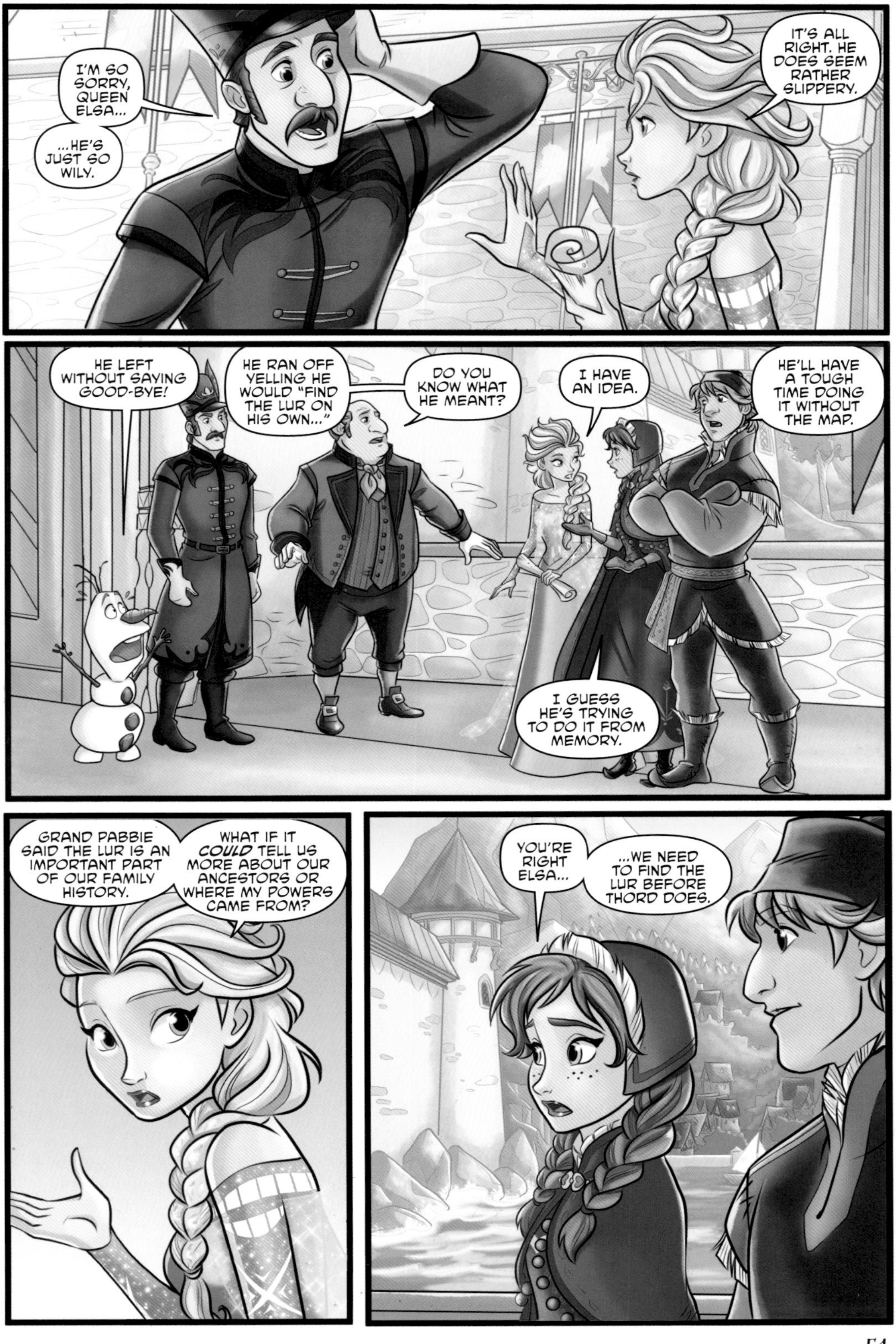
I'M SO SORRY, QUEEN ELSA...
...HE'S JUST SO WILY.
IT'S ALL RIGHT. HE DOES SEEM RATHER SLIPPERY.
HE LEFT WITHOUT SAYING GOOD-BYE!
HE RAN OFF YELLING HE WOULD "FIND THE LUR ON HIS OWN..."
DO YOU KNOW WHAT HE MEANT?
I HAVE AN IDEA.
HE'LL HAVE A TOUGH TIME DOING IT WITHOUT THE MAP.
I GUESS HE'S TRYING TO DO IT FROM MEMORY.
GRAND PABBIE SAID THE LUR IS AN IMPORTANT PART OF OUR FAMILY HISTORY.
WHAT IF IT COULD TELL US MORE ABOUT OUR ANCESTORS OR WHERE MY POWERS CAME FROM?
YOU'RE RIGHT ELSA...
...WE NEED TO FIND THE LUR BEFORE THORD DOES.

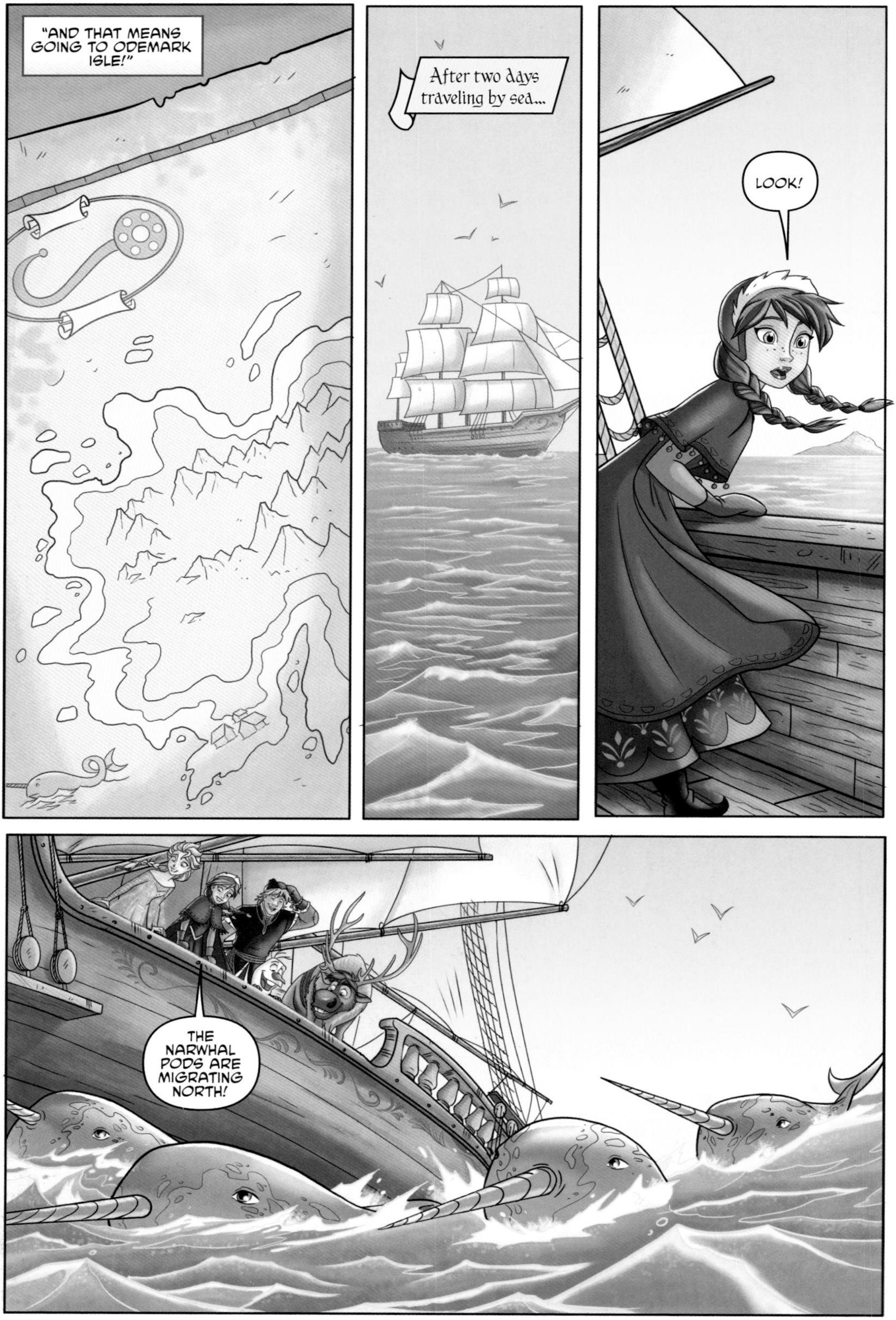
"AND THAT MEANS GOING TO ODEMARK ISLE!"
After two days traveling by sea...
LOOK!
THE NARWHAL PODS ARE MIGRATING NORTH!

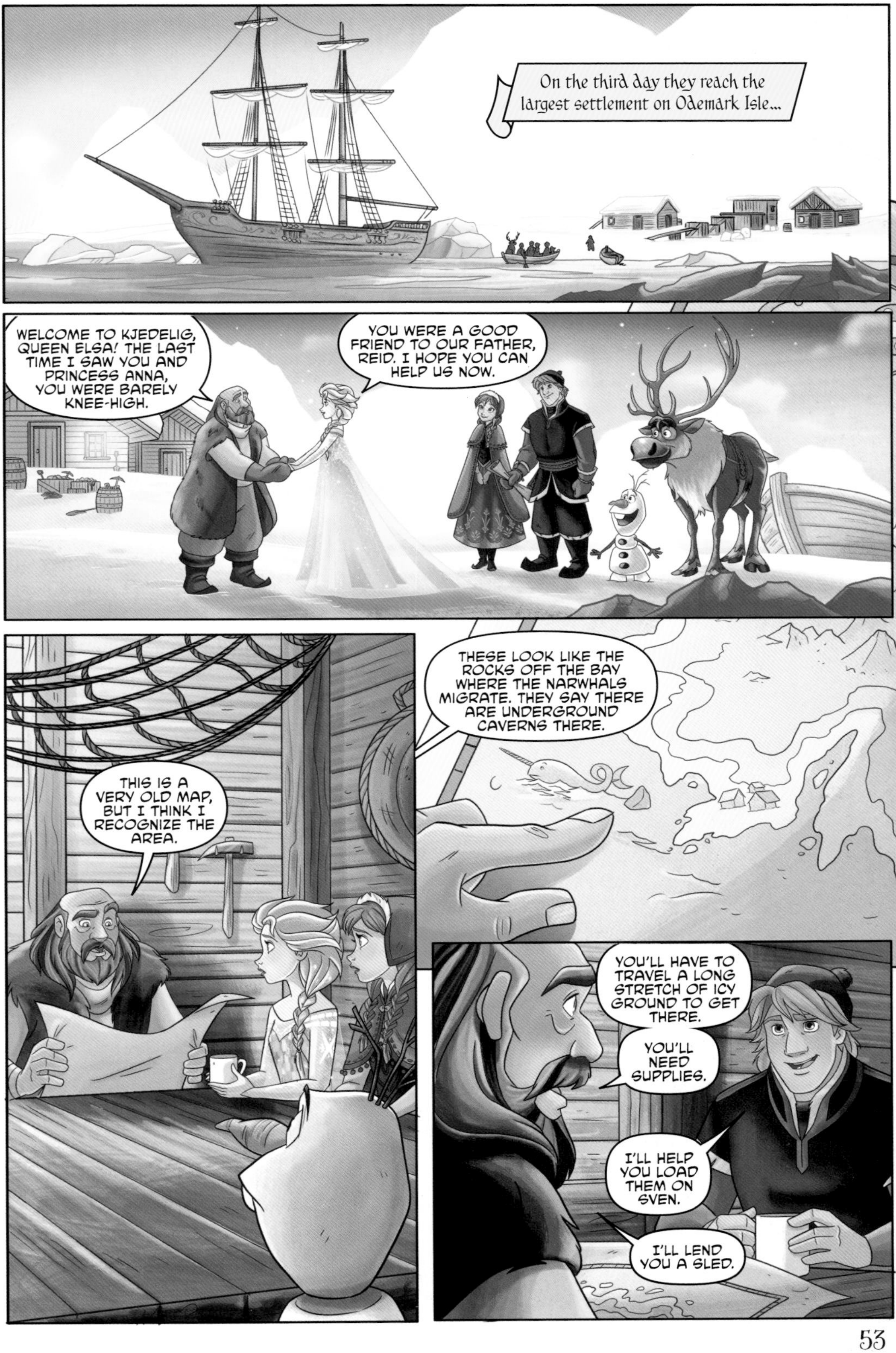
On the third day they reach the largest settlement on Odemark Isle...
WELCOME TO KJEDELIG, QUEEN ELSA! THE LAST TIME I SAW YOU AND PRINCESS ANNA, YOU WERE BARELY KNEE-HIGH.
YOU WERE A GOOD FRIEND TO OUR FATHER, REID. I HOPE YOU CAN HELP US NOW.
THIS IS A VERY OLD MAP, BUT I THINK I RECOGNIZE THE AREA.
THESE LOOK LIKE THE ROCKS OFF THE BAY WHERE THE NARWHALS MIGRATE. THEY SAY THERE ARE UNDERGROUND CAVERNS THERE.
YOU'LL HAVE TO TRAVEL A LONG STRETCH OF ICY GROUND TO GET THERE.
YOU'LL NEED SUPPLIES.
I'LL HELP YOU LOAD THEM ON SVEN.
I'LL LEND YOU A SLED.

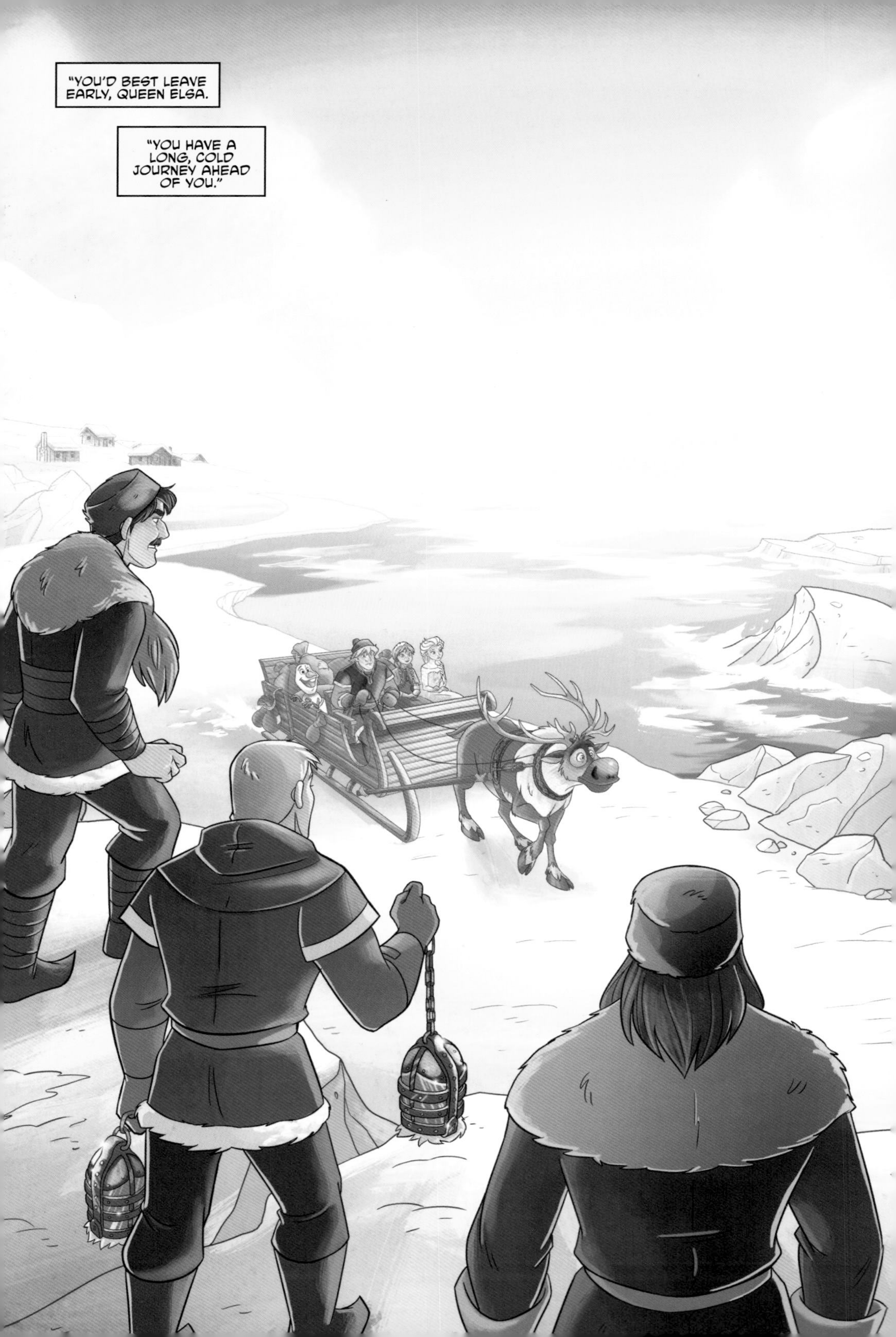
"YOU'D BEST LEAVE EARLY, QUEEN ELSA.
"YOU HAVE A LONG, COLD JOURNEY AHEAD OF YOU."

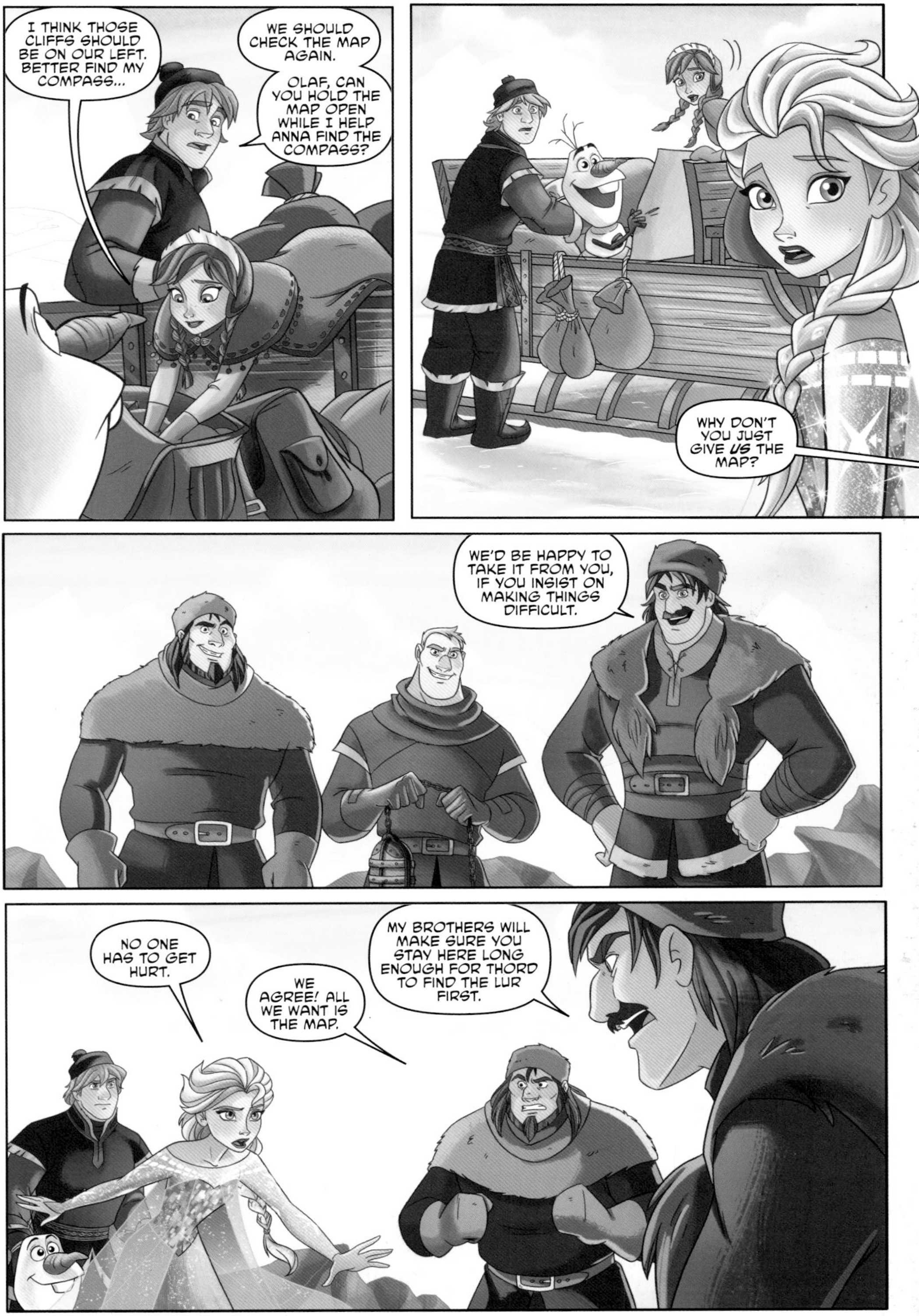
I THINK THOSE CLIFFS SHOULD BE ON OUR LEFT. BETTER FIND MY COMPASS...
WE SHOULD CHECK THE MAP AGAIN.
OLAF, CAN YOU HOLD THE MAP OPEN WHILE I HELP ANNA FIND THE COMPASS?
WHY DON'T YOU JUST GIVE *US* THE MAP?
WE'D BE HAPPY TO TAKE IT FROM YOU, IF YOU INSIST ON MAKING THINGS DIFFICULT.
NO ONE HAS TO GET HURT.
WE AGREE! ALL WE WANT IS THE MAP.
MY BROTHERS WILL MAKE SURE YOU STAY HERE LONG ENOUGH FOR THORD TO FIND THE LUR FIRST.

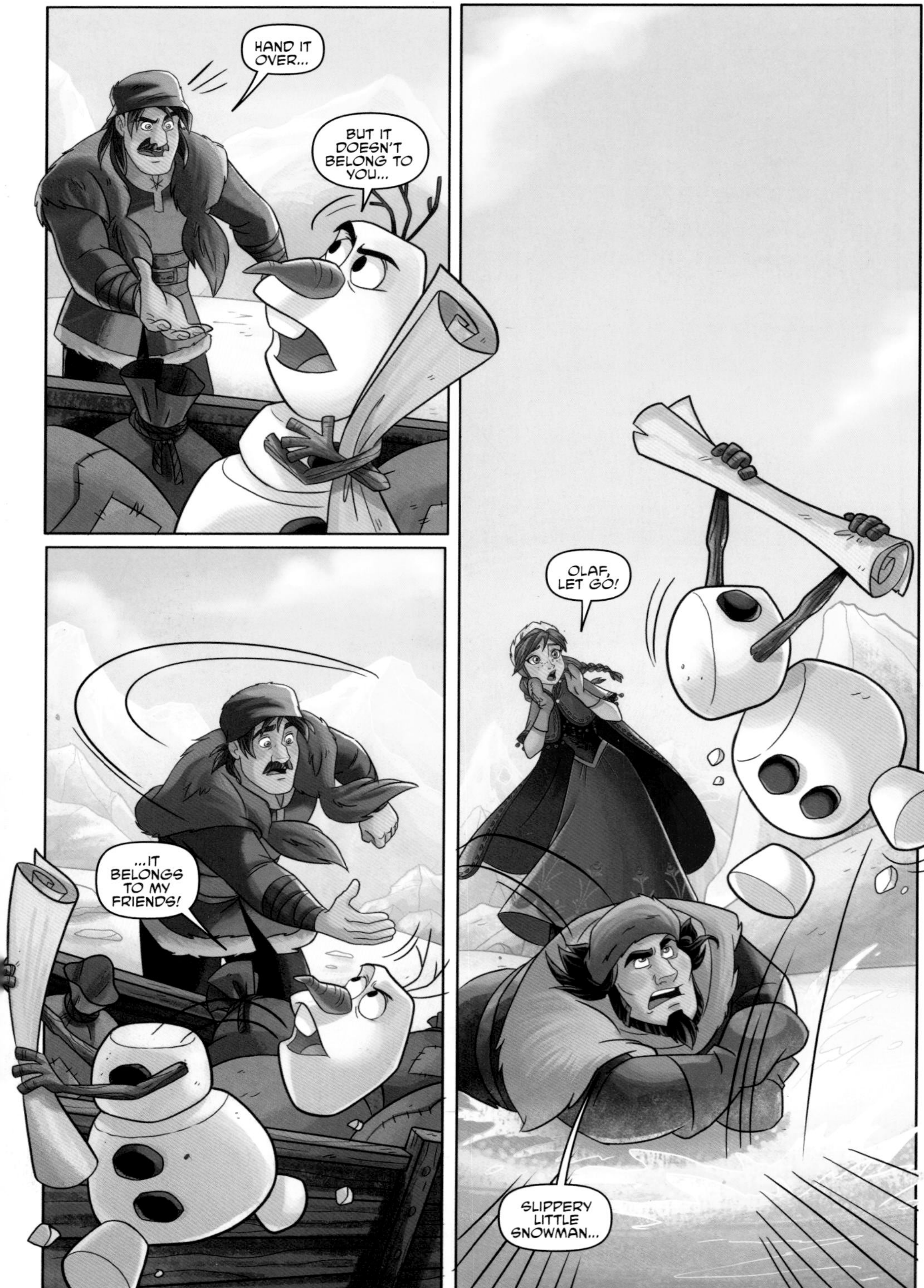
HAND IT OVER...
BUT IT DOESN'T BELONG TO YOU...
...IT BELONGS TO MY FRIENDS!
OLAF, LET GO!
SLIPPERY LITTLE SNOWMAN...

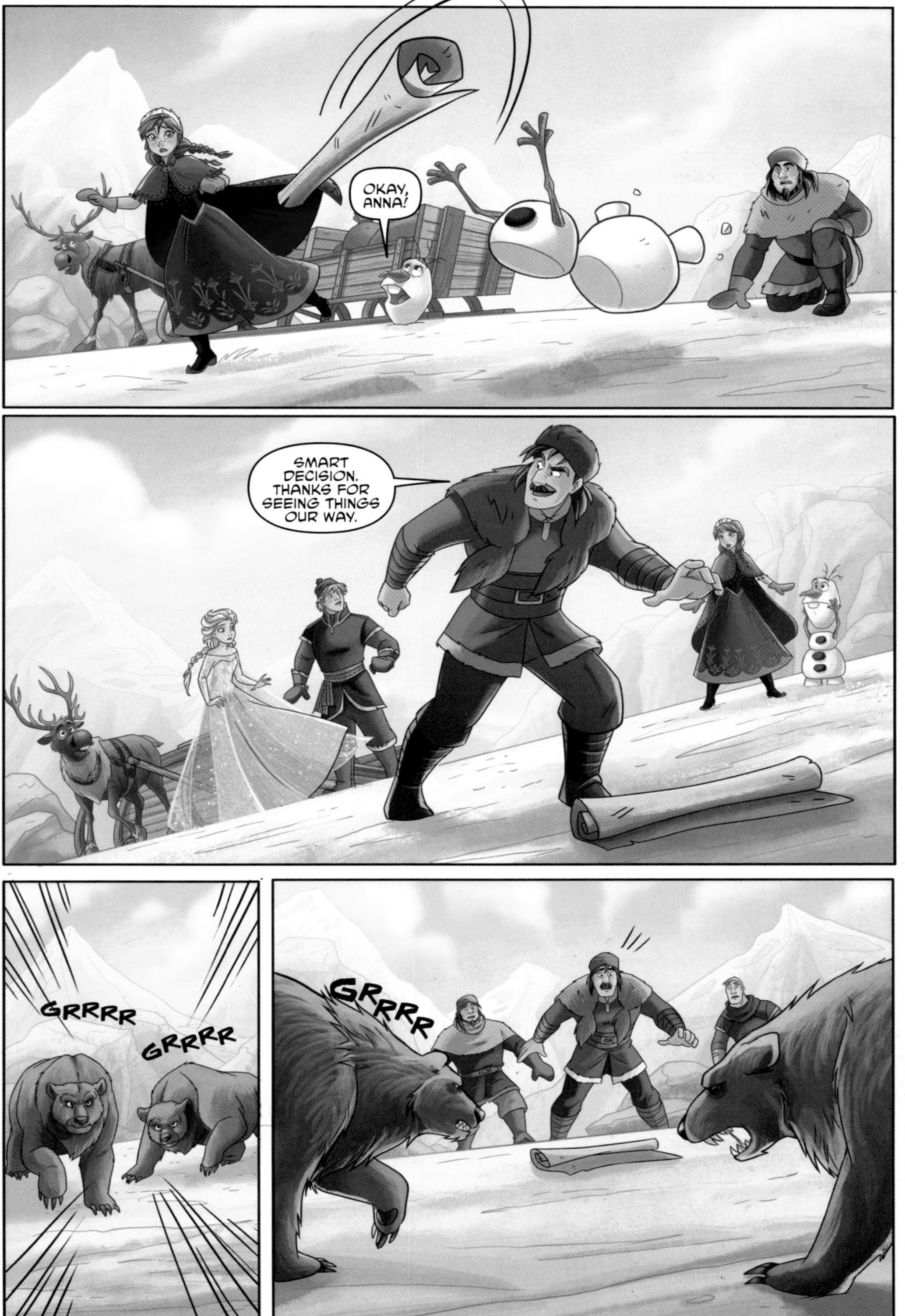
OKAY, ANNA!
SMART DECISION. THANKS FOR SEEING THINGS OUR WAY.
GRRRR
GRRRR
GRRRR

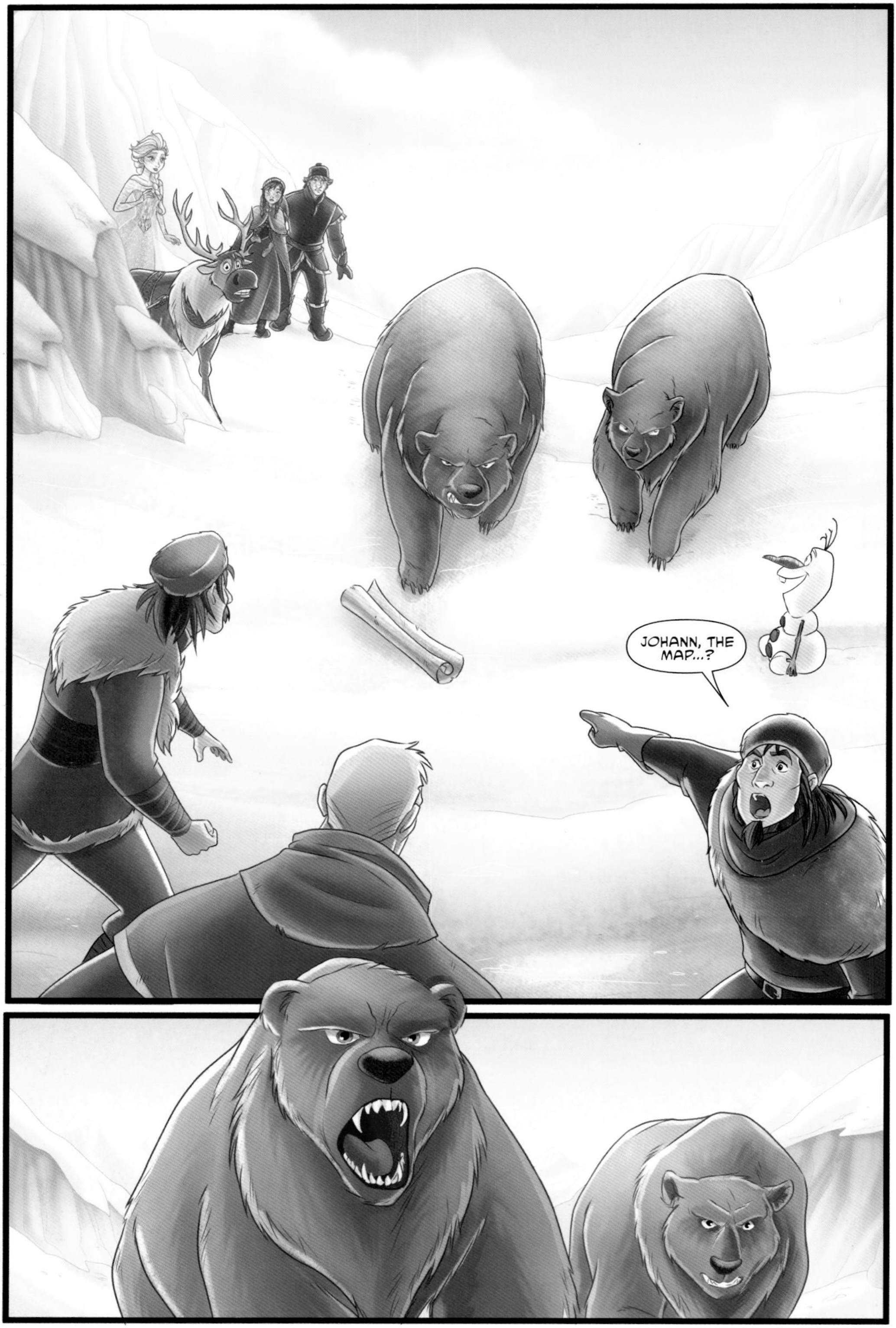
JOHANN, THE MAP...?

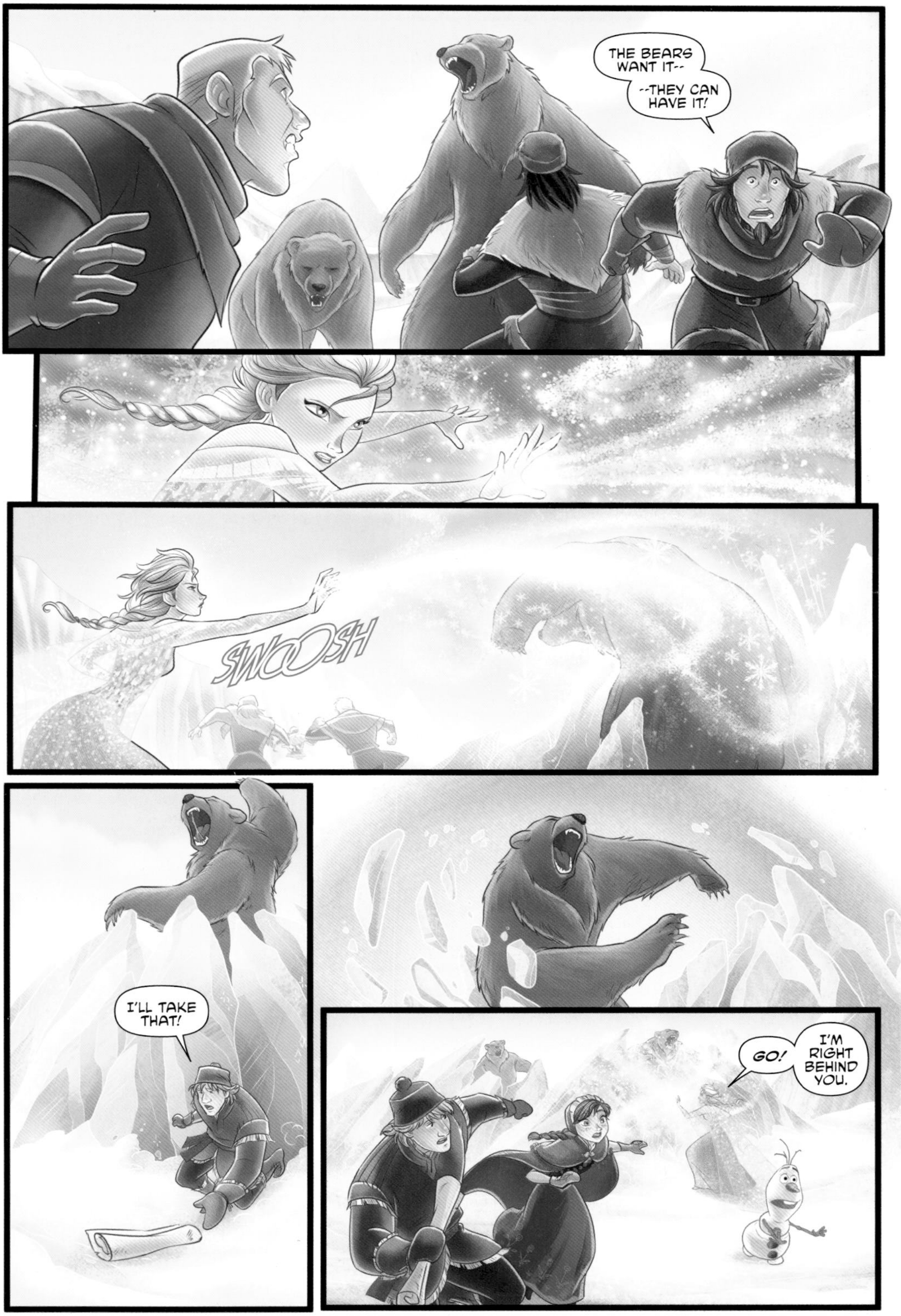
THE BEARS WANT IT--
--THEY CAN HAVE IT!
SWOOSH
I'LL TAKE THAT!
GO!
I'M RIGHT BEHIND YOU.

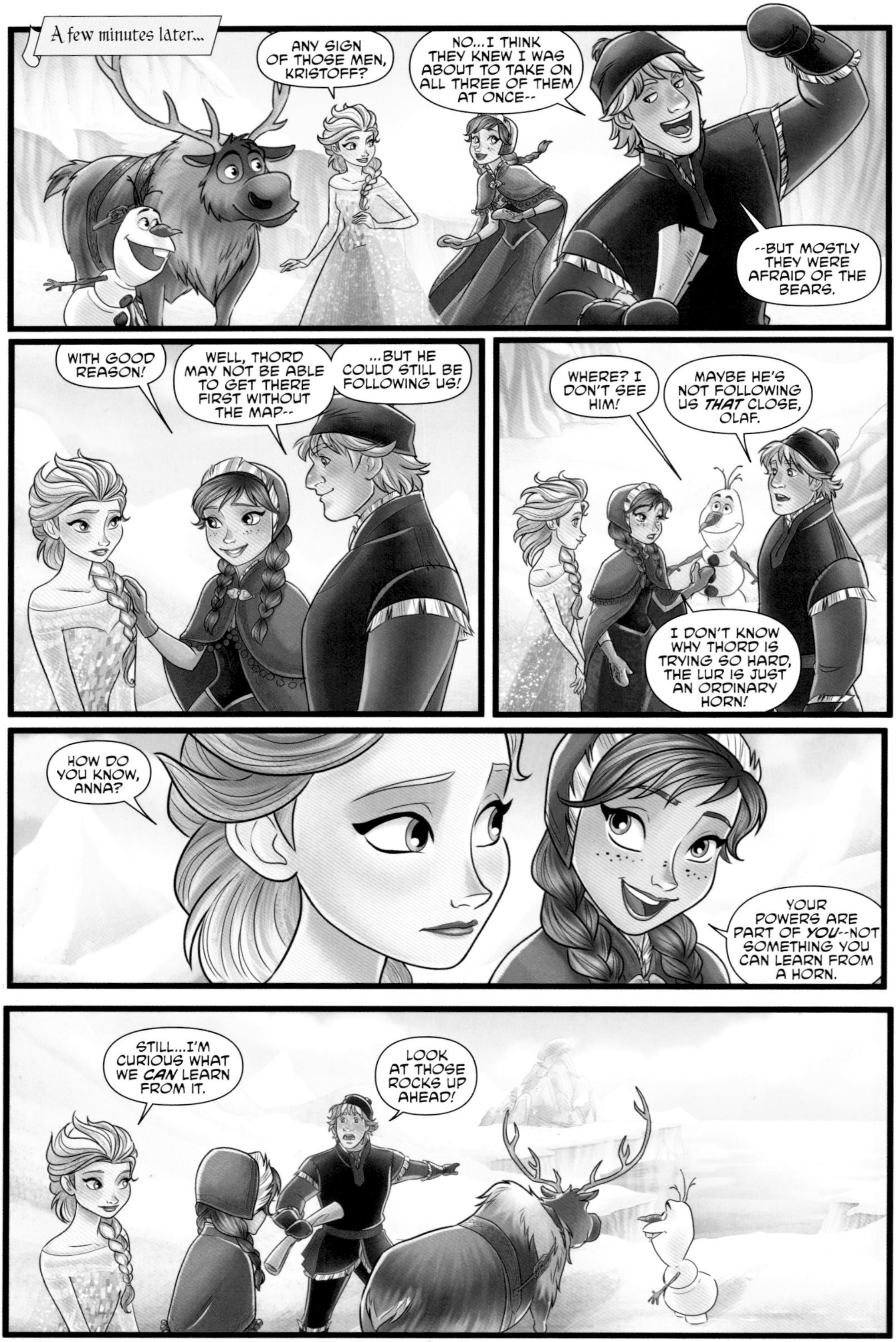
A few minutes later...
ANY SIGN OF THOSE MEN, KRISTOFF?
NO...I THINK THEY KNEW I WAS ABOUT TO TAKE ON ALL THREE OF THEM AT ONCE--
--BUT MOSTLY THEY WERE AFRAID OF THE BEARS.
WITH GOOD REASON!
WELL, THORD MAY NOT BE ABLE TO GET THERE FIRST WITHOUT THE MAP--
...BUT HE COULD STILL BE FOLLOWING US!
WHERE? I DON'T SEE HIM!
MAYBE HE'S NOT FOLLOWING US *THAT* CLOSE, OLAF.
I DON'T KNOW WHY THORD IS TRYING SO HARD, THE LUR IS JUST AN ORDINARY HORN!
HOW DO YOU KNOW, ANNA?
YOUR POWERS ARE PART OF *YOU*--NOT SOMETHING YOU CAN LEARN FROM A HORN.
STILL...I'M CURIOUS WHAT WE *CAN* LEARN FROM IT.
LOOK AT THOSE ROCKS UP AHEAD!

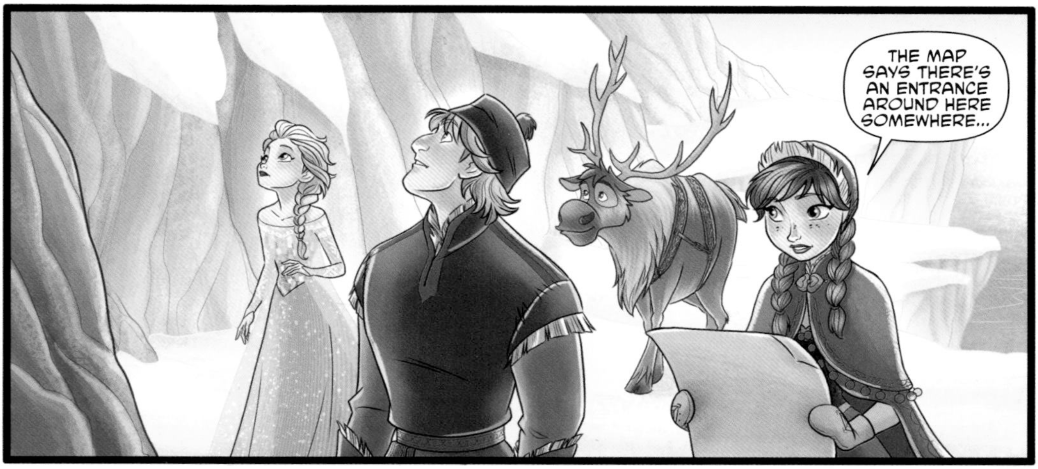
THE MAP SAYS THERE'S AN ENTRANCE AROUND HERE SOMEWHERE...

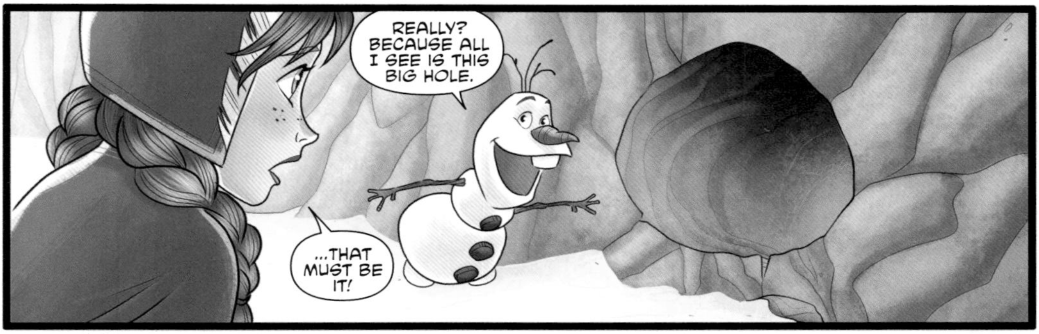
REALLY? BECAUSE ALL I SEE IS THIS BIG HOLE.
...THAT MUST BE IT!

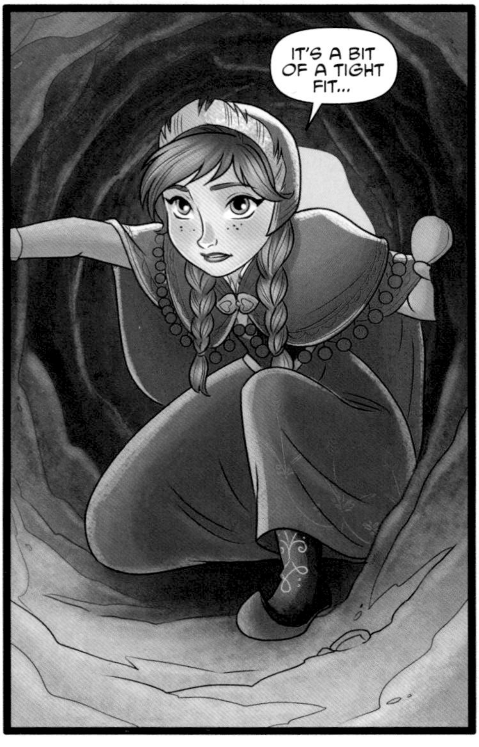
IT'S A BIT OF A TIGHT FIT...

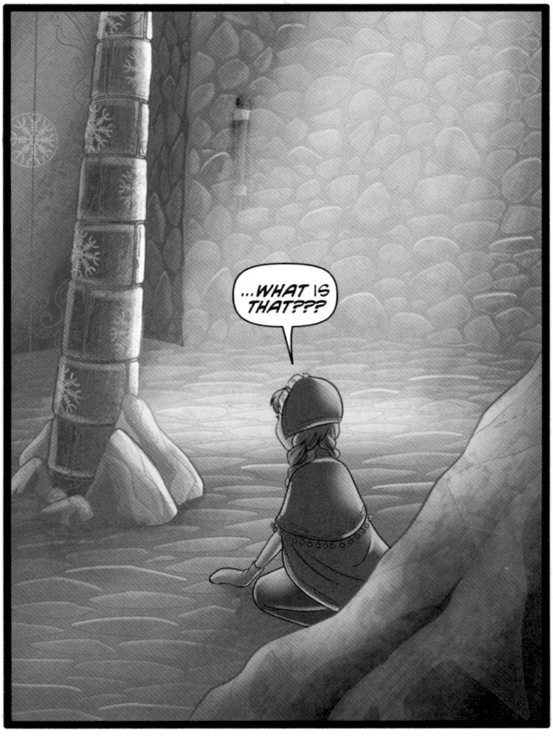
...*WHAT* IS *THAT???*

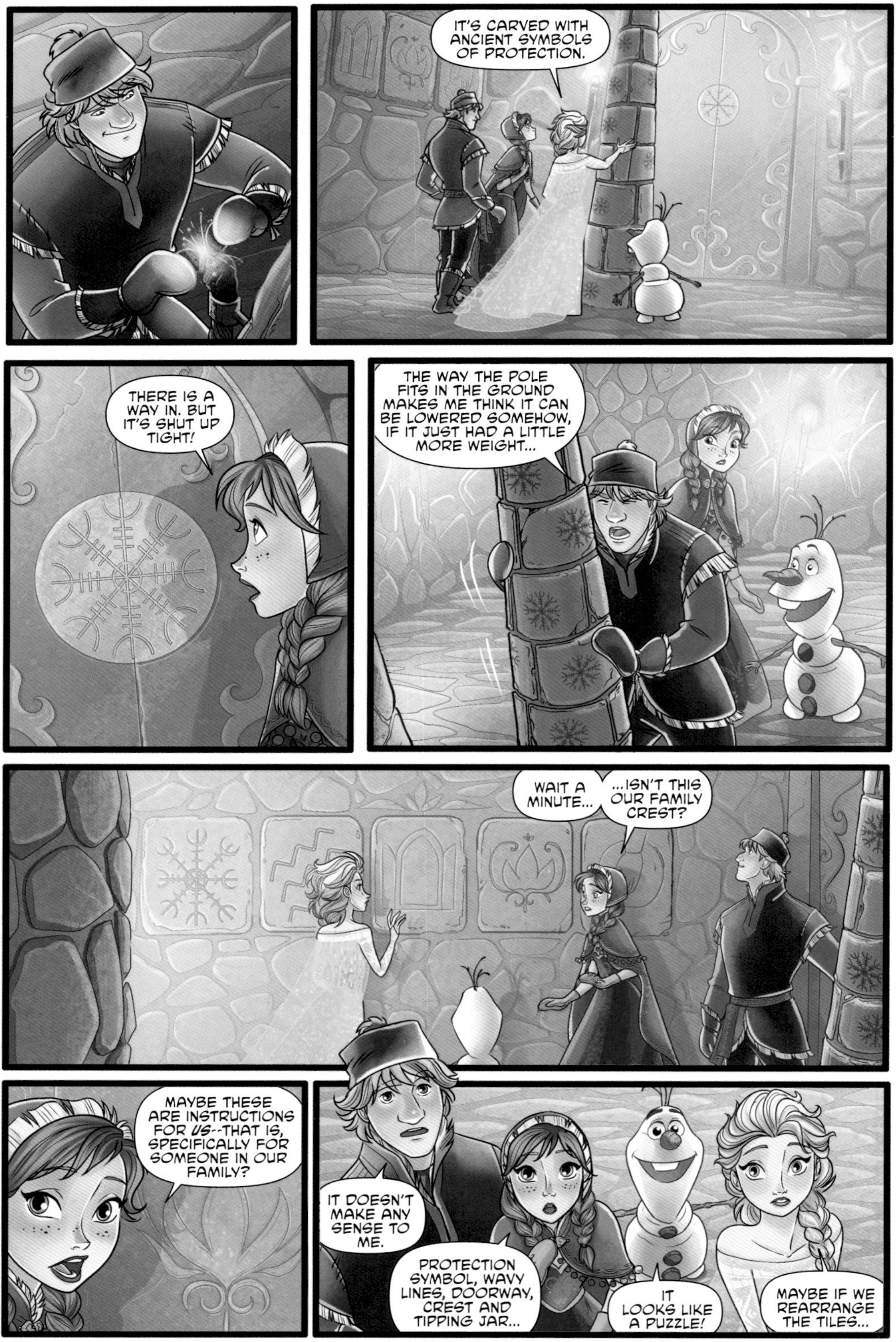
IT'S CARVED WITH ANCIENT SYMBOLS OF PROTECTION.
THERE IS A WAY IN. BUT IT'S SHUT UP TIGHT!
THE WAY THE POLE FITS IN THE GROUND MAKES ME THINK IT CAN BE LOWERED SOMEHOW, IF IT JUST HAD A LITTLE MORE WEIGHT...
WAIT A MINUTE...
...ISN'T THIS OUR FAMILY CREST?
MAYBE THESE ARE INSTRUCTIONS FOR US--THAT IS, SPECIFICALLY FOR SOMEONE IN OUR FAMILY?
IT DOESN'T MAKE ANY SENSE TO ME.
PROTECTION SYMBOL, WAVY LINES, DOORWAY, CREST AND TIPPING JAR...
IT LOOKS LIKE A PUZZLE!
MAYBE IF WE REARRANGE THE TILES...

...LET'S START WITH THE CREST!

THE WAVY LINES LOOK LIKE WATER. I'LL PLACE THAT NEXT TO THE TIPPING JAR.

I PLACED THE PROTECTION SYMBOL--THE ONE THAT APPEARS ALL OVER THE POLE.

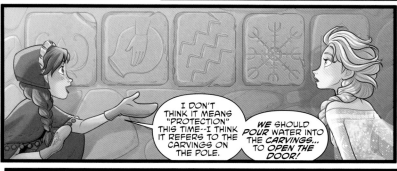

I DON'T THINK IT MEANS "PROTECTION" THIS TIME--I THINK IT REFERS TO THE CARVINGS ON THE POLE.

WE SHOULD POUR WATER INTO THE CARVINGS... TO OPEN THE DOOR!

BUT THE POLE IS UPRIGHT. HOW ARE WE GOING TO GET WATER INTO VERTICAL CARVINGS?

I THINK I KNOW!

RAINBOWS!

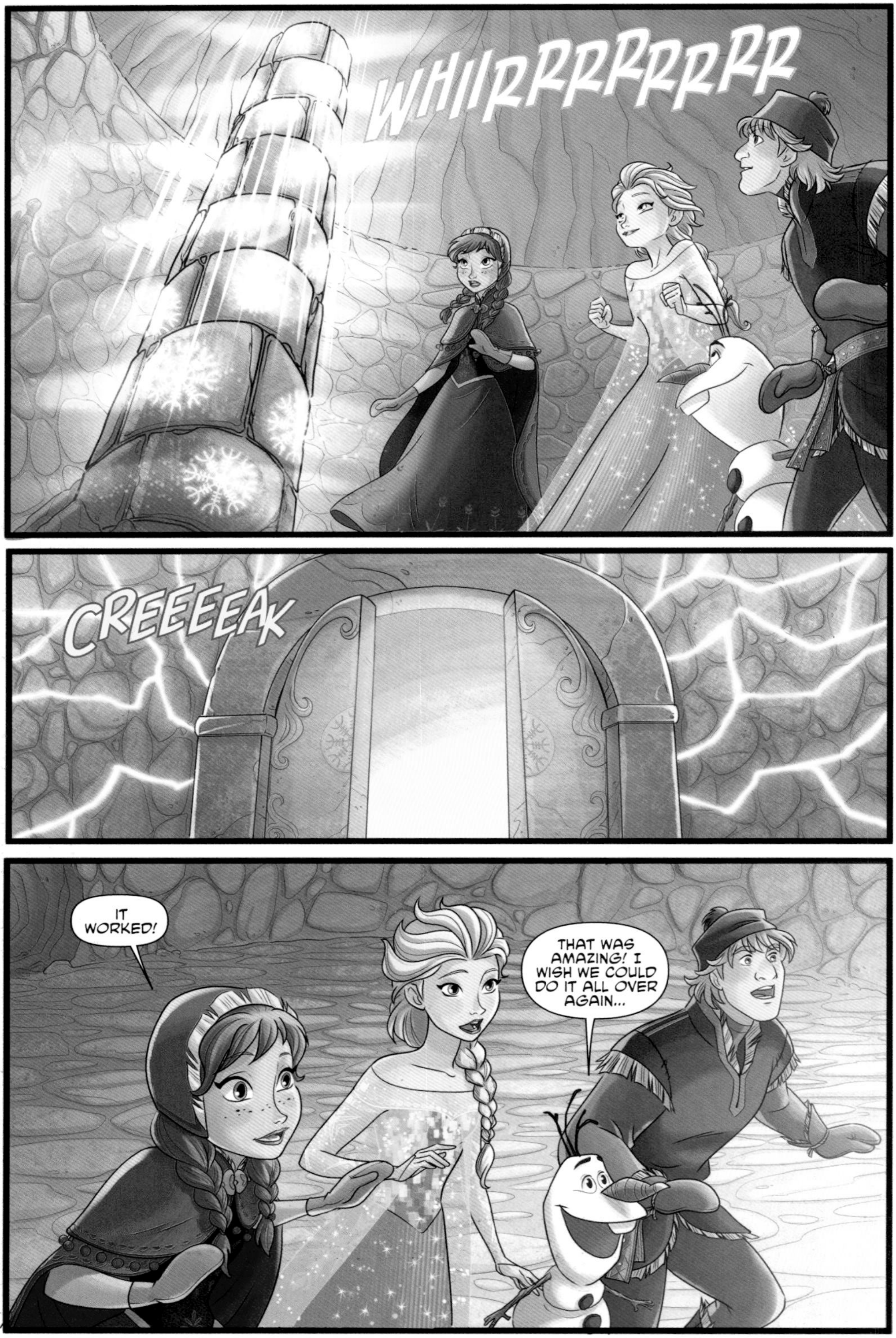
WHIIRRRRRRRR
CREEEEAK
IT WORKED!
THAT WAS AMAZING! I WISH WE COULD DO IT ALL OVER AGAIN...

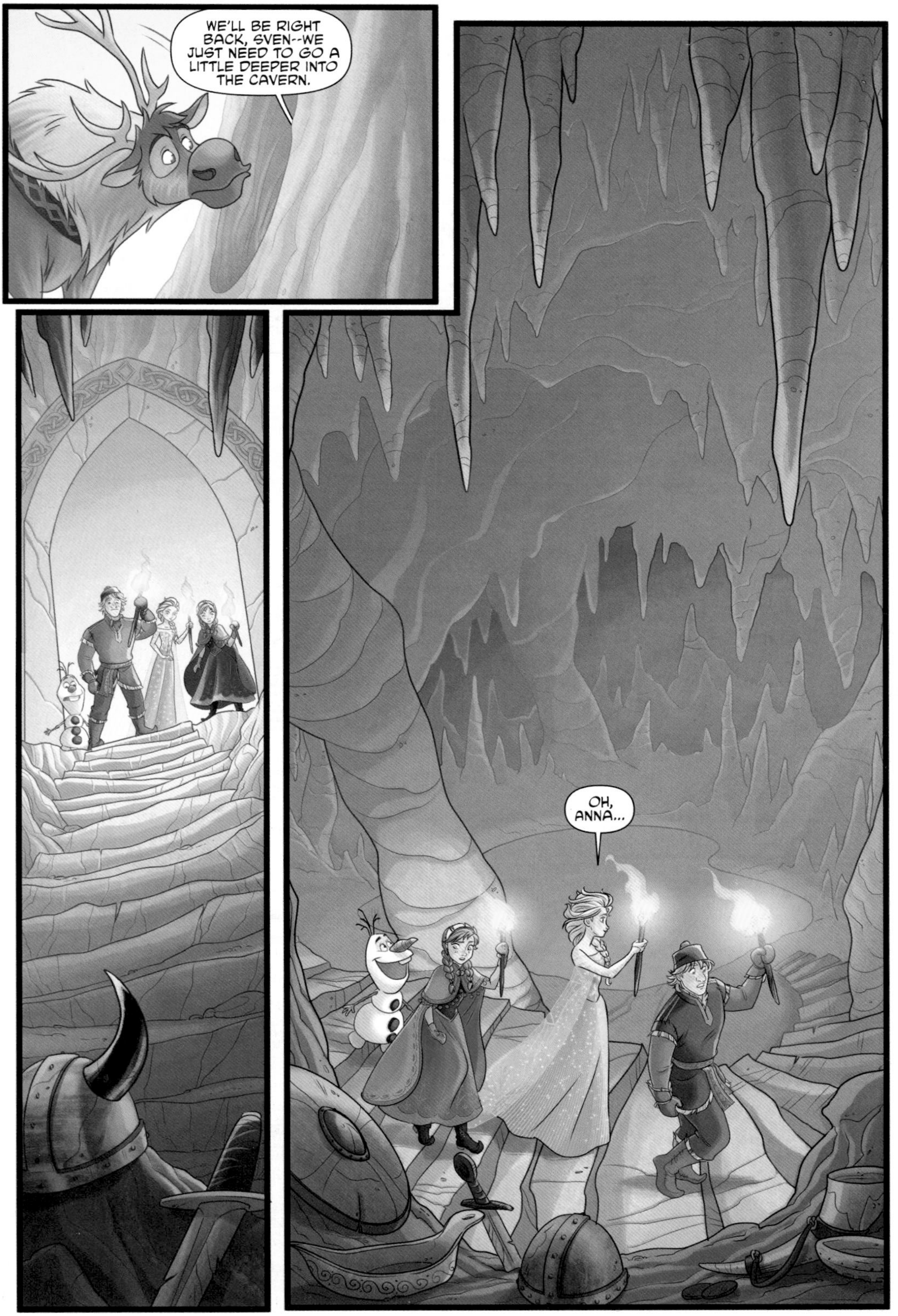
WE'LL BE RIGHT BACK, SVEN--WE JUST NEED TO GO A LITTLE DEEPER INTO THE CAVERN.
OH, ANNA...

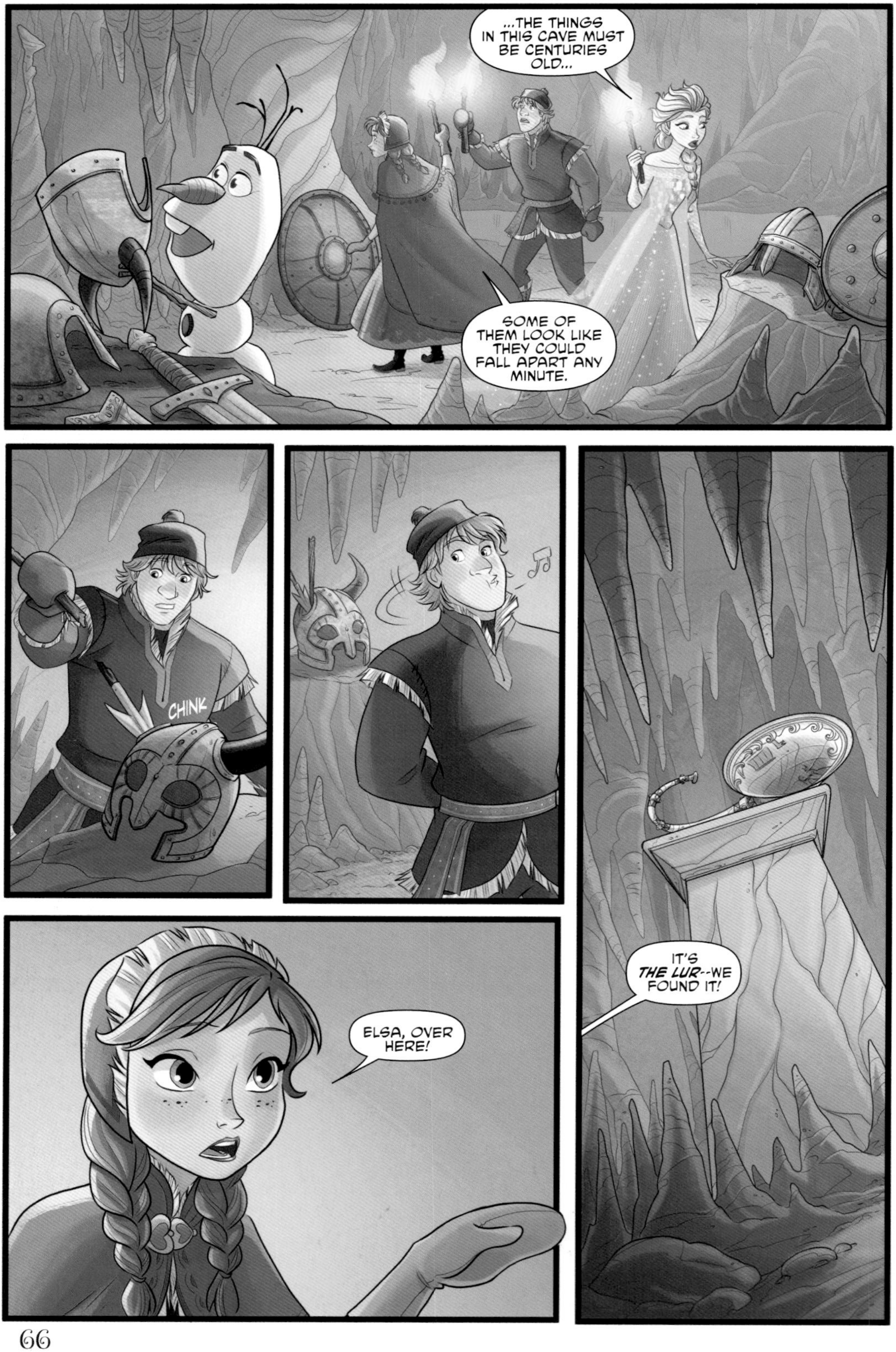
...THE THINGS IN THIS CAVE MUST BE CENTURIES OLD...
SOME OF THEM LOOK LIKE THEY COULD FALL APART ANY MINUTE.
CHINK
ELSA, OVER HERE!
IT'S *THE LUR*--WE FOUND IT!

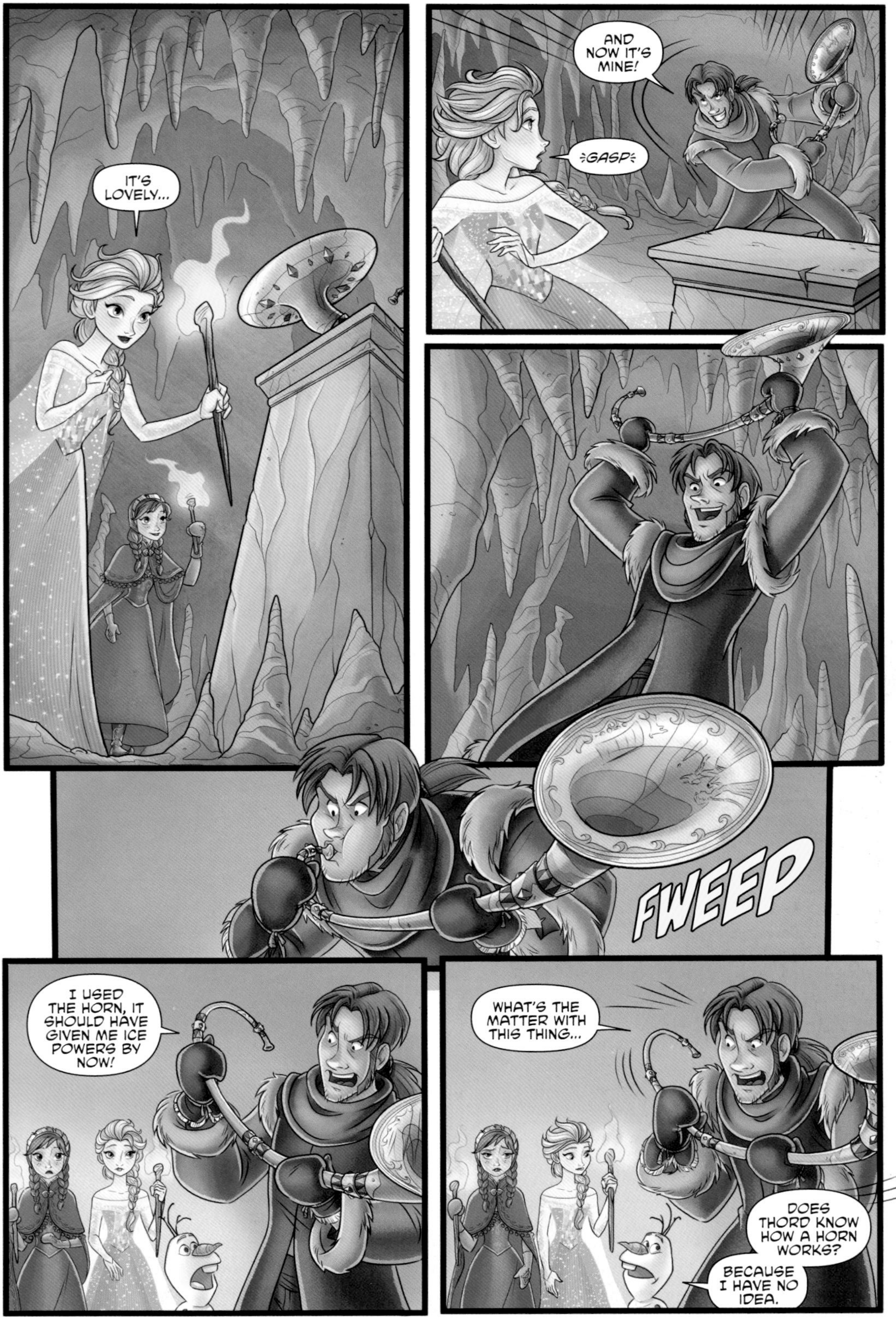
IT'S LOVELY...
AND NOW IT'S MINE!
GASP
FWEEP
I USED THE HORN, IT SHOULD HAVE GIVEN ME ICE POWERS BY NOW!
WHAT'S THE MATTER WITH THIS THING...
DOES THORD KNOW HOW A HORN WORKS?
BECAUSE I HAVE NO IDEA.

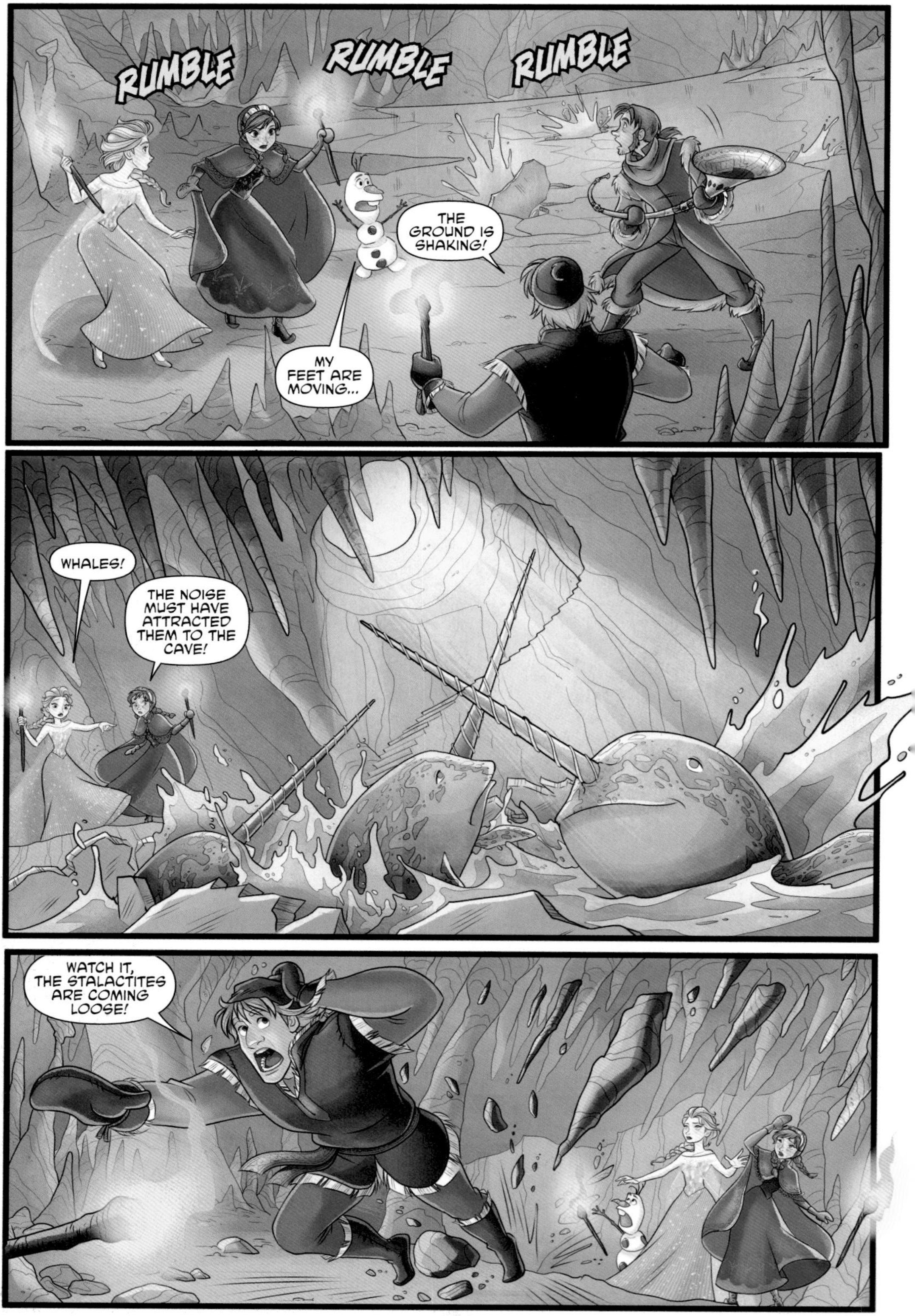
RUMBLE
RUMBLE
RUMBLE
THE GROUND IS SHAKING!
MY FEET ARE MOVING...
WHALES!
THE NOISE MUST HAVE ATTRACTED THEM TO THE CAVE!
WATCH IT, THE STALACTITES ARE COMING LOOSE!

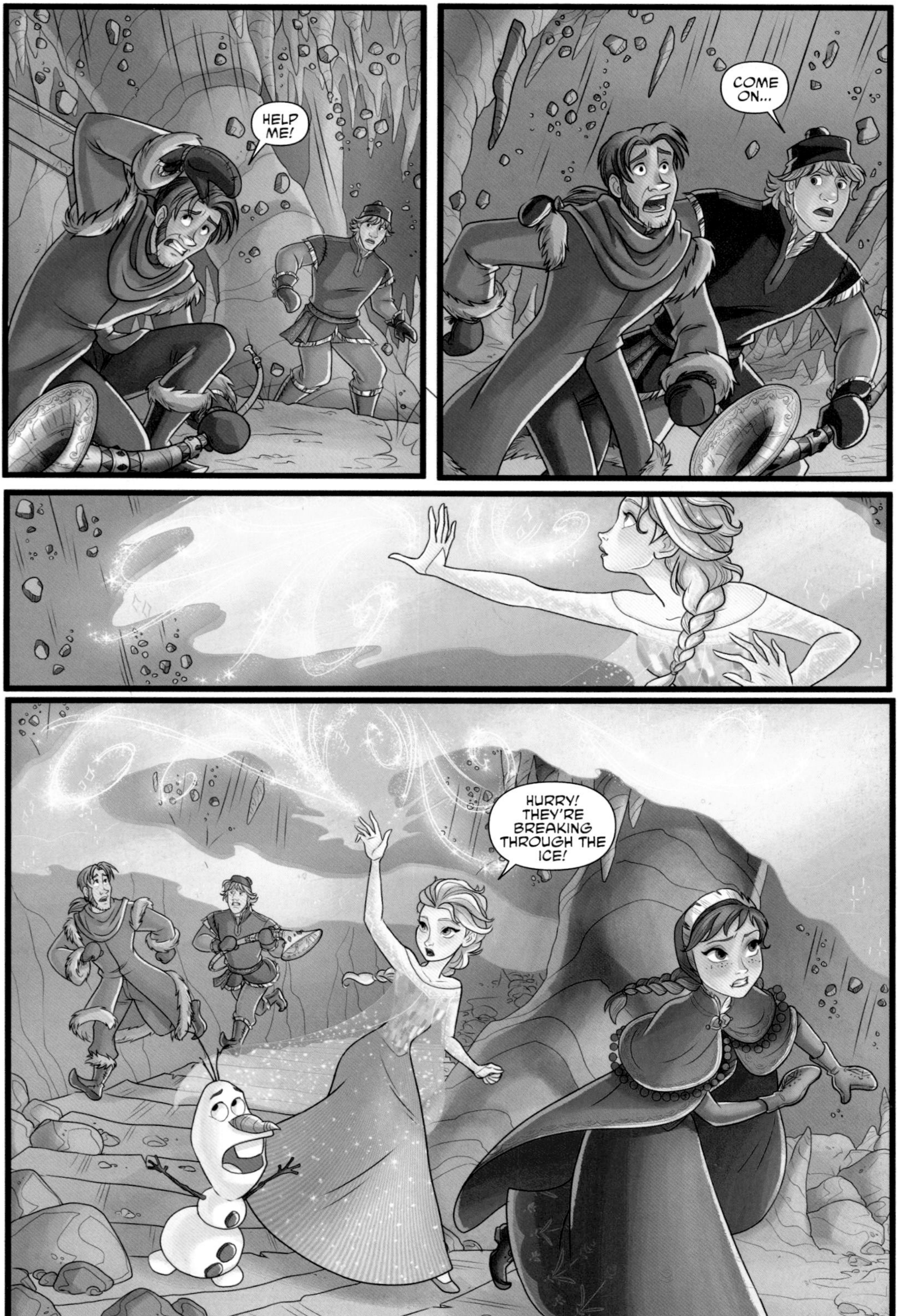
HELP ME!
COME ON...
HURRY! THEY'RE BREAKING THROUGH THE ICE!

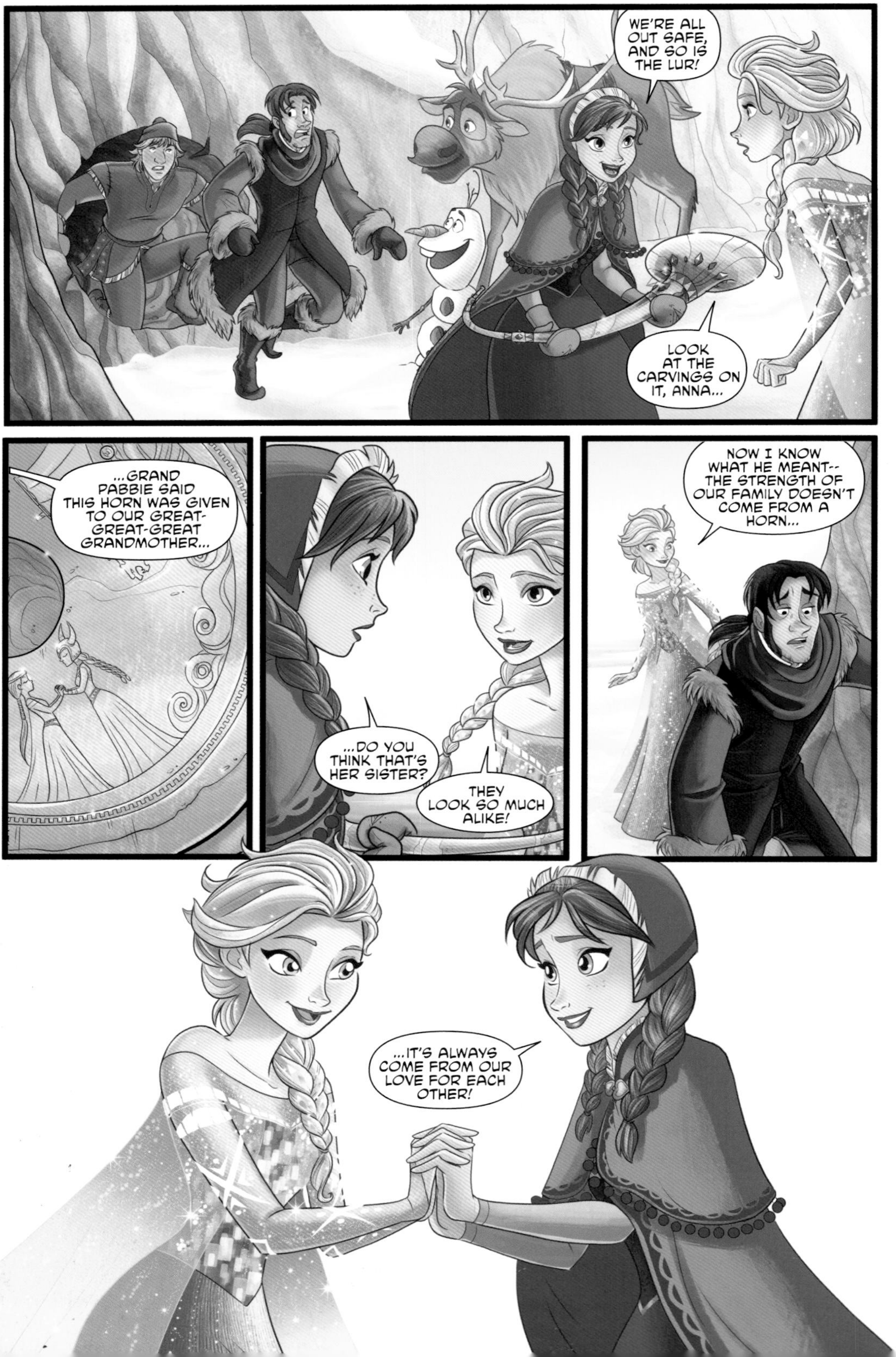
WE'RE ALL OUT SAFE, AND SO IS THE LUR!
LOOK AT THE CARVINGS ON IT, ANNA...
...GRAND PABBIE SAID THIS HORN WAS GIVEN TO OUR GREAT-GREAT-GREAT GRANDMOTHER...
...DO YOU THINK THAT'S HER SISTER?
THEY LOOK SO MUCH ALIKE!
NOW I KNOW WHAT HE MEANT-- THE STRENGTH OF OUR FAMILY DOESN'T COME FROM A HORN...
...IT'S ALWAYS COME FROM OUR LOVE FOR EACH OTHER!

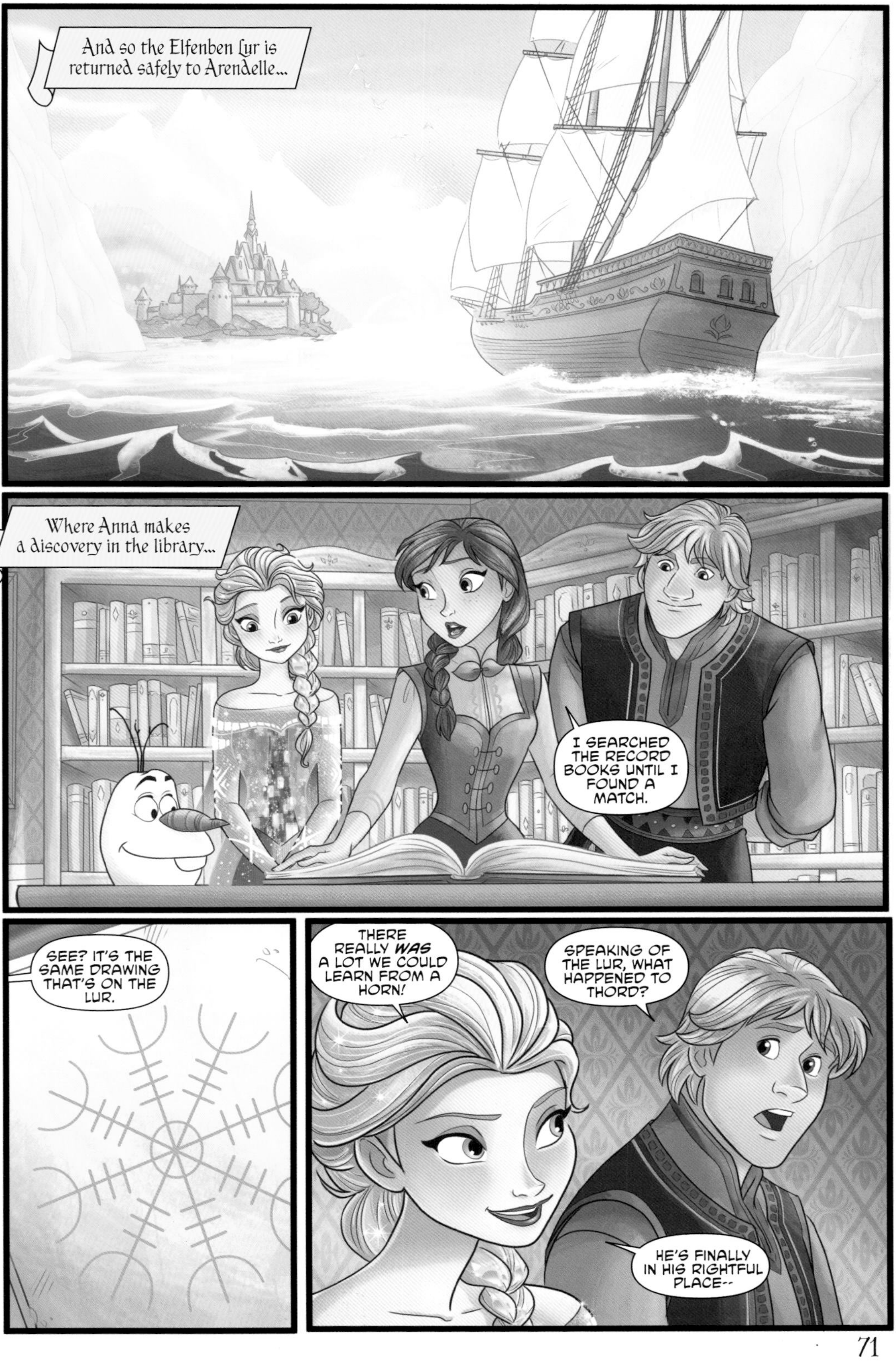
And so the Elfenben Lur is returned safely to Arendelle...
Where Anna makes a discovery in the library...
I SEARCHED THE RECORD BOOKS UNTIL I FOUND A MATCH.
SEE? IT'S THE SAME DRAWING THAT'S ON THE LUR.
THERE REALLY *WAS* A LOT WE COULD LEARN FROM A HORN!
SPEAKING OF THE LUR, WHAT HAPPENED TO THORD?
HE'S FINALLY IN HIS RIGHTFUL PLACE--

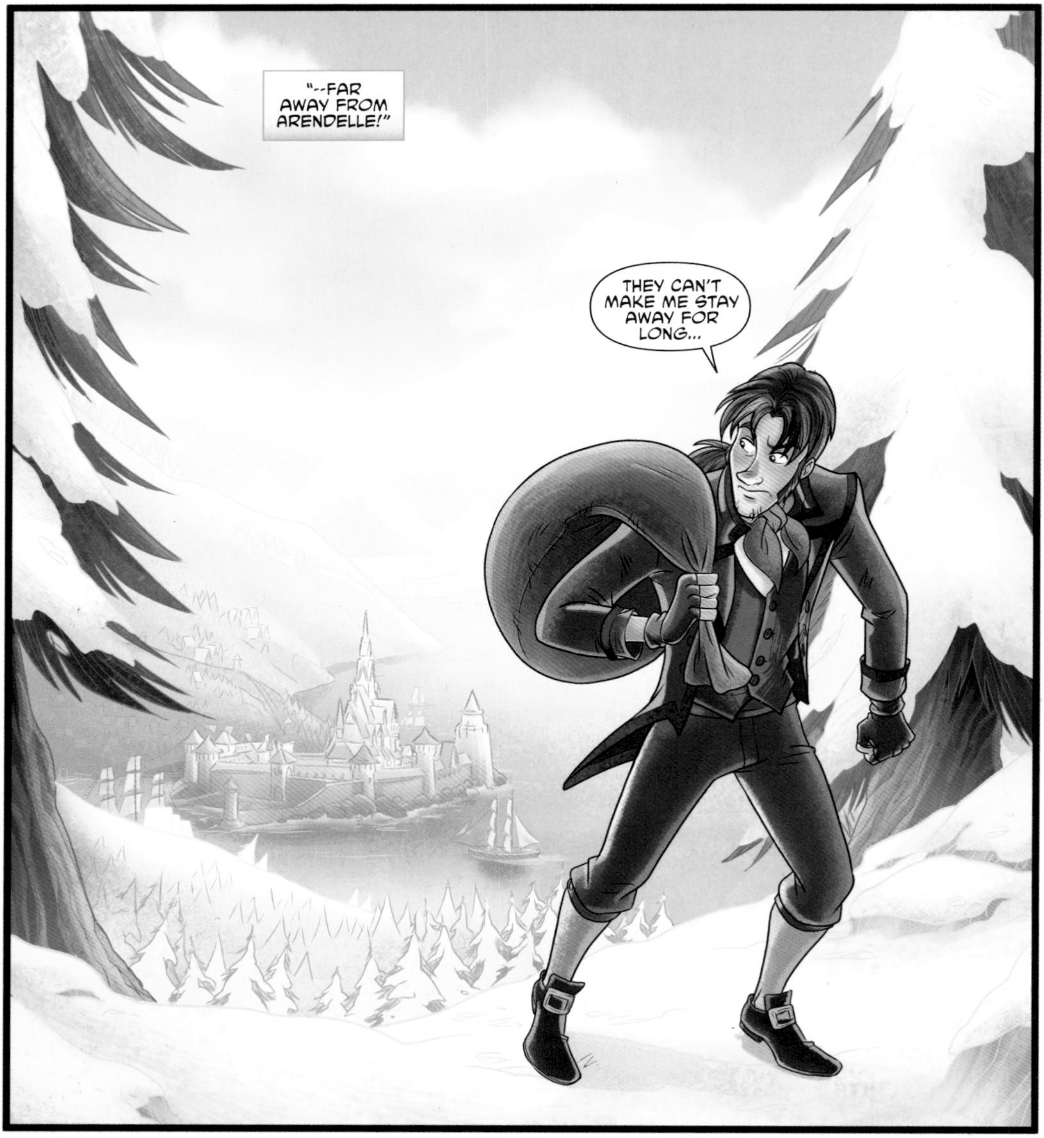
"--FAR AWAY FROM ARENDELLE!"
THEY CAN'T MAKE ME STAY AWAY FOR LONG...

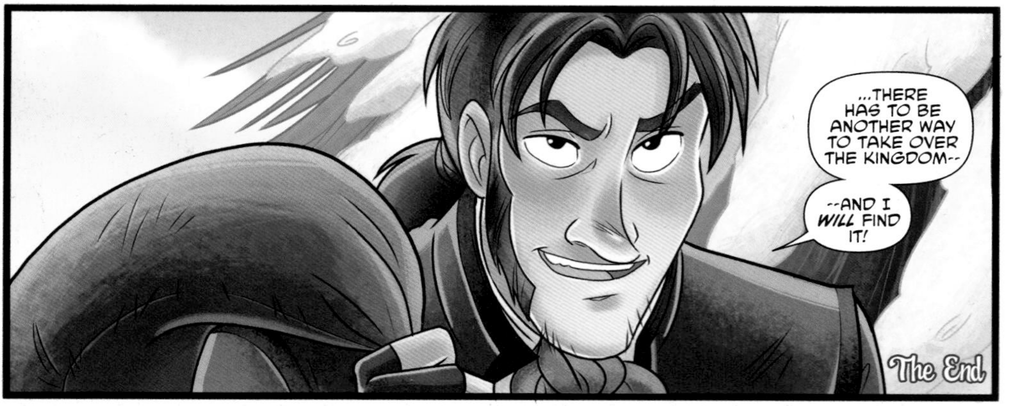
...THERE HAS TO BE ANOTHER WAY TO TAKE OVER THE KINGDOM--
--AND I *WILL* FIND IT!
The End

This Land Is Our Land

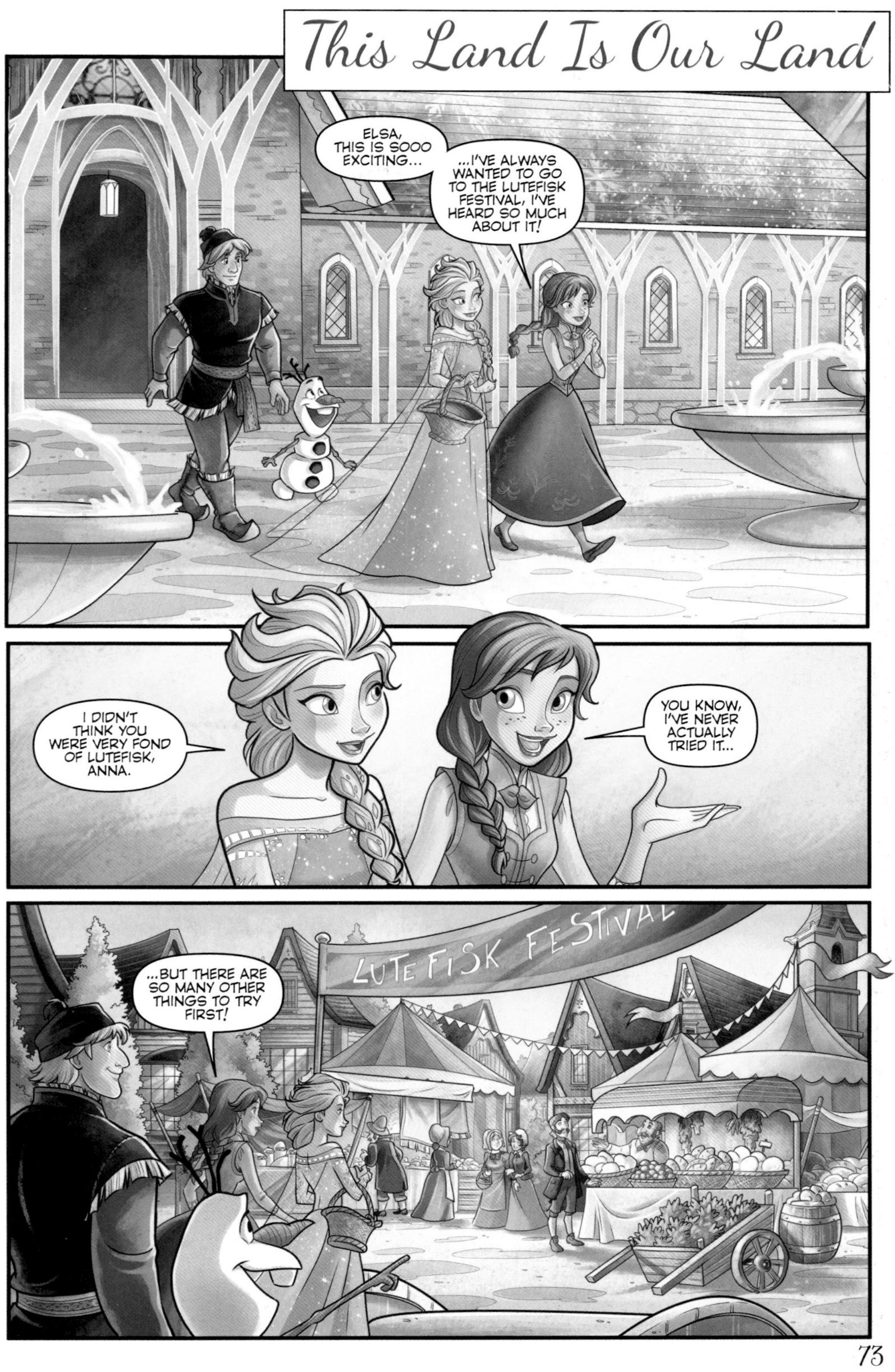
ELSA, THIS IS SOOO EXCITING...
...I'VE ALWAYS WANTED TO GO TO THE LUTEFISK FESTIVAL, I'VE HEARD SO MUCH ABOUT IT!
I DIDN'T THINK YOU WERE VERY FOND OF LUTEFISK, ANNA.
YOU KNOW, I'VE NEVER ACTUALLY TRIED IT...
LUTEFISK FESTIVAL
...BUT THERE ARE SO MANY OTHER THINGS TO TRY FIRST!

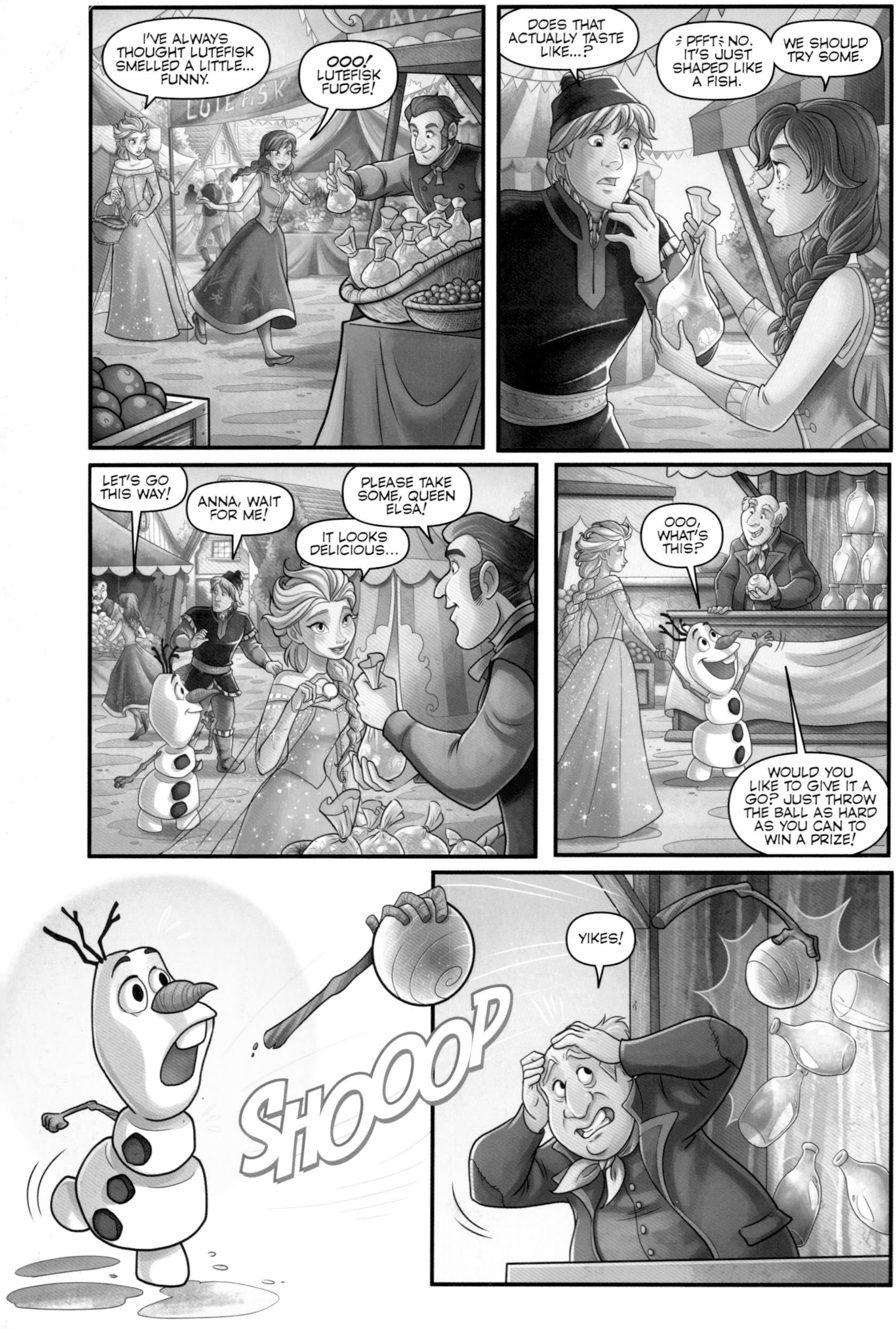
I'VE ALWAYS THOUGHT LUTEFISK SMELLED A LITTLE... FUNNY.
LUTEFISK
OOO! LUTEFISK FUDGE!
DOES THAT ACTUALLY TASTE LIKE...?
PFFT! NO. IT'S JUST SHAPED LIKE A FISH.
WE SHOULD TRY SOME.
LET'S GO THIS WAY!
ANNA, WAIT FOR ME!
PLEASE TAKE SOME, QUEEN ELSA!
IT LOOKS DELICIOUS...
OOO, WHAT'S THIS?
WOULD YOU LIKE TO GIVE IT A GO? JUST THROW THE BALL AS HARD AS YOU CAN TO WIN A PRIZE!
SHOOOP
YIKES!

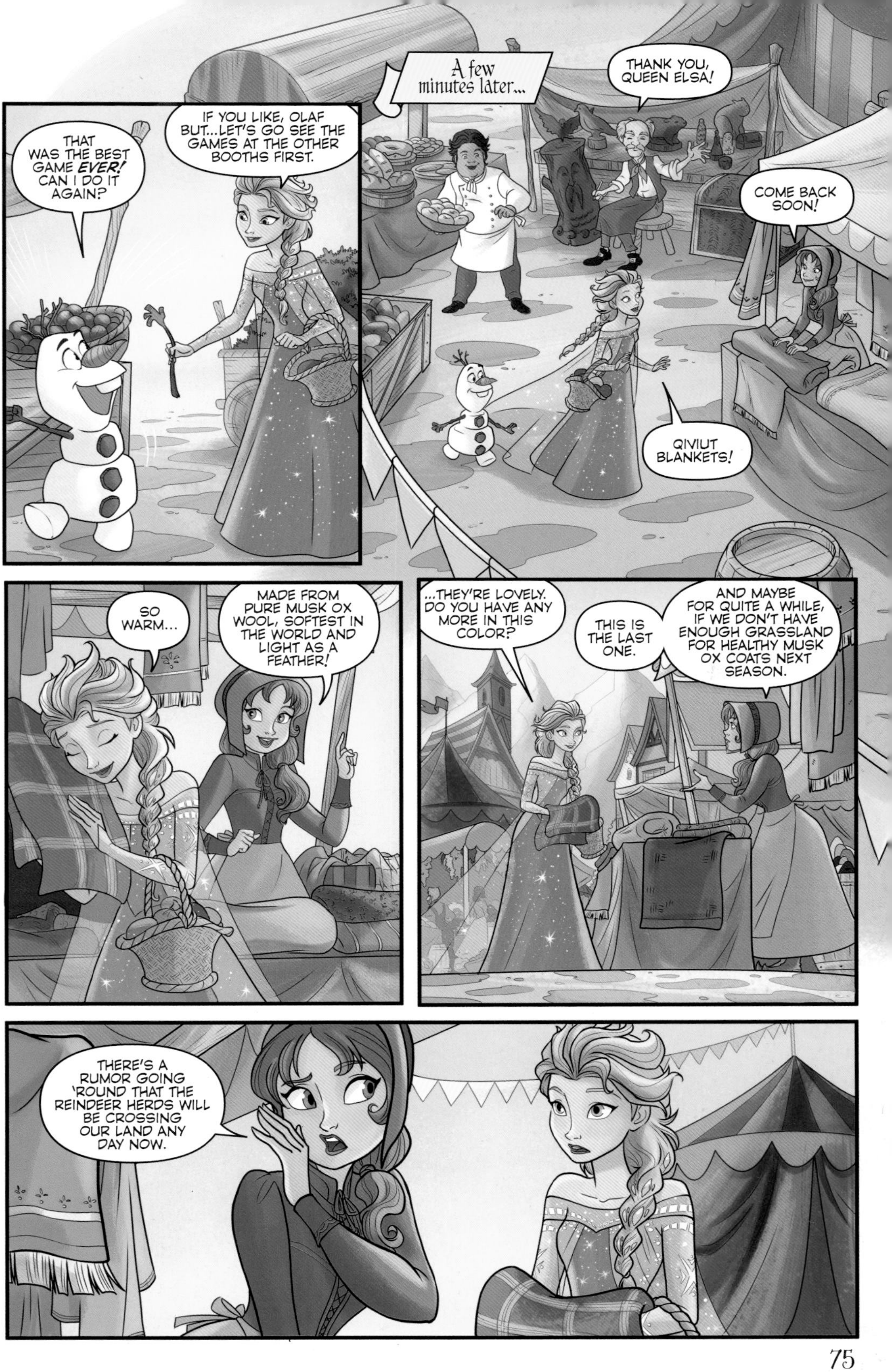
A few minutes later...
THAT WAS THE BEST GAME EVER! CAN I DO IT AGAIN?
IF YOU LIKE, OLAF BUT...LET'S GO SEE THE GAMES AT THE OTHER BOOTHS FIRST.
THANK YOU, QUEEN ELSA!
COME BACK SOON!
QIVIUT BLANKETS!
SO WARM...
MADE FROM PURE MUSK OX WOOL, SOFTEST IN THE WORLD AND LIGHT AS A FEATHER!
...THEY'RE LOVELY. DO YOU HAVE ANY MORE IN THIS COLOR?
THIS IS THE LAST ONE.
AND MAYBE FOR QUITE A WHILE, IF WE DON'T HAVE ENOUGH GRASSLAND FOR HEALTHY MUSK OX COATS NEXT SEASON.
THERE'S A RUMOR GOING 'ROUND THAT THE REINDEER HERDS WILL BE CROSSING OUR LAND ANY DAY NOW.

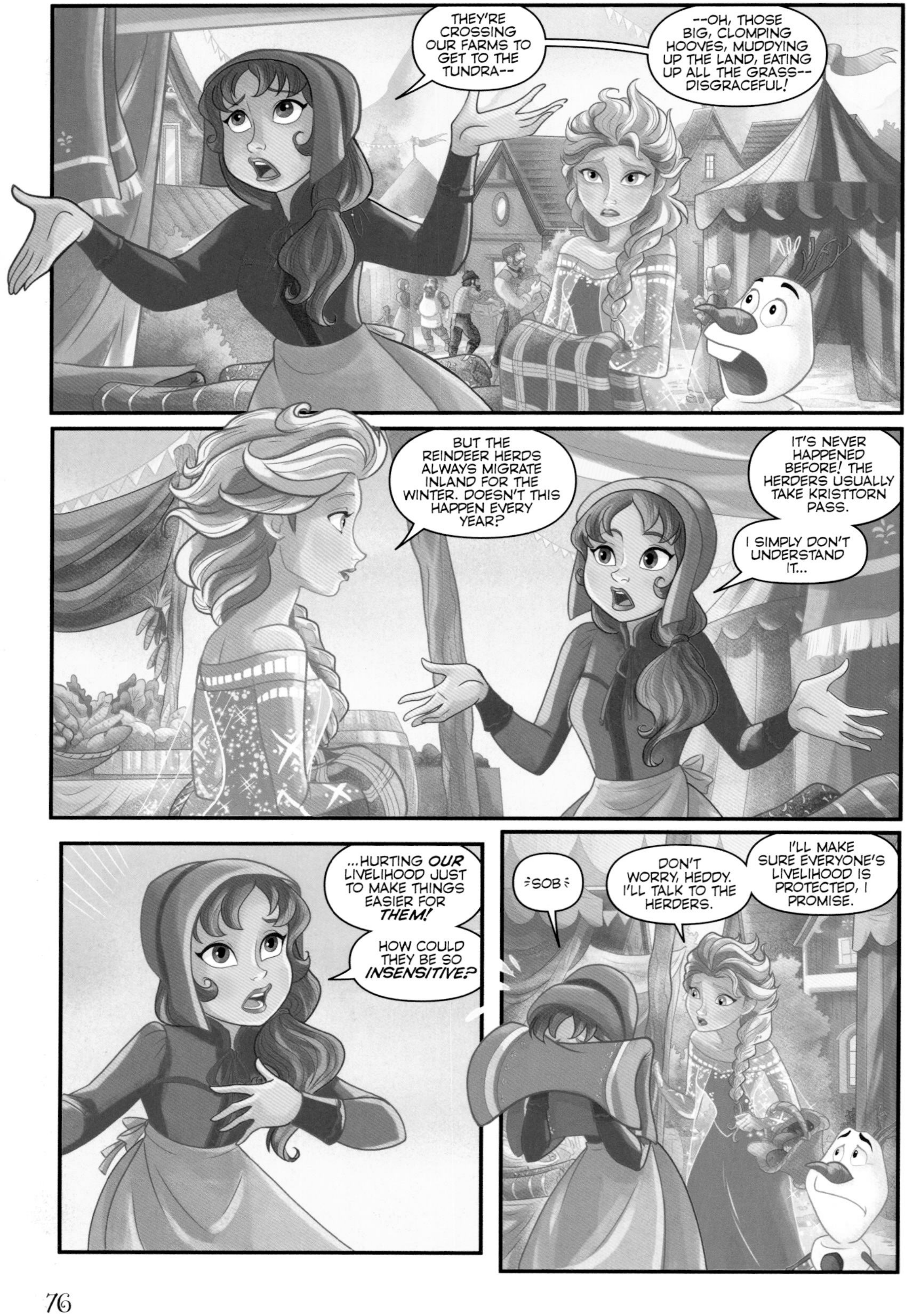
THEY'RE CROSSING OUR FARMS TO GET TO THE TUNDRA--
--OH, THOSE BIG, CLOMPING HOOVES, MUDDYING UP THE LAND, EATING UP ALL THE GRASS-- DISGRACEFUL!
BUT THE REINDEER HERDS ALWAYS MIGRATE INLAND FOR THE WINTER. DOESN'T THIS HAPPEN EVERY YEAR?
IT'S NEVER HAPPENED BEFORE! THE HERDERS USUALLY TAKE KRISTTORN PASS.
I SIMPLY DON'T UNDERSTAND IT...
...HURTING OUR LIVELIHOOD JUST TO MAKE THINGS EASIER FOR THEM!
HOW COULD THEY BE SO INSENSITIVE?
SOB
DON'T WORRY, HEDDY. I'LL TALK TO THE HERDERS.
I'LL MAKE SURE EVERYONE'S LIVELIHOOD IS PROTECTED, I PROMISE.

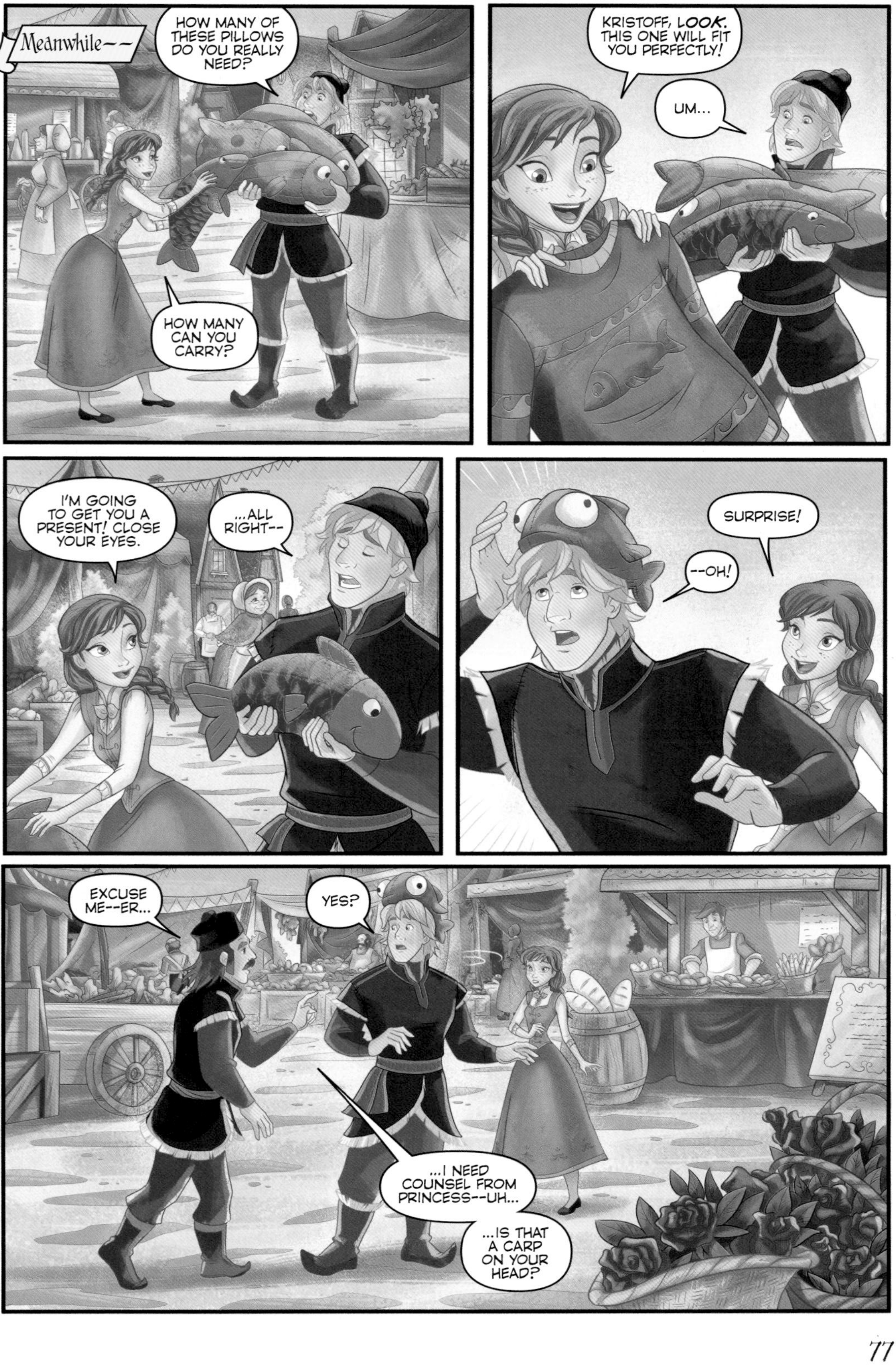

Meanwhile--
HOW MANY OF THESE PILLOWS DO YOU REALLY NEED?
HOW MANY CAN YOU CARRY?
KRISTOFF, LOOK. THIS ONE WILL FIT YOU PERFECTLY!
UM...
I'M GOING TO GET YOU A PRESENT! CLOSE YOUR EYES.
...ALL RIGHT--
SURPRISE!
--OH!
EXCUSE ME--ER...
YES?
...I NEED COUNSEL FROM PRINCESS--UH...
...IS THAT A CARP ON YOUR HEAD?

LOOKS MORE LIKE A SALMON TO ME.

WHAT CAN I DO FOR YOU?

MY APOLOGIES FOR DISTURBING YOU, PRINCESS ANNA. I AM ERET, A REINDEER HERDER. THE REST OF THE REINDEER HERDERS HAVE ASKED ME TO FIND YOU AND SPEAK FOR US ALL.

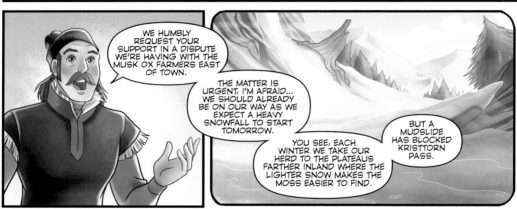

WE HUMBLY REQUEST YOUR SUPPORT IN A DISPUTE WE'RE HAVING WITH THE MUSK OX FARMERS EAST OF TOWN.

THE MATTER IS URGENT, I'M AFRAID... WE SHOULD ALREADY BE ON OUR WAY AS WE EXPECT A HEAVY SNOWFALL TO START TOMORROW.

YOU SEE, EACH WINTER WE TAKE OUR HERD TO THE PLATEAUS FARTHER INLAND WHERE THE LIGHTER SNOW MAKES THE MOSS EASIER TO FIND.

BUT A MUDSLIDE HAS BLOCKED KRISTTORN PASS.

WE MUST CROSS THE FARMERS' PASTURES INSTEAD. THEY'RE ANGRY WITH US BUT WE HAVE NO CHOICE.

WE'VE TRIED TO EXPLAIN BUT THEY WON'T STOP SHOUTING LONG ENOUGH TO LISTEN. MANY OF THEM ARE BUSY WITH THE FESTIVAL TODAY AND THERE'S NO MORE TIME TO ARGUE.

HOW TERRIBLE! I'M SURE QUEEN ELSA WILL HELP.

WE HAVE TO ACT QUICKLY.

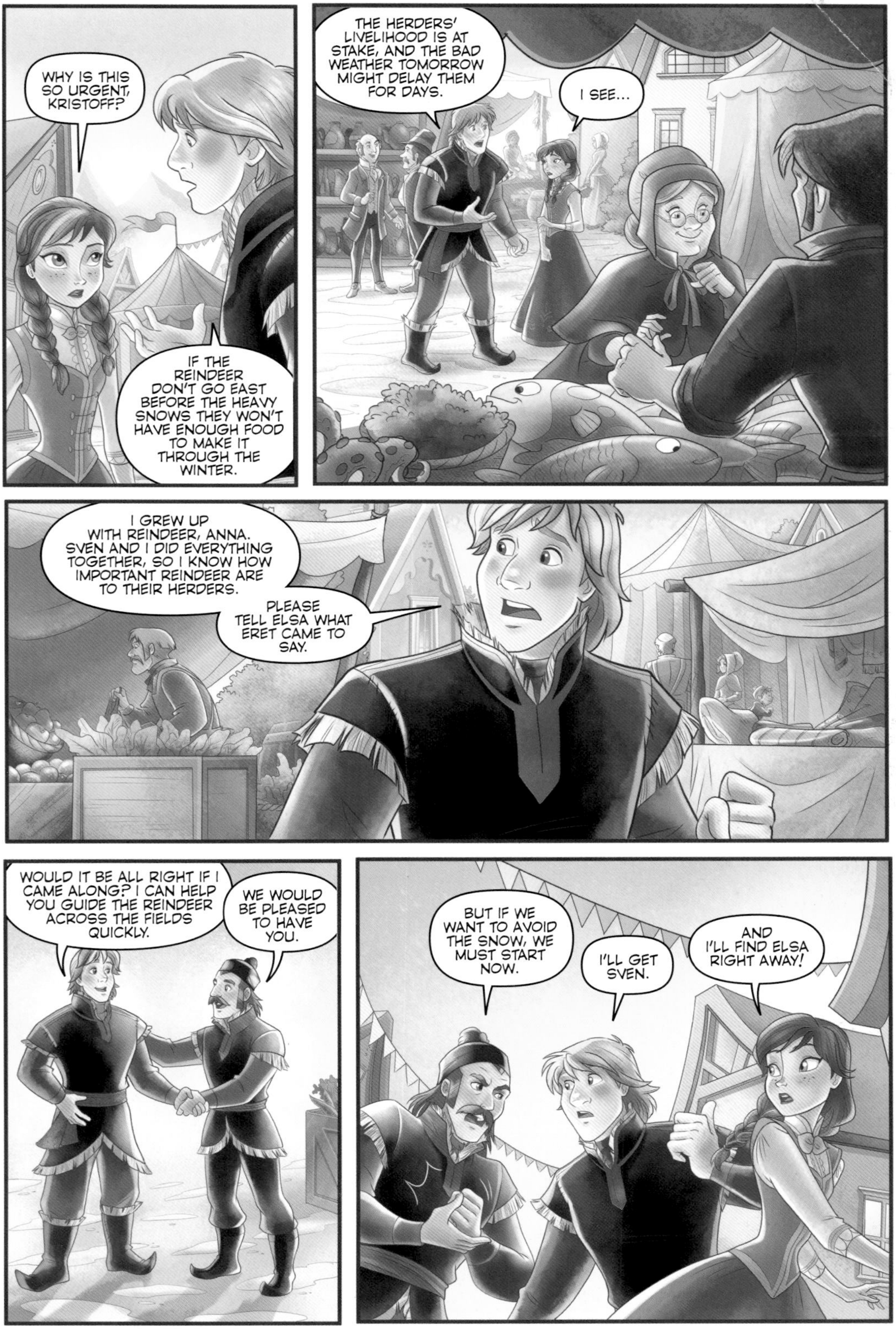
WHY IS THIS SO URGENT, KRISTOFF?
IF THE REINDEER DON'T GO EAST BEFORE THE HEAVY SNOWS THEY WON'T HAVE ENOUGH FOOD TO MAKE IT THROUGH THE WINTER.
THE HERDERS' LIVELIHOOD IS AT STAKE, AND THE BAD WEATHER TOMORROW MIGHT DELAY THEM FOR DAYS.
I SEE...
I GREW UP WITH REINDEER, ANNA. SVEN AND I DID EVERYTHING TOGETHER, SO I KNOW HOW IMPORTANT REINDEER ARE TO THEIR HERDERS.
PLEASE TELL ELSA WHAT ERET CAME TO SAY.
WOULD IT BE ALL RIGHT IF I CAME ALONG? I CAN HELP YOU GUIDE THE REINDEER ACROSS THE FIELDS QUICKLY.
WE WOULD BE PLEASED TO HAVE YOU.
BUT IF WE WANT TO AVOID THE SNOW, WE MUST START NOW.
I'LL GET SVEN.
AND I'LL FIND ELSA RIGHT AWAY!

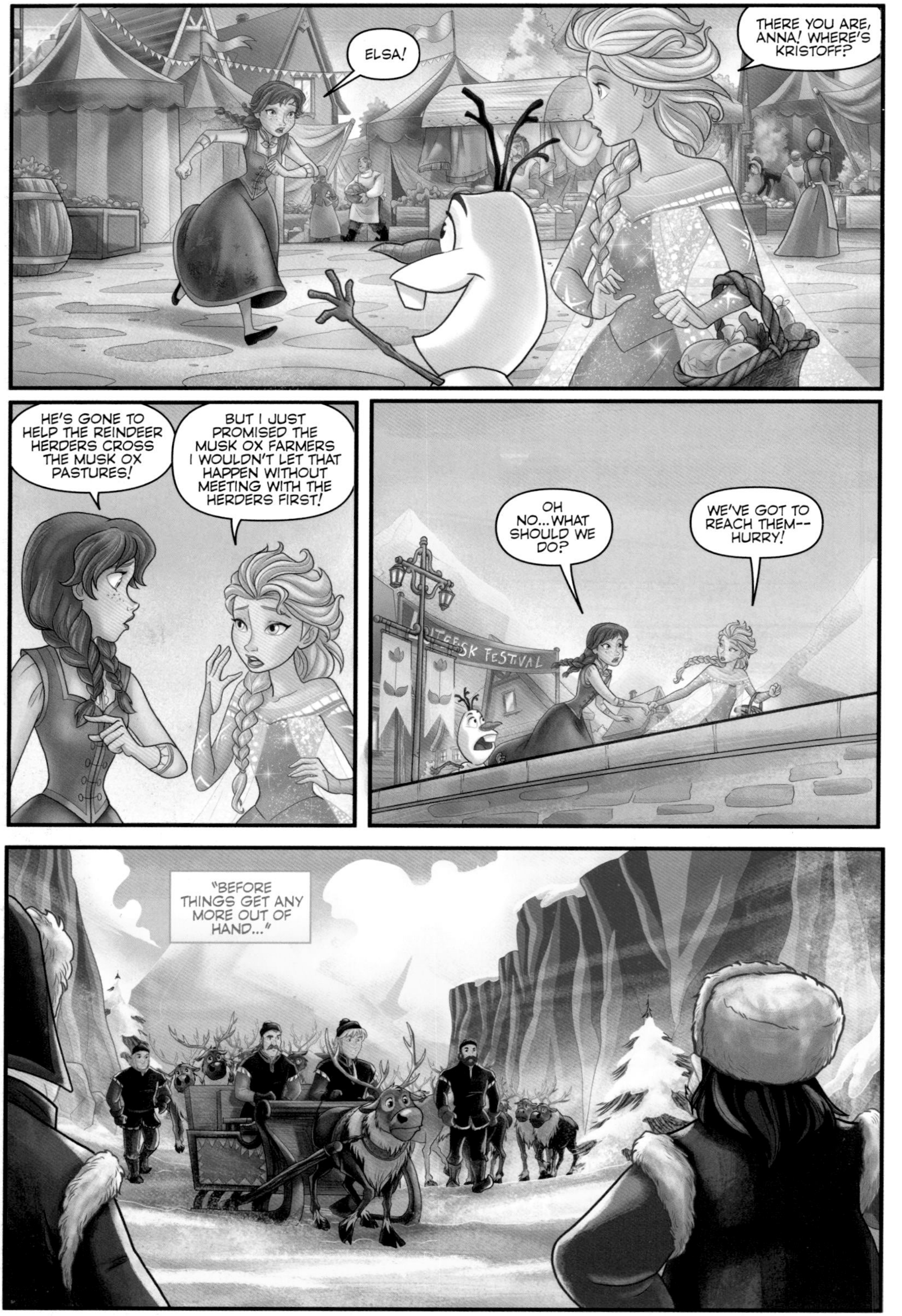
ELSA!
THERE YOU ARE, ANNA! WHERE'S KRISTOFF?
HE'S GONE TO HELP THE REINDEER HERDERS CROSS THE MUSK OX PASTURES!
BUT I JUST PROMISED THE MUSK OX FARMERS I WOULDN'T LET THAT HAPPEN WITHOUT MEETING WITH THE HERDERS FIRST!
OH NO...WHAT SHOULD WE DO?
WE'VE GOT TO REACH THEM--HURRY!
"BEFORE THINGS GET ANY MORE OUT OF HAND..."

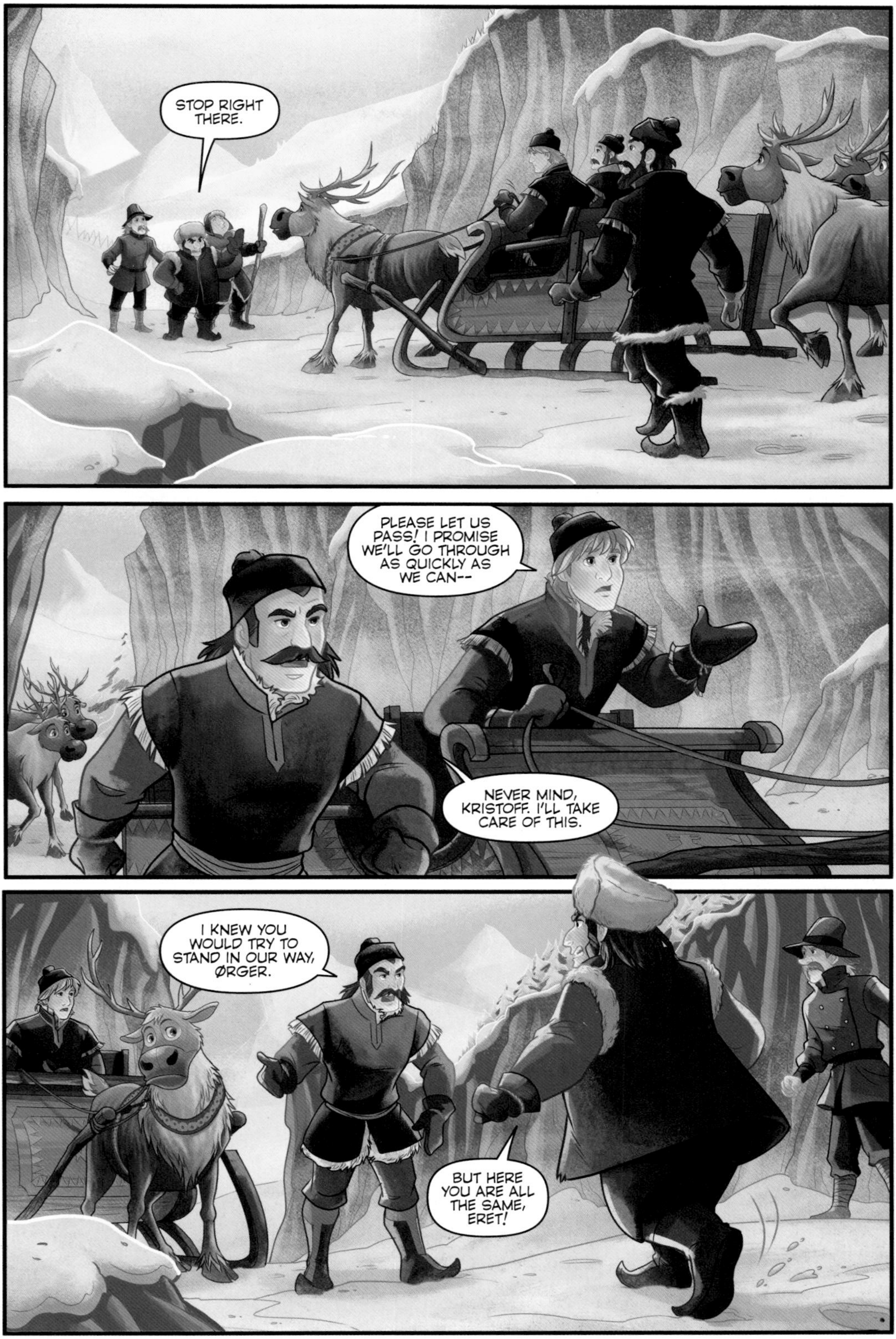
STOP RIGHT THERE.
PLEASE LET US PASS! I PROMISE WE'LL GO THROUGH AS QUICKLY AS WE CAN--
NEVER MIND, KRISTOFF. I'LL TAKE CARE OF THIS.
I KNEW YOU WOULD TRY TO STAND IN OUR WAY, ØRGER.
BUT HERE YOU ARE ALL THE SAME, ERET!

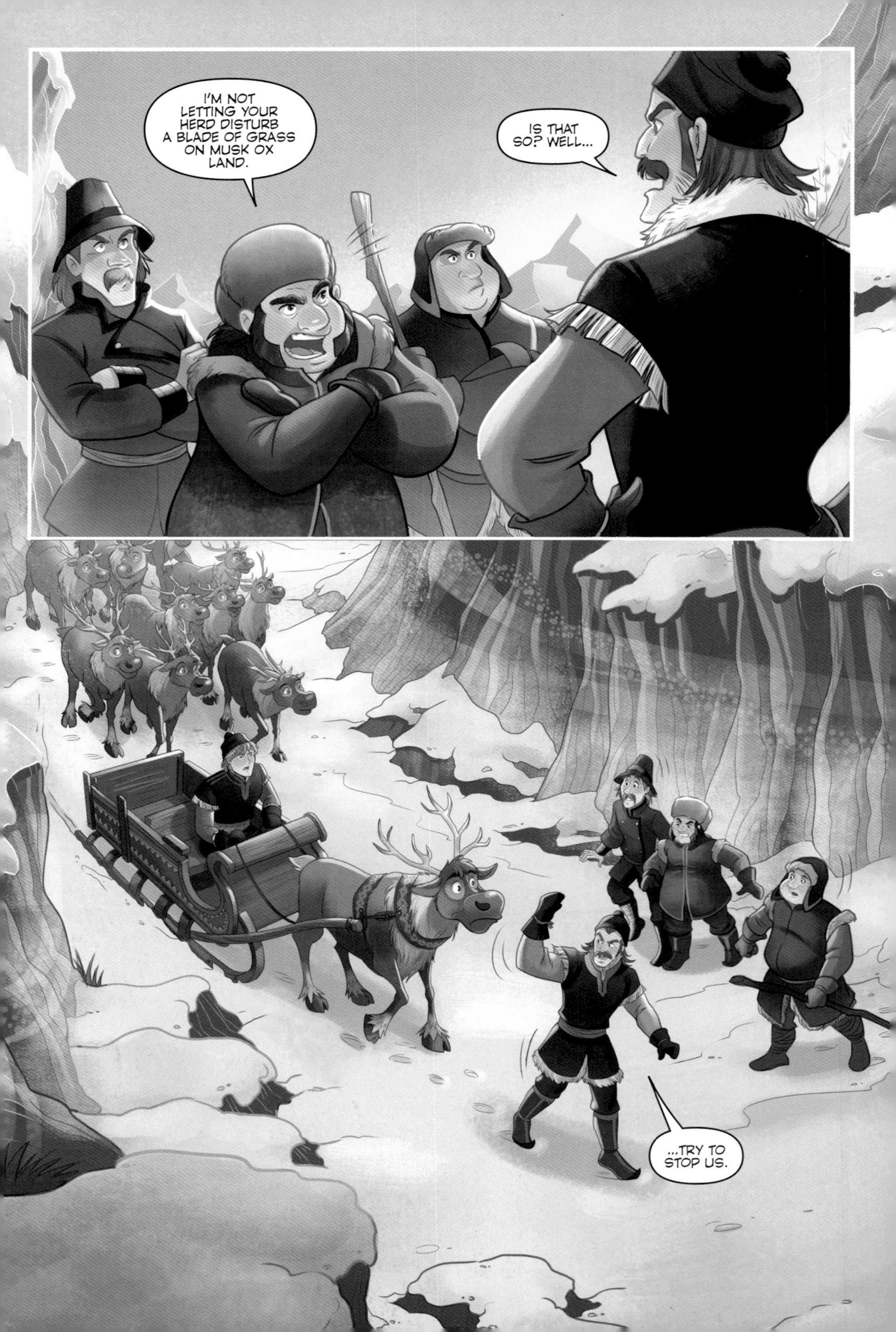
I'M NOT LETTING YOUR HERD DISTURB A BLADE OF GRASS ON MUSK OX LAND.
IS THAT SO? WELL...
...TRY TO STOP US.

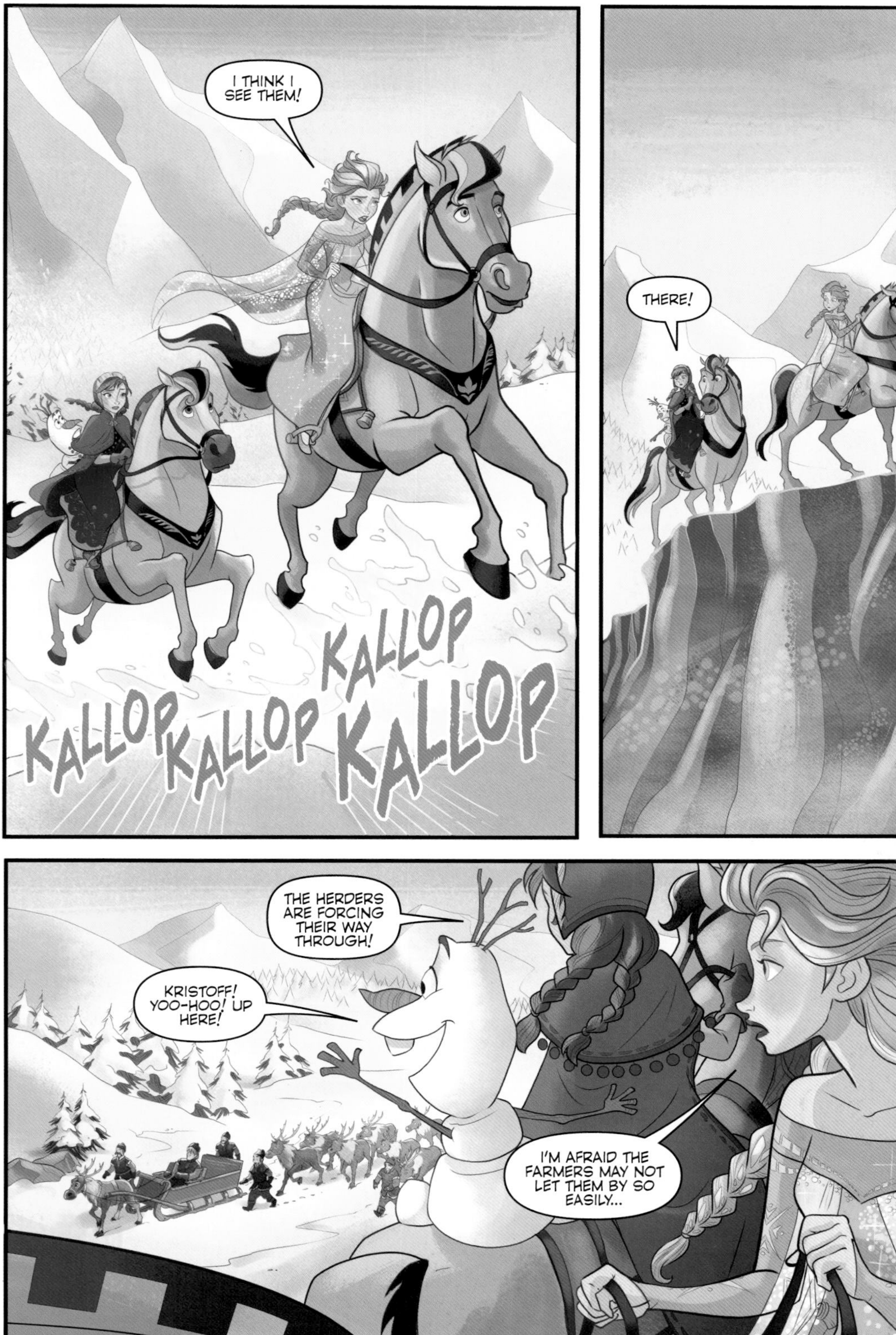
I THINK I SEE THEM!
KALLOP KALLOP KALLOP KALLOP
THERE!
THE HERDERS ARE FORCING THEIR WAY THROUGH!
KRISTOFF! YOO-HOO! UP HERE!
I'M AFRAID THE FARMERS MAY NOT LET THEM BY SO EASILY...

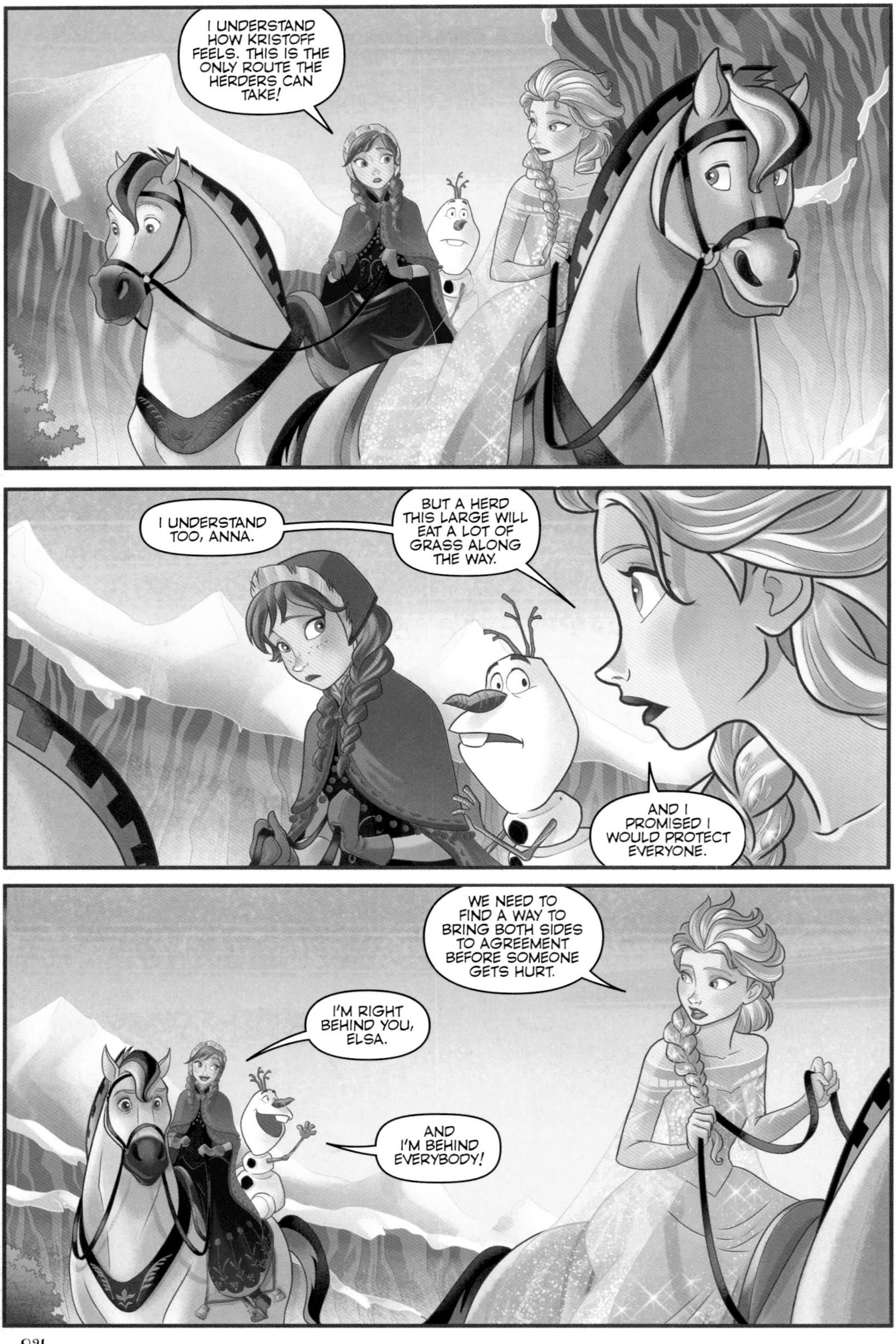
I UNDERSTAND HOW KRISTOFF FEELS. THIS IS THE ONLY ROUTE THE HERDERS CAN TAKE!
I UNDERSTAND TOO, ANNA.
BUT A HERD THIS LARGE WILL EAT A LOT OF GRASS ALONG THE WAY.
AND I PROMISED I WOULD PROTECT EVERYONE.
WE NEED TO FIND A WAY TO BRING BOTH SIDES TO AGREEMENT BEFORE SOMEONE GETS HURT.
I'M RIGHT BEHIND YOU, ELSA.
AND I'M BEHIND EVERYBODY!

DO THEY THINK WE'RE JUST GOING TO LET THEM WALK ALL OVER US?

DROP THE STONES TO BLOCK THEIR WAY!

DROP THE STONES TO BLOCK THEIR WAY!

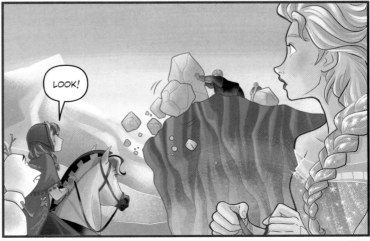

LOOK!

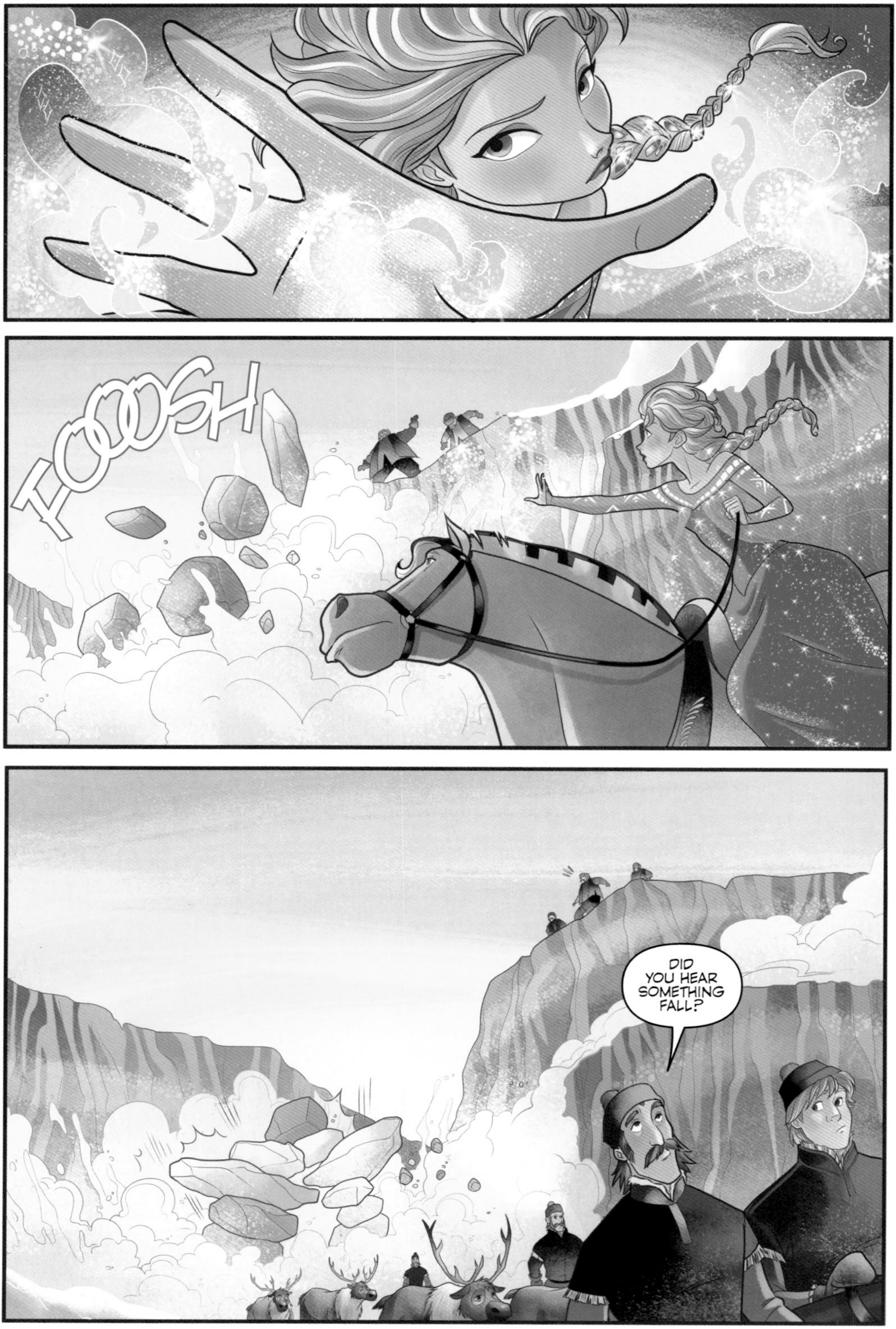
FOOOSH
DID YOU HEAR SOMETHING FALL?

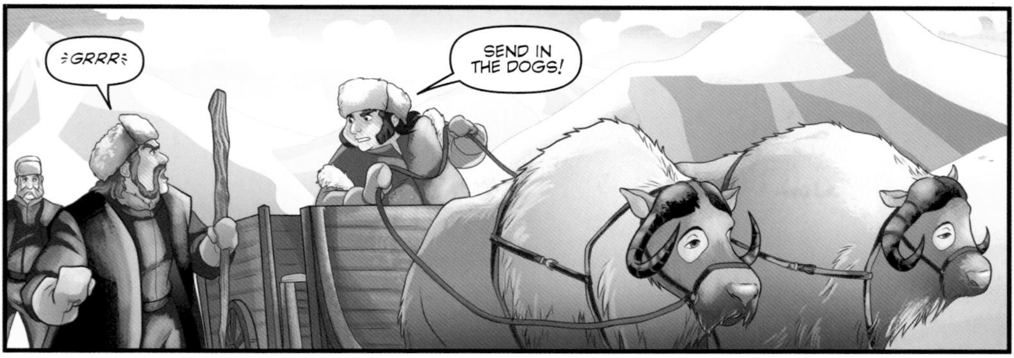

GRRR
SEND IN THE DOGS!

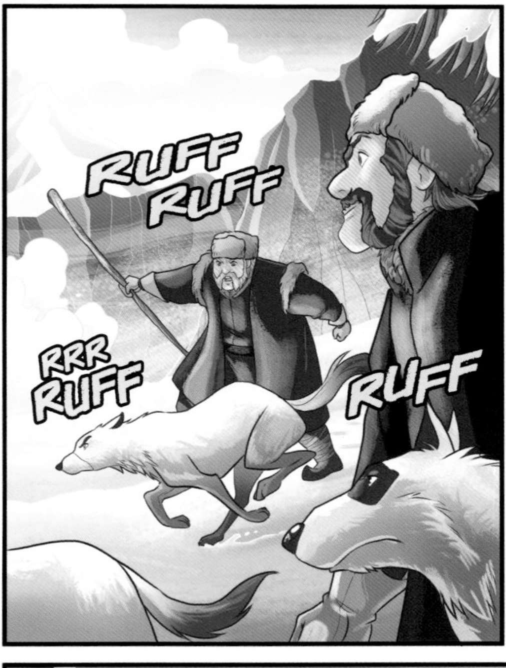

RUFF RUFF
RRR RUFF
RUFF

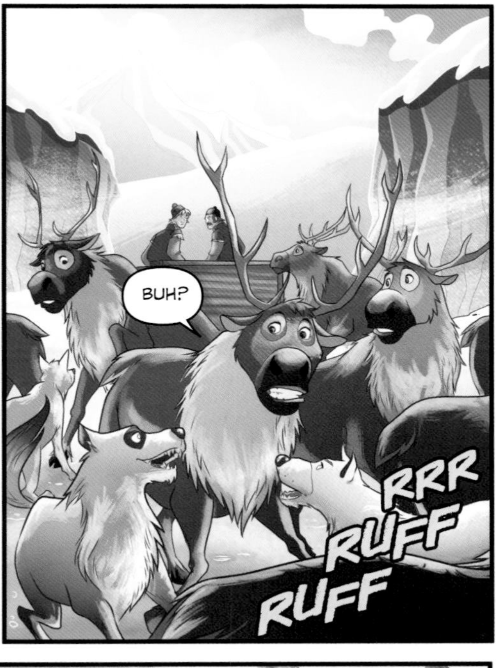

BUH?
RRR RUFF RUFF

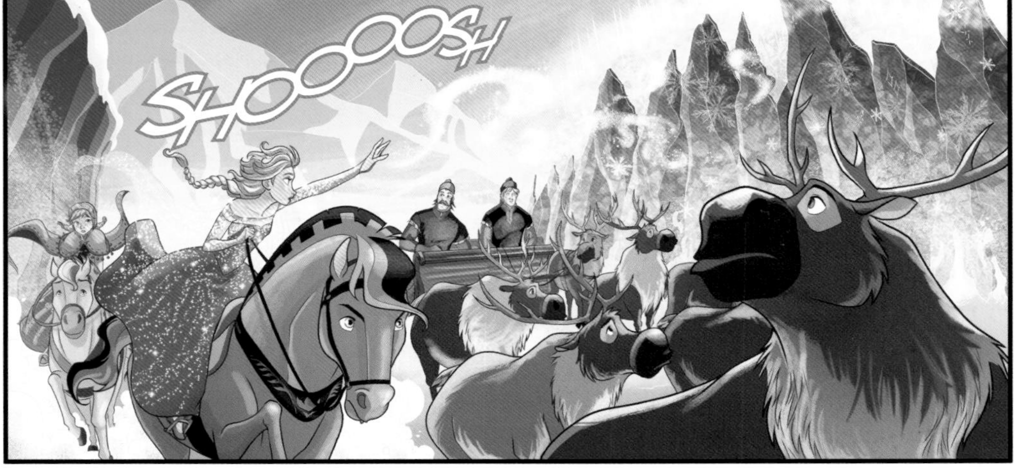

SHOOOOSH

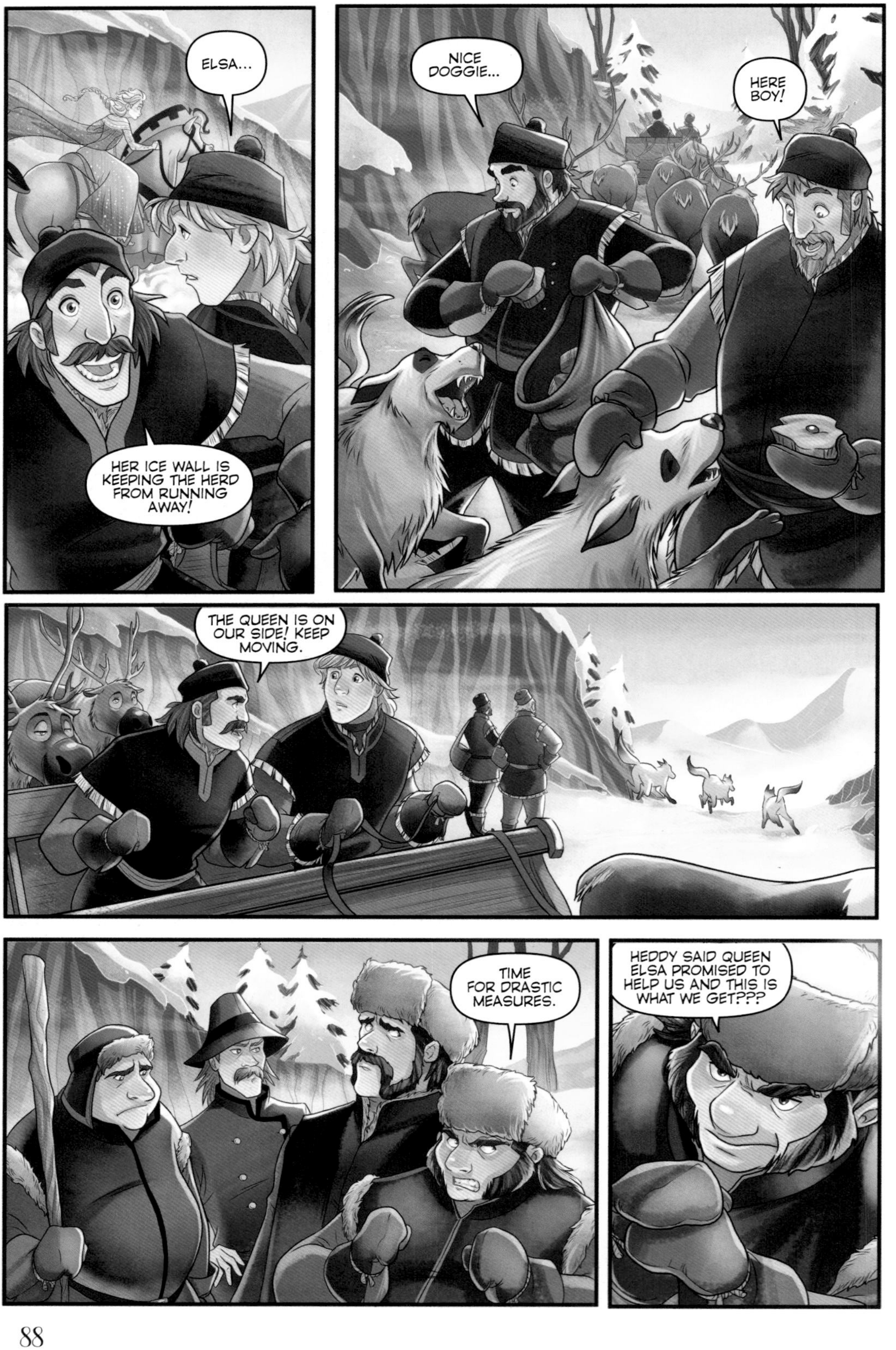
ELSA...
HER ICE WALL IS KEEPING THE HERD FROM RUNNING AWAY!
NICE DOGGIE...
HERE BOY!
THE QUEEN IS ON OUR SIDE! KEEP MOVING.
TIME FOR DRASTIC MEASURES.
HEDDY SAID QUEEN ELSA PROMISED TO HELP US AND THIS IS WHAT WE GET???

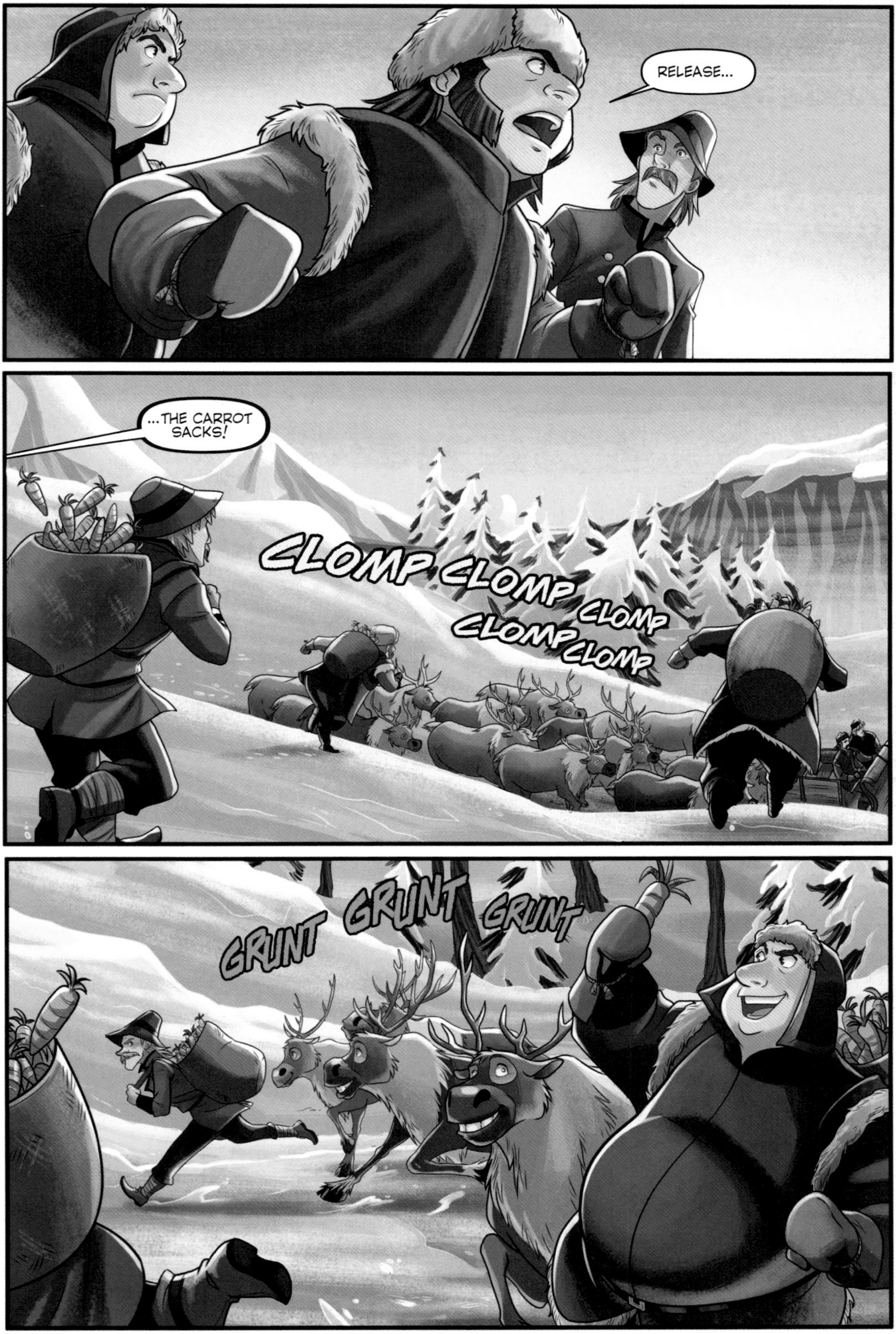
RELEASE...
...THE CARROT SACKS!
CLOMP CLOMP CLOMP
CLOMP CLOMP
GRUNT GRUNT GRUNT

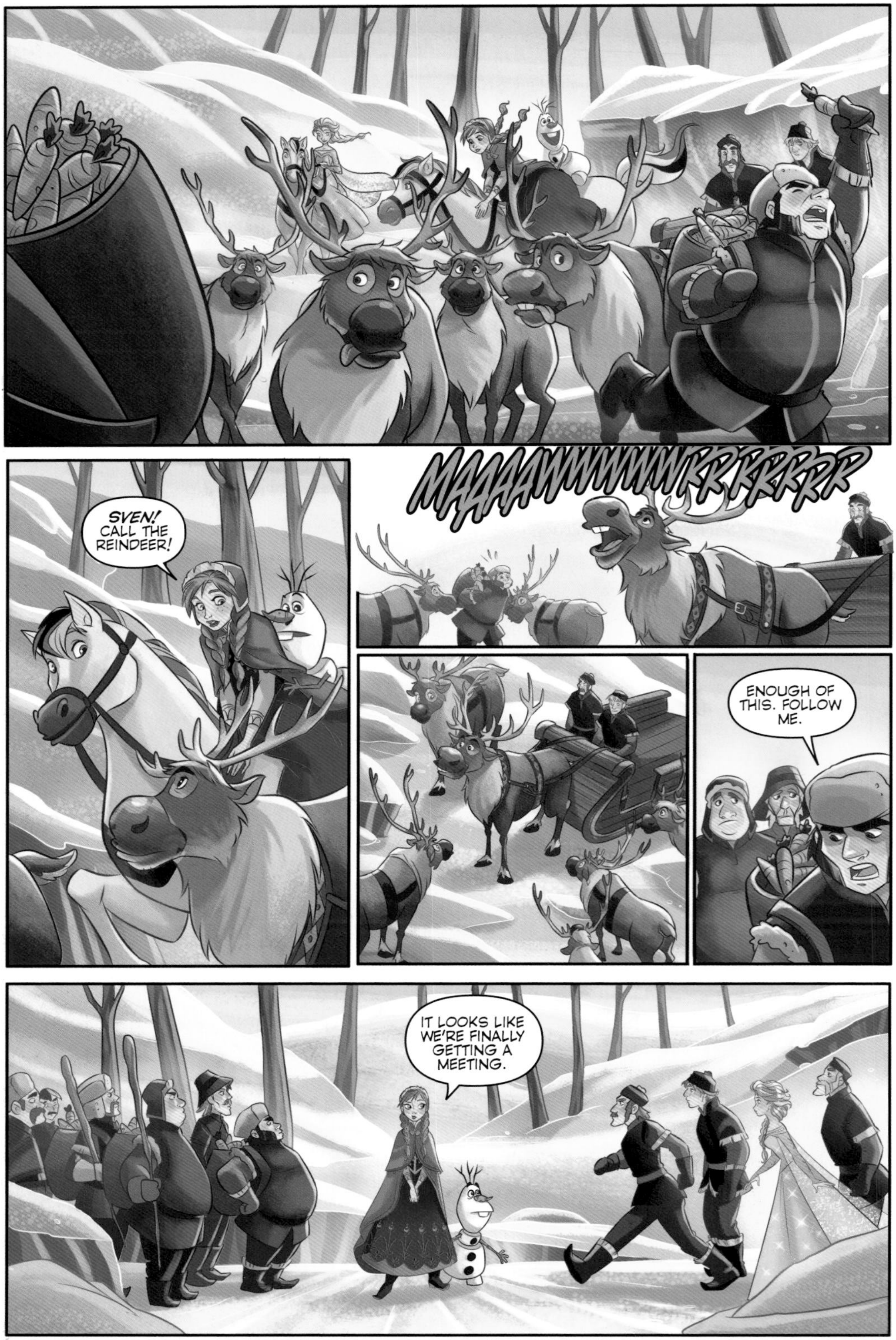
SVEN! CALL THE REINDEER!
MAAAAWWWWWKRRKRRR
ENOUGH OF THIS. FOLLOW ME.
IT LOOKS LIKE WE'RE FINALLY GETTING A MEETING.

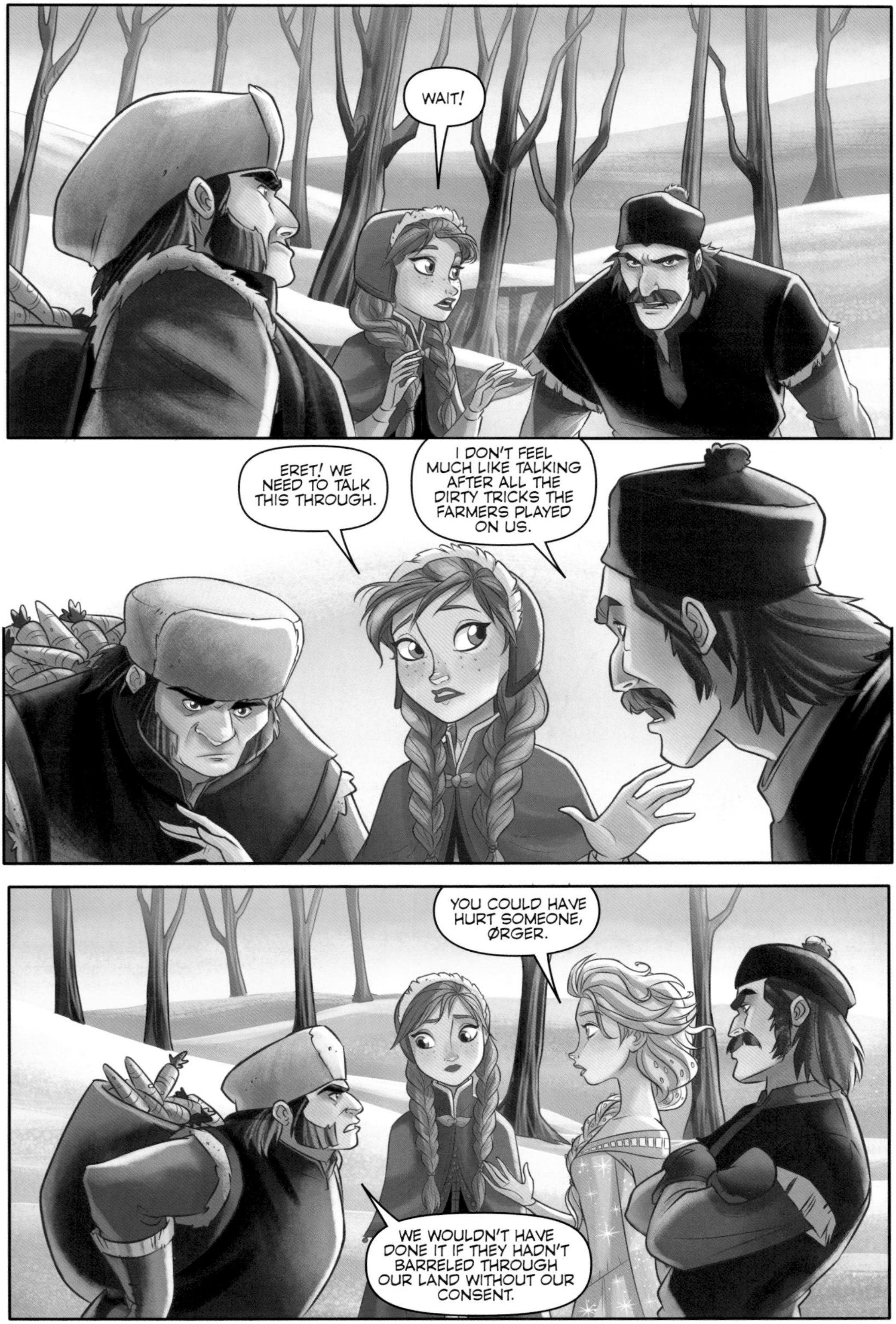

WAIT!
ERET! WE NEED TO TALK THIS THROUGH.
I DON'T FEEL MUCH LIKE TALKING AFTER ALL THE DIRTY TRICKS THE FARMERS PLAYED ON US.
YOU COULD HAVE HURT SOMEONE, ØRGER.
WE WOULDN'T HAVE DONE IT IF THEY HADN'T BARRELED THROUGH OUR LAND WITHOUT OUR CONSENT.

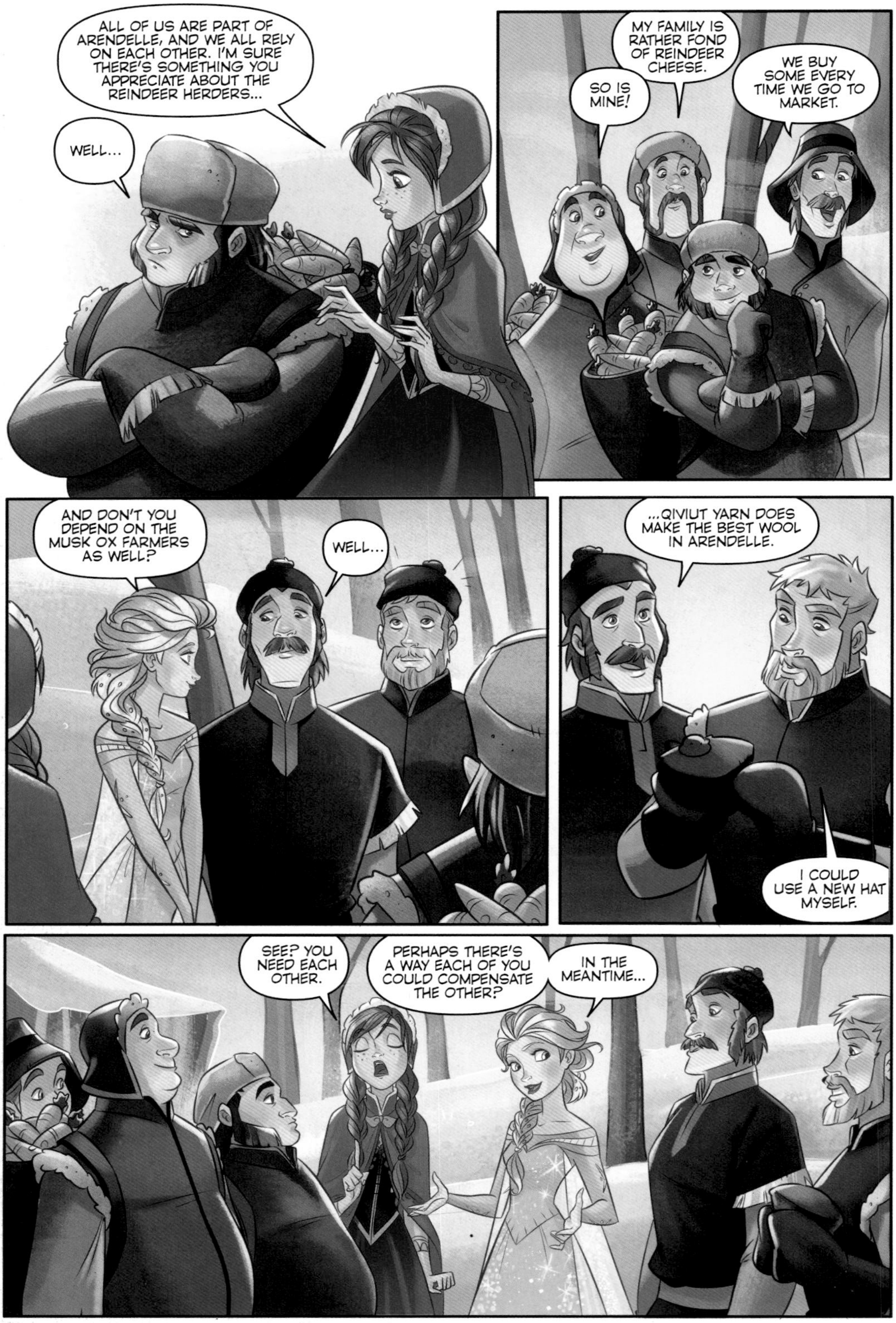
ALL OF US ARE PART OF ARENDELLE, AND WE ALL RELY ON EACH OTHER. I'M SURE THERE'S SOMETHING YOU APPRECIATE ABOUT THE REINDEER HERDERS...
WELL...
MY FAMILY IS RATHER FOND OF REINDEER CHEESE.
SO IS MINE!
WE BUY SOME EVERY TIME WE GO TO MARKET.
AND DON'T YOU DEPEND ON THE MUSK OX FARMERS AS WELL?
WELL...
...QIVIUT YARN DOES MAKE THE BEST WOOL IN ARENDELLE.
I COULD USE A NEW HAT MYSELF.
SEE? YOU NEED EACH OTHER.
PERHAPS THERE'S A WAY EACH OF YOU COULD COMPENSATE THE OTHER?
IN THE MEANTIME...

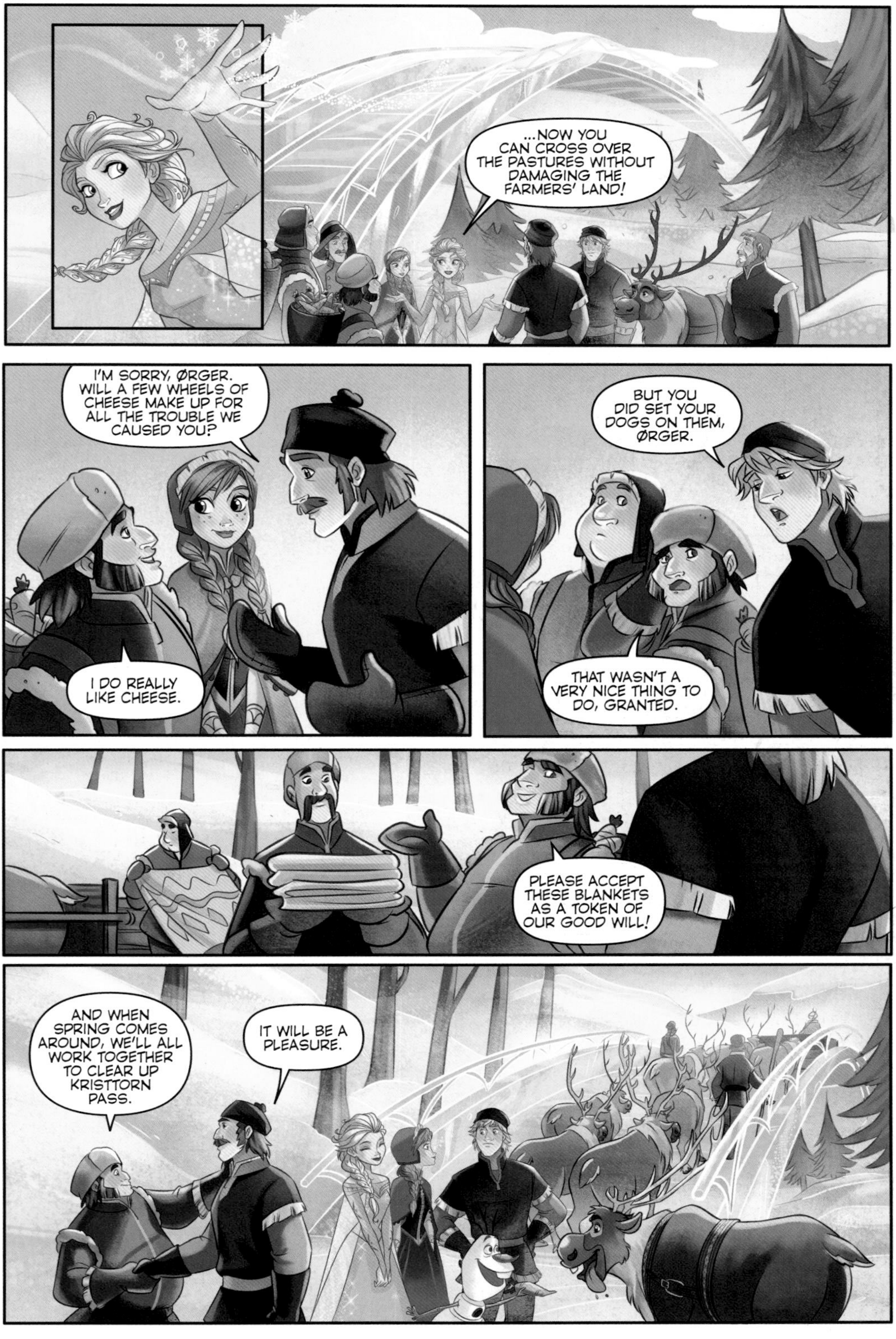
...NOW YOU CAN CROSS OVER THE PASTURES WITHOUT DAMAGING THE FARMERS' LAND!
I'M SORRY, ØRGER. WILL A FEW WHEELS OF CHEESE MAKE UP FOR ALL THE TROUBLE WE CAUSED YOU?
I DO REALLY LIKE CHEESE.
BUT YOU DID SET YOUR DOGS ON THEM, ØRGER.
THAT WASN'T A VERY NICE THING TO DO, GRANTED.
PLEASE ACCEPT THESE BLANKETS AS A TOKEN OF OUR GOOD WILL!
AND WHEN SPRING COMES AROUND, WE'LL ALL WORK TOGETHER TO CLEAR UP KRISTTORN PASS.
IT WILL BE A PLEASURE.

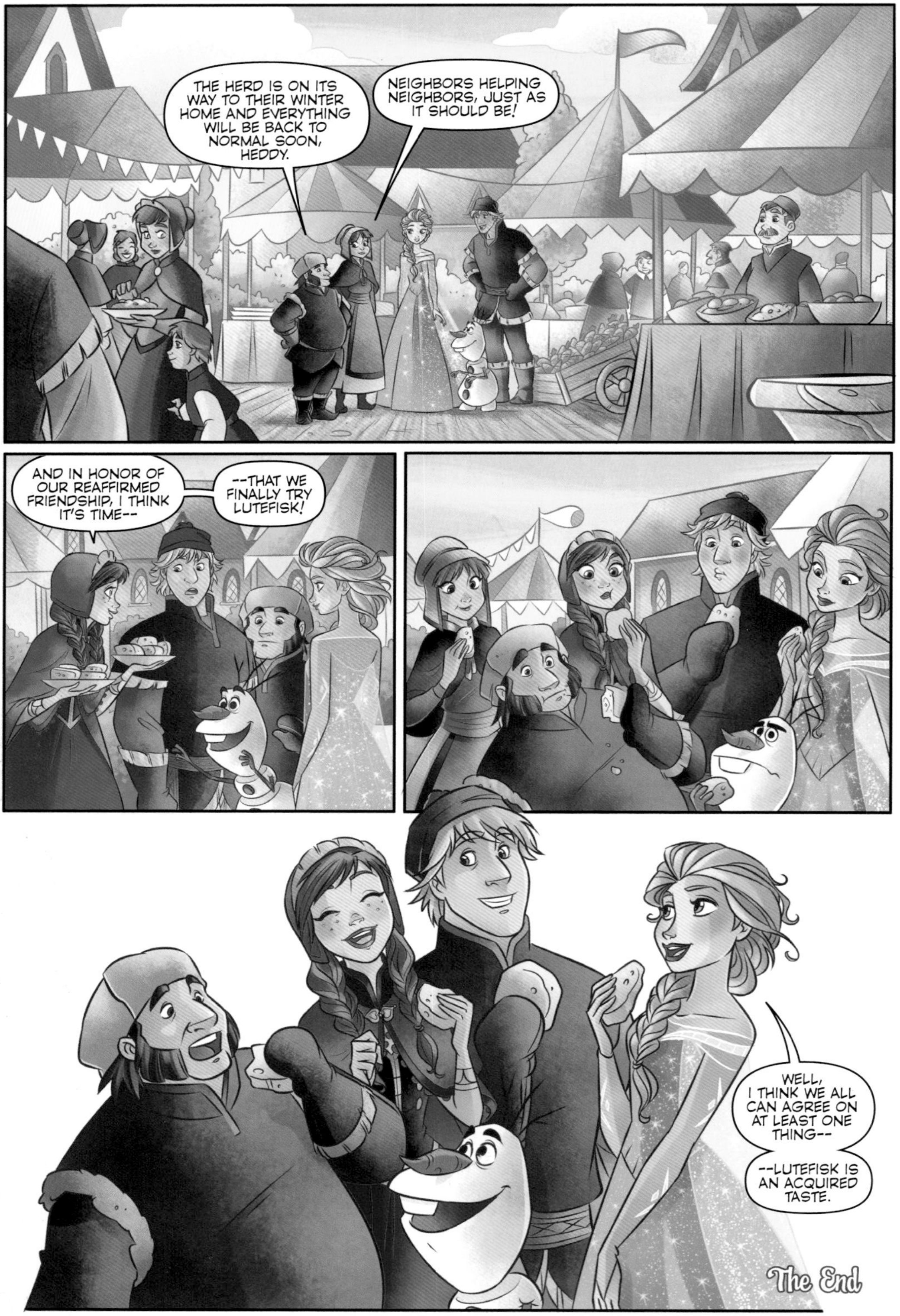
THE HERD IS ON ITS WAY TO THEIR WINTER HOME AND EVERYTHING WILL BE BACK TO NORMAL SOON, HEDDY.
NEIGHBORS HELPING NEIGHBORS, JUST AS IT SHOULD BE!
AND IN HONOR OF OUR REAFFIRMED FRIENDSHIP, I THINK IT'S TIME--
--THAT WE FINALLY TRY LUTEFISK!
WELL, I THINK WE ALL CAN AGREE ON AT LEAST ONE THING--
--LUTEFISK IS AN ACQUIRED TASTE.
The End

CREDITS

Travel Arendelle
Script by Georgia Ball
Layouts by Grafimated, Michela Cacciatore
Inks by Michela Cacciatore, Monica Catalano,
Veronica Di Lorenzo
Colors by Kat Maximenko, Vita Efremov,
Alesya Barsukova, Hanna Chinstova,
Anastasiia Belousova, Jackie Lee

The Shifting Shores of Sankershus
Script by Georgia Ball
Layouts by Benedetta Barone
Inks by Veronica Di Lorenzo
Colors by Cecilia Giumento, Manuela Nerolini,
Kat Maximenko, Julia Pinchuk,
Hanna Chinstova, Nastia Beloushova

The Lur Thief
Script by Georgia Ball
Layouts by Benedetta Barone
Inks by Michela Cacciatore, Elisabetta Melaranci
Colors by Kat Maximenko, Manuela Nerolini,
Cecilia Giumento, Alessandra Bracaglia,
Alessandro Russato, Julia Pinchuk

This Land Is Our Land
Script by Georgia Ball
Layouts by Benedetta Barone
Inks by Michela Cacciatore, Rosa La Barbera
Colors by Kat Maximenko, Jackie Lee, Manuela
Nerolini, Sara Spano, Luca Merli, Anastasiia
Belousova, Yana Chintsova

Cover by Benedetta Barone
Edited by Jennifer Hale
Lettered by AndWorld Design
Special thanks to Jessica Julius, Peter Del Vecho, Mike Giaimo, Julie Dorris,
Manny Mederos, Chris Troise, Eugene Paraszczuk, and Tea Orsi.

BRILLIANT ADVENTURES AWAIT

Experience the wonders of adventure with Elsa, Anna, Kristoff, Sven, and Olaf as they travel through Arendelle exploring the wilderness, helping save the flooding village of Sankershus, embarking on a search for a precious family heirloom, and celebrating at the Lutefisk Festival. With teamwork and the gift of friendship, they quickly learn that anything is possible!

Includes original art and stories from the *Disney Frozen* comic series.

JOE BOOKS LTD

Vol. 2

$9.99 US |$12.99 CAN

ISBN 978-1-77275-332-5

P7-EVF-790